Mi...
app...

"D...
manded of Aurora.

"How can I see what you are about if I do not?" she replied.

"As you will," he sighed and drew her to him.

"That's it?" Her tone was mildly derisive.

"No," he said huskily, pulling her into his arms again. "Now shut your eyes, and part your lips," he whispered thickly into her hair, his fingers trailing seductively over her jawline. "Pretend that I am Walsh."

She gasped at his suggestion. He took advantage of her surprise, kissing her half-opened mouth. She gasped again, this time with pleasure.

"You should know that the French have some interesting variations of this theme," he whispered and proceeded to push the kissing lesson a step further.

Aurora had known that Miles would be an expert teacher of the art of love. But she had not imagined how eager a student _____ be.

The Love Knot

by

Elisabeth Fairchild

A SIGNET BOOK

SIGNET
Published by the Penguin Group
Penguin Books USA Inc., 375 Hudson Street,
New York, New York 10014, U.S.A.
Penguin Books Ltd, 27 Wrights Lane,
London W8 5TZ, England
Penguin Books Australia Ltd, Ringwood,
Victoria, Australia
Penguin Books Canada Ltd, 10 Alcorn Avenue,
Toronto, Ontario, Canada M4V 3B2
Penguin Books (N.Z.) Ltd, 182-190 Wairau Road,
Auckland 10, New Zealand

Penguin Books Ltd, Registered Offices:
Harmondsworth, Middlesex, England

First published by Signet, an imprint of Dutton Signet,
a division of Penguin Books USA Inc.

First Printing, November 1995
10 9 8 7 6 5 4 3 2 1

This book is dedicated to those who have been most instrumental in supporting and furthering my passion for writing: Jim Kerr, Denise Marcil, Hilary Ross, and the Greater Dallas Writers' Association.

ACKNOWLEDGMENT

Special thanks to the personnel at Holkham Hall, for providing me with detailed knowledge of the estate.

AUTHOR'S NOTE

The love knot, or countryman's favor, is an intricate knot woven of plaited cornstalks, in a loose, doubled loop resembling a heart, bound at the bottom with a twist of ribbon grass to several stalks of golden grain. A fertility symbol, the number of stalks indicates the number of babies to come to a couple. The handwoven love knot was offered by a young man to his beloved as a blessing.

Prologue

Miles Fletcher suffered not the slightest premonition that a page in his life had quietly turned in the hands of Fate. Sunk in one of the comfortable leather chairs at the Travellers' club, he was leafing through a book of maps, making careful notes—Hertfordshire, Essex, Cambridgeshire and Norfolk—a seasoned traveler preparing for yet another journey. Miles liked to be prepared. He liked his travels, his very life, to go according to plan.

It was a quiet, mild, rain-scented evening perfumed by the promise of spring, but Miles had closed the door on the smell of freshly turned soil and green things. Here, no matter the season, the odor that met one's nostrils was that of cigar smoke and colza oil, traveler's pie and a strangely piquant blend of exotic colognes from every corner of the globe. It was a comforting and familiar bouquet.

The languages of at least five different nations could be heard drifting from the card room, but this evening number 106 Pall Mall was neither crowded nor noisy. In fact, the bas relief characters in the Roman frieze that encircled the ceiling evidenced more animation than was to be witnessed between the rows of stylish Corinthian columns in the library.

One of the waiters bent to whisper discreetly. "Lord Ware, sir, is here to fetch you."

Miles quietly closed the book of maps. Unhurried, he returned the volume to its proper spot in the shelves that lined the walls. His calm, collected expression evidenced no trace of alarm. Ware had come to fetch him where he knew he would not be admitted, because club members were required to have traversed at least five hundred miles from London in a straight line before they were allowed into the inner sanctum. Ware had never set foot outside of the British Isles. A good and tactful man, he never bothered to "fetch" Miles unless Lester had become quite unmanageable.

"I hope I did not keep you waiting," Miles said politely, his manner deceptively unruffled as he joined Ware in the entry to the club.

Ware had a worried look. "Sorry to interrupt."

"No need for apology." Miles calmly accepted assistance from a porter in sliding into the fashionably confining coat he could not have donned otherwise. "I daresay my uncle is enjoying a far more lively evening than I am."

Ware's lips tightened. He refrained from answering until the door was opened for them and they had stepped out onto the gaslit steps. There he waited until the door was firmly closed behind them before, with customary verbal economy, he confirmed Miles's worst fears.

"The damned fool is bent on killing himself."

Brooks's Club, Lester Fletcher's favorite haunt, was a livelier, less orderly spot than the somnolent Travellers'. Smoke and conversation hung almost as thick as the refined air of expectancy peculiar to a club where the stakes ran high. Whist, faro, macao, and hazard were the games of choice. There were, of course, clubs where one might more speedily dispose of a fortune, but at Brooks's one might do so in the elegant comfort of what appeared to be a rich relative's country home. The Whigs who played here were serious about the gaming that went on in the Great Subscription Room. No Roman friezes enlivened the swagged simplicity of the ceiling at Brooks's. Cavorting gods and goddesses, after all, might distract one from one's cards.

Lester Fletcher was in fine form. Miles was no more than halfway up the white marble stairs to the first floor when he was assailed by the carrying rumble of his uncle's phlegmy laugh. The laugh inevitably turned into a fit of coughing. Miles looked up as he took the risers with a nonchalant haste that left Ware puffing in his wake. Lester's cough sounded worse than usual.

A tall, handsome, freckled fellow with tousled red hair paused at the head of the stairs, as arrested by the cough as Miles had been. His scowling disapproval of the noise was more pronounced.

"Oh, dear," Ware murmured breathlessly. "The game is finished."

The gentleman above turned his freckled face in their direction and started down the stairs, still scowling. Miles recognized him. "Rakehell" he was called, "Rakehell" Ramsay. Lester had lost many a hand of faro to the man. He was a serious gamester, a reckless bettor, and a dangerous companion for Lester Fletcher in his current condition.

Ramsay ignored Miles as he passed, but to Ware he drawled with bitter sarcasm, "A pity your friend will not live to enjoy the fortune he has won tonight."

"Winning or losing, Uncle?" Miles said with a studied calmness when he had crossed to the table where his uncle sat laughing and coughing and puffing a cheroot.

"Harumph! Winning, my boy, winning. I would not have it any other way." As he spoke, Lester Fletcher, who knew how unhappy it made his nephew that he so consistently ignored his physician's direction that he stop drinking and smoking to excess, made a game attempt to hide his cigar and swallow the cloud he was puffing. The result was another coughing spell and a spiral of smoke that issued rather dangerously from the pocket of his waistcoat.

"Here." Miles swept a glass of water from a passing tray and held it above his uncle's pudgy, palsied hand.

"You do not expect me to drink that stuff, do you?" Lester blustered.

"Your pocket is thirsty." Miles coolly dashed the contents of the glass onto the smoking fabric.

"Oh, my! Am I on fire then?" Lester began to laugh. The

attendant coughing attack was more pronounced than before, but Lester was still smiling and wheezing "Oh my," when its severity abated.

Miles summoned up a glass of brandy. "Here, take a sip, and see if you cannot still that nasty cough."

Lester Fletcher took the glass without comment. When he had swallowed a sip as instructed, he smacked his lips in appreciation and tipped up the glass to drink it dry. The glass empty, he wagged a finger at Miles. "You know my leech has instructed me to forgo brandy, my boy. There are those who will say you mean to claim your inheritance sooner rather than later."

Miles could not smile, though he knew it was his uncle's intention to provoke humor with his remark. "If you are done here," he said, "I would be happy to see you home."

"Home? So early? The night is too young to waste, lad."

Miles drew forth his gold pocket watch and consulted the time. "Grace and I are off at first light."

Lester's bloodshot eyes widened. "Ah, yes, the shearing! Completely slipped my mind. Are you packed?"

Miles nodded. The watch found its way back into his pocket. "The carriage stands waiting."

"I shall miss you, my boy." The brightness of Lester's smile dimmed. His face went slack, but only for a moment, and then the jaw beneath his drooping jowls set itself with surprising firmness. "I've the strongest premonition I shall be setting off on my own unavoidable jaunt soon."

Troubled by the change of his uncle's tone, Miles allowed no hint of his feeling to evidence itself. Lester did not like to be fussed over, even when it came to the matter of his imminent demise. Mildly Miles suggested, "The trip to Holkham might best be postponed."

Lester would not hear of it. "Do not delay on my account! I would not stay any man's progress in the life I've left me, you know that."

"I do not like to think you so bold as to set off alone, Uncle."

His uncle grabbed urgently at his hand. "Never mind tearful good-byes, lad, and bedside vigils. I do not care for them. There's more reason than ever that you should go to the shearing. I cannot set off comfortably either to Heaven or to Hell, until I am sure an innocent lamb has not been fleeced by this evening's good fortune."

"A lamb, sir?"

Lester winked at him. "A devilish pretty lamb, my boy, do not mistake me. A lamb in fox's clothing."

Chapter One

A thing of beauty tested Miles Fletcher's penchant for arriving promptly wherever he was due. It first manifested itself as an uneven thud, a muffled beating like a heart whose pace has gone awry. This sound was curious enough to divert Fletcher's attention from the prospect of arriving at Holkham Hall precisely on time, as was his strict habit. This pleasing prospect he had regularly contemplated in the glassy face of his elegant gold watch. Again and again, like a mechanical flower, it bloomed in the palm of his hand. How gratifying to arrive exactly as scheduled when one came so far, over unfamiliar roads!

The ticking metal blossom was initially drawn forth as his dust-covered coach passed beneath the Triumphal Arch marking the edge of their host's vast holdings. A second time it filled his palm as his team clattered past a half-moon cluster of cottages alongside the straight avenue that forced them up a gentle rise, where the tall, pale needle of an obelisk cut the sky. For a third time, on the far side of that rise, the watch was consulted. Holkham Hall loomed in the distance, the sun glittering on the water of its man-made canal and the picturesque panorama of white sheep and gamboling lambs scattered across green pasturage.

Ffft. Ta-dum. The thudding noise, curiously out-of-keeping with pastoral vistas, especially followed as it was by the polite flutter of applause and the high lilt of feminine laughter, was distraction enough to convince Miles he must click shut the face of his timepiece and tuck it away. But he did not immediately order the coach to slow.

Instead, lifting a crisp, monogrammed handkerchief to

his nose, he braved the cloud of dust it raised and leaned his head a little out of the window in the gracefully liquid manner that was distinctly his own. He meant to identify the thudding noise, nothing more. It sounded vaguely familiar.

Through the trees to his right, a flash of white caught his eye: white columns against creamy yellow brick, white muslin fluttering against the lush green backdrop of newly leafed trees. Almost hidden among the greenery was a hint of Greece in the midst of the English countryside: a Doric style temple—a thing of beauty. Before it stood a row of female archers, caught by Mr. Fletcher's passing eye, poised in the moment before arrows were loosed—beauty before beauty. The uneven thud made sense to him now, as the row of longbows released a quicksilver gleaming of feathered shafts at a cluster of pasteboard and cloth targets set back amongst the trees.

There was a beauty in the moment, an elegance in the setting, in the activity and its participants. Beauty and elegance never failed to give Miles Fletcher serious pause.

"Hold!" he called, punctuality abandoned. Withdrawing into the coach, he took up his walking stick. It too was a thing of beauty. The shaft was ebony wood, the top an exquisitely rendered marble fist. With this fist as an extension of his own arm, he knocked a brisk tattoo against the carriage roof.

The coach was promptly pulled to a stop.

"What? We are not there, are we?" The young woman who nestled in the squabs beside him sleepily raised her head.

One corner of Miles's mouth lifted. He returned his attention to the window. "Not quite." He leaned out of the window to direct the coachman to pull off the main avenue, onto the grassy, shaded track that led to the temple. "Sorry to wake you, Grace," he said, when the coach rumbled onto the rutted track, throwing them both about. "I think you might like to see this."

Grace yawned like a kitten as she shoved herself into a more comfortable position. "Very pretty, if one does not mind the bruises required to approach the thing." She rubbed her hip. "Tell me Miles, is it the temple caught your eye, or the women in front of it?"

"You wound me, Gracie," Miles murmured as he drew forth, not his watch this time, but a gold-rimmed pince-nez, which he polished on his handkerchief with thorough precision despite the inconvenience of being thrown against the squabs yet again.

Gracie laughed dryly. "I am on target then. Spy you some fair Diana? Have you not enough female conquests in London that you must add another bruised heart to your list?"

"Bruised heart? What tender creature have I so injured?" Miles arched a dark brow and narrowed his eyes to examine through the window, with the aid of his sparkling ogler, the armed rank of women, who stood, bows raised and drawn again.

"I know enough"—Grace laughed—"to know you love all women and favor none. There are dozens who go to great lengths to win your attention."

"So many?" Miles could not smother the grin that leapt to his lips and was as swiftly gone. "Forgive me, my dear, if I appear inattentive, but I cannot resist the sight of beauty, no matter its form."

"Am I not beautiful then?"

His grin broadened. "Without question, but it does not do to stare at one's sister, no matter how beautifully she snores."

"I do not snore!" the Honorable Grace Fletcher insisted, and as quickly lost her serene certainty. "I do not. Do I?"

Miles absently turned his quizzing glass on his youngest sister. She was a fetching creature and she knew it well enough. They were plagued by her admirers wherever they went. "Of course not, my dear. But, your bonnet has been knocked askew and your lace tucker requires attention."

As she adjusted the tilt of her bonnet, the arrows flew like a flock of birds, drawing both their heads in the same direction. A chorus of cheers rose from the picturesque gathering among the trees.

"Drat!" Grace exclaimed, withdrawing from the window.

"Walsh is here! Quick, turn the coach and drive on. I would not have him see me." She ducked to the floor in a rustle of starched petticoats.

"I do not see him." Miles languidly studied the crowd. Lord Walsh was no cause for serious alarm. He was but one of the many unappreciated young men who dangled after Grace. Miles could not remember if Walsh had actually made Grace an offer. It was certainly his intention, but his chances of an affirmative response were slim either way. She had turned down half a dozen suitors, determined, she had told her brother, not to marry at all if not for love, even if it meant marrying a pauper and living in a garret. Painters commonly lived in garrets, did they not? Grace fancied herself a serious artist because she had a knack with watercolors. She was a romantic creature with very high ideals. A garret appealed to those ideals. Miles loved her for her passionate expectations, but he was not about to turn the coach around and head back to London just to avoid one spurned suitor.

"Ah, I see him now," he admitted as Walsh hailed him.

"Why did you not tell me he was to number among the guests?" Grace hissed from her ignominious seat on the floor. "I would never have come had I the slightest inkling. I shall not have a moment's peace to paint with Walsh hovering at my elbow."

"I thought you liked Walsh."

"I do."

"I thought you liked him better than any of that pack of dogs that hounds you."

"Perhaps I do," she said. "But, the man wants to marry me, and I do not think I like any man well enough for that."

"Well, if you like him enough to be civil, you had best dust yourself off and sit up," Miles suggested. "His Grace is headed this way."

Walsh was moving purposefully toward them.

"Ooh!" Grace muttered as she shifted to the far side of the coach and rose to the seat, straightening her rumpled skirts. "You are insufferably cruel, Miles, not to order the coachman onward."

"I do apologize." Miles smiled at her. "But, it would be insufferably rude in me to leave a peer of the realm standing in a cloud of dust when he has made it clear he means to have a word with us."

As he spoke, the volume of his voice dropped. Walsh was almost upon them. Beyond him the archers were lined up for another go at the targets. The ranks of competitors had been thinned. Only those who had hit a golden center ring were requested to knock arrow for a shot at the cleared targets once again. As this smaller number of females adjusted stance and raised their bows, Walsh arrived to engage Grace in unwanted conversation, but Miles no more than nodded to the earl. He was too caught up in the scene playing itself out behind him.

For a brief moment, it was as though the heavens meant to produce a living canvas before the little Doric temple. A shaft of light filtered through the lush green of the trees, glancing off the graceful columns and catching in the pale, white muslin dresses that belled and wafted in the breeze like the wings of a flock of pale butterflies. In the midst of this weightless gathering, one young woman, tall and trim and shapely, seemed almost rooted to the earth by the dark weight of the distinctive hunter's-green outfit she wore. The sun played on the white fur that trimmed its neckline and the buff slash insets at shoulder, cuff and ankle-high hem. It gleamed too, in the white feather that graced the brim of the archer's green hat, marking her a member of the Royal British Bowmen's Society.

Miles Fletcher had seen countless beautiful women in his travels throughout Europe and the Far East, but he had never been as intrigued by a woman as he was by this one—a woman who looked like a fox hiding in the undergrowth of her clothing. More than anywhere else, the light shifted and glittered like fire in the wispy red tendrils that had freed themselves from a heavy braid coiled at the nape of her neck.

He leaned forward as though drawn by a string.

As if she felt the intensity of his gaze, she turned her face in his direction for the breadth of a moment. Her cheeks were heavily freckled, lending this fair young woman's complexion a rare, golden cast. This was, Miles decided, a feral and intriguing sort of beauty.

She looked away, her attention on the targets.

As different as the young woman was in her attire, so too was she different in the manner in which she drew arrow. Almost as one, the other archers raised and drew in one single, sweeping motion. This was the commonly accepted method in which a woman took aim. It was a graceful move, a flattering move. But the dark green silhouette chose a more difficult and less graceful approach—one that required more strength. Her bow arm rose above the others, then drew string to gilded cheek, aiming at the heavens before lowering to sight upon the target. For a heartbeat, her gaze, stance, and focus were steady and self-assured. Miles held his breath. For that single heartbeat, the sculptural line of arm, the careful positioning of shoulder, the soft curve of breast echoing the taut curve of the bow, was a thing of such perfect beauty, symmetry, and grace that Miles was struck by the sensation that art and myth had come to life. Diana the Huntress had sprung from the forest floor, in the form of this fiery archer who would as blithely shoot down a cloud as she might shoot at ringed targets. For an instant, it seemed as though an architect designed her stance—for an instant as if the light of a Heaven she had pierced poured heavy and honey-gold upon her head.

"So, you are the reason I am here," Miles murmured under his breath.

Chapter Two

The arrows were launched.

Miles willed *her* arrow to find the center ring. He willed her to turn and look his way, that he might see the whole of her face.

Of course, her arrow struck center. Of course, this fair huntress must be proclaimed the winner. He had expected nothing less. The only thing that surprised Miles was that she did turn in the moment the arrow sank home, her face suffused with the satisfaction of a job perfectly executed, to look in his direction, as if she was in some way moved by his desire that she should do so. Her pleasure in the moment had her smiling, teeth and dimples flashing amid the tawny freckling of her skin. The wind stirred her bright hair like a candle flickering in a draft.

Ye gods, she was breathtaking! He had not expected to encounter such beauty in the fulfillment of his promise to Lester.

The light changed. The fire in her hair died down. The stirring crowd hid her from his view.

"A goddess sublime," he murmured, as he took the first truly steady breath he had managed since catching sight of the archer whose brilliance cast all others into the shade.

Grace knew of whom he spoke. She had been watching the archers as well, but Walsh had his back to the targets. In talking to Grace, who had been smiling vapidly and answering in monosyllables in hopes of cutting short their conversation, he had missed the conclusion of the competition.

"A goddess is it?" He turned to observe the crowd and

saw nothing remarkable. "Really, Miles, old man, which goddess is it who has shown herself to you?"

Miles smiled politely. "Diana, of course. The huntress," he said mildly, unwilling to point the girl out. Pulling forth his watch, he pleased Grace no end by announcing, "Goddesses aside, it is high time we made our way to Holkham Hall. Our host is expecting us."

Walsh took himself off, with a parting promise to secure a dance or two from Grace that evening.

Miles bade the coachman, "Walk on."

The coach lurched forward. They rode in silence a moment, enjoying the view.

Then came the interrogation Miles had been expecting, voiced in the innocent tone that marked Gracie's most delving questions. "Do you know," she said sweetly, "I do not recall ever having heard you refer to any of your other goddesses as sublime." She toyed with the ribbons of her bonnet. "That compliment is one you normally reserve for oils or marble or architecture. Tell me, can a woman with so many freckles truly be judged so? I think not! Her hair is far too forward a color to be greatly admired."

Miles laughed, the sound welling up from deep within his chest. Grace meant to test him with her words. Grace always set about discovering things by indirect methods, and in honeyed tones.

"You are too severe," he said lightly. "Both in your opinion of me and in judging the attraction of your own sex. Yon fair Diana was undeniably sublime. It was her hair and freckles, and the bow in her hand that made her so."

Grace studied him very carefully from beneath the brim of her bonnet. "*This* is what I thought you would find sublime, Miles." She waved her hand toward the view of Holkham Hall as the road bent westward and they were afforded a better aspect of the large and very striking Palladian country house their host's ancestor had built in the middle of the Norfolk wilderness half a century ago. With a gusty sigh she sank back against the cushions. "It is even more beautiful than I had imagined it from Kent's drawings, a delightful combination of Greek and Roman influences. A sight worth seeing, Miles. I am pleased you talked me into coming with you, Walsh or no. I must have out my watercolors and paint the place before the day is done."

Miles was pleased to indulge his sister's passion for the Classical style. It never occurred to him to destroy her joy in the sight of Holkham Hall by telling her that he found the Palladian style a trifle austere, almost severe in the cleanliness of its lines. "I look forward to viewing the Italian landscapes and Roman marbles that the late Lord Leicester gathered in his Grand Tour of Europe," was what he said by way of an answer.

"This place is a treasure trove!" Grace was never so passionate as when she spoke of her love of art. No man had ever lit her eyes and brought color to her cheeks in such a way. "Do you see the large, central block of the building?" She pointed. "There, beneath the Corinthian portico? I am told Coke devotes the whole of that part of the Hall to the display of his collection. The layout of the buildings is modeled—"

"After Palladio's Villa Mocenigo." Miles tried to suppress a smile and failed.

Grace's lips pursed. She would not smile back at him. "Have I been boring you with architectural detail throughout the entirety of the journey with which you are already familiar, Miles?"

One raven's wing brow flew upward. "No, Grace. I have not been bored. It is a rare pleasure to spend time with someone as immersed in an appreciation of art and antiquities as I am. I do not know that I would have made this trip at all without you to accompany me."

"Pish!" She shoved at his arm. "Your real reason for being here has nothing to do with me."

Miles shrugged, his gaze focused on the approaching view of symmetrical rooftops, dun-colored brick, massive Corinthean columns, and arched or porticoed window-frames. The image of a real-life Diana, posed with bow before her temple in the woods, blotted out the architectural eyeful. Grace was quite right of course. His reasons for coming were many and varied and none of them had much to do with his sister.

"You are come to this sheep shearing fortnight so that you might see a flock denuded. Admit it," she teased him.

Miles splayed his hands in acquiescence. He preferred not to divulge all of his true reasons. To explain meant discussing their Uncle Lester's impending death, and he had no desire to contemplate too thoroughly such a reality. For the present, he would let Grace believe what she would.

"As you say, I have come to see how one goes about undressing a sheep. I have come to see a flock defrocked. I must understand this business of fleecing and being fleeced much better than I do." He spoke lightly, though his thoughts weighed heavy.

She laughed and then frowned as she plucked at the lace that hung down over her wrists. "You could have gone to Matthew for the information you seek and saved yourself this trip."

Miles sighed. Grace sought his confidences by back-door methods again. Matthew would have been no help at all in the matter at hand. "Matthew, I am sorry to say, is rather annoyed with me at the moment."

"Annoyed? Whatever for?"

"He is displeased that I am to inherit Uncle Lester's land and properties."

"What?" She laughed at the absurdity of it. "Matthew begrudges you Loughdon Hall, and a town house inferior to his own when he is already in possession of more land and property than he can personally oversee?"

Miles shrugged and tried to keep the conversation light. "Perhaps it is the hunting box he covets."

She pursed her lips. "How absurd! How selfish! Yet, how typical. Matthew has always seen himself, alone among us, in the role of lord and master of all he surveys."

Miles allowed himself a tight little smile. "Yes. He was brought up with no other expectation to trouble him."

"And you, as second son, were not, any more than I was," Grace said gently, voicing far more understanding than Miles had expected, even from his nearest and dearest sibling.

"So Matthew was quick to point out to me." He altered the tilt of his head and the pitch of his voice to give a fair impression of Matthew's condescending tone. "Whatever will you do with land, Miles? I advise you to sell before your overseer has much chance to cheat you. After all, you haven't the vaguest idea what to do when it comes to looking after an estate, now have you?"

"Did he really suggest that you sell? Matthew? Who would never part with so much as a handful of his own soil? What cheek!"

Miles stroked the fisted end of his cane. "Honest cheek. He is dead-on accurate. I've not the least notion how to manage the land Uncle saw fit to entrust to me."

Grace laughed and reached out to pat his arm in a comforting manner. "Uncle Lester believes otherwise, else he would not be so set on leaving you Loughdon and its acreage. You've brought the world to his drawing room, Miles. It is no wonder he means to give it all back to you. Never fear your ignorance of land management. I have seen you poring over agricultural texts and pamphlets. Here, where the most informed agriculturalists in England have gathered, you will soon understand the handling of your properties every bit as well as you understand the handling of a Grecian urn or a Roman marble."

He smiled at her. "It would be satisfying to disappoint Matthew's expectations of me."

She laughed and nodded. "Sublimely so."

Chapter Three

Miles Fletcher's second encounter with Lester's lamb, his goddess sublime, was something of a surprise. He had been on the lookout for the young woman all evening. He had, in fact, taken great pains to look his best, determined that she should be impressed by his irreproachable style. His cravat was flawlessly tied, his swallow-tailed coat fit him like a glove. His waistcoat was a favorite.

It was difficult to find anyone in the absolute crush of people that crowded the dining hall at dinner. There was certainly no fair Diana to be seen, for so he had begun to think of her. He must have passed right over her. Dressed much like any other young woman in the room, with her magnificent hair pulled away from her face and tightly constricted in a twist at the crown of her head, the glow of her was almost extinguished. When he recognized her at last, in the statue gallery, where a chamber orchestra tucked away in the north tribune kept the dance floor filled, she was virtually unrecognizable. Could this be his red-haired huntress?

Gone was the defining weight of the dark green Bowman's Society outfit that suited her so well. The pale, high-waisted, round-necked satin and gauze she now wore did not in the least become her. Her coloring was too vivid for pastels, her figure too buxom for a dress bound just beneath the breasts. She looked as if she had pulled on a satin sack and tied it in the middle. Whoever had the dressing of her should have known better. Her hairdresser, too, was in need of a scolding. The fiery, curling hair was pulled too severely back from a face heavily powdered in a vain attempt to disguise indisguisable freckles. The graceful huntress looked a pale and uncertain ghost of herself. Among the crush of glittering ladies and gentlemen, the girl was not at ease in her ill-chosen finery. She frequently looked down at her neckline to check the lace tucker that saved her bosom from overexposure. She plucked and fiddled with the ribbons on her sleeves.

Determined to verify her identity and reconcile his boundless expectations of a goddess with reality, Miles negotiated his way around the crowded room, keeping his gaze carefully pinned on her.

She stood alone, uncomfortably framed on one side by the whirl of dancers and on the other by a cluster of young men and women determined to exclude newcomers from their conversation. She edged away from the whirl and the laughter with the guilty sideways glance of someone who has arrived without an invitation at a function where they are familiar with no one. Gone was the self-assurance that had added grace and agility to her every movement out-of-doors. Approached by a balding and bespectacled gentleman almost as retiring as she, Lester's lamb had the look about her of a nervous creature ready to bolt. To Miles's chagrin, just as he managed to break through the crush that separated him from his prize, the gentleman convinced her to dance.

It was a shame really, that the young woman agreed to take the floor. She was no great dancer. Her partner proved equally awkward. Between them, they were clumsy and inept, managing to bump into one another and the couples around them more than once. The young lady's foot was compromised. Her expression registered shock and then pain as her partner swung her near. The gentleman apologized, contrition written all over his face. She smiled and gamely made the best of her predicament.

It was disturbing for Miles to watch the two of them.

"The bounder should never trouble any poor female to trip about the floor with him if he can do no better than that." It was Thomas Coke, his host, who dared make such a cutting remark.

Miles turned to greet him as though they picked up a conversation interrupted only moments before, when in fact, it had been months since their last encounter. "Tell me, who is the lovely creature the clod keeps treading on?"

Coke laughed. "Fancy redheads do you? Aurora Ramsay's not your style, young man."

Ramsay! So she *was* the Ramsay he came in search of, the innocent lamb his uncle would not see fleeced. He had suspected as much from the moment he had set eyes on her. His uncle had described the color of her hair exactly. It was amusing really, that of all the women gathered here at Holkham Hall, he should be attracted to this one. "Speaking of paintings," he said, "I am looking forward to examining your landscapes at my leisure. Rumor has it there are several treasures stashed away in your attic."

Coke directed his gaze toward the ceiling. "There are a few canvases upstairs—none of them landscapes, but you are welcome to have a peek if you like. Your sister, too, if she is not easily shocked by the excesses of art. She tells me she means to do several watercolors of the Hall while she is here. Nice girl. Fine, light touch with her paintbrush. I'm glad you brought her with you. She is good company for my girls. I see Lord Walsh wastes no time in dancing with her."

Miles drew forth his quizzing glass and studied the dancers. A well-built, handsome fellow of impressive stature, Walsh was not easy to miss. A vigorous dancer, he galloped Grace about the floor with admirable enthusiasm.

As the couple swept past them in a wind of their own making, Grace shot her brother a desperate look. Miles understood. She required rescuing. He smiled and nodded. Time enough to save his little sister when the music stopped. In the meantime, there was more to be found out about the canvases in the attic.

"Do you not care for the paintings? I am sure I could find a buyer for you if they do not suit."

"Care for them? They're first-rate, lad. I would not dream of parting with them." Coke lowered his voice. "They are, however, a trifle suggestive. In the Classical mode of course, but I've impressionable daughters. As a man of the world, I'm sure you understand. My wife will not have them hanging about, putting romantic notions in the girls' heads."

"I see," Miles said, without really seeing at all. The nudes lining the gallery in which they stood might be labeled suggestive and the tapestry wall hangings in his rooms were none too prudish. The paintings in the attic must be striking indeed to be banned from view! Miles allowed no hint of disappointment to surface in his expression at the news Coke had no inclination to sell. He had heard that the canvases were excellent. A list of potential buyers was filed away in his head. A peek in the attic was a welcome invitation. If these suggestive paintings were as good as rumored, Tom might yet be coaxed around to the idea of selling them. If not, Miles would enjoy the viewing, pay rapt attention to a sheep shearing, do his best, as his sister suggested, to learn in a fortnight what it took to run an estate, and perhaps most important of all, he would introduce himself to Aurora Ramsay.

He returned his attention to the graceless antics of his anything-but-sublime goddess of the dance floor. Coke could tell him more about the girl he was sure, if only the matter were approached in the right way. "The Ramsay. Is she cut from the same rough cloth as her brothers 'Rakehell' and what is it the brother is called who has the pox? 'Rogue'? No it is 'Rogering' Ramsay, isn't it?"

"Is Aurora anything like her brothers? By no means. I would not allow her near my girls if that were the case. The girl takes after Rue, if she takes after any Ramsay. He comes here as her escort, though he hasn't the slightest interest in sheep, dear boy. Aurora makes him bring her every year. She likes to stay abreast of the latest agricultural and stock-raising trends. Remarkably informed young woman. Has a love of the soil, Aurora does. Not at all afraid to get her hands dirty. Her brothers would not have an acre left between them did she not manage the tenants and fields now that their father is gone. A pity, but she may not be able to hold on to what little is left if her siblings continue to indulge themselves with wine, women, dice, and cards."

Miles's eyes narrowed. How like his Uncle Lester these Ramsays sounded. "Losing heavy and riding life hard, are they?"

"No more than usual, if I am to take Rue at his word. Holed up as usual, in the library, on account of his peg leg. He is perhaps the best of the lot, other than Aurora, judging reputation by the foolish nicknames they are all of them saddled with."

"Do tell." Miles winced as he continued to observe, through his quizzing glass, the gyrations of the couple who plowed their way across the floor. This Aurora Ramsay was in need of rescuing far more than his sister—and in more ways than one.

Coke counted them off on his fingers. "Let me see if I can keep them straight. 'Rash' Ramsay, the eldest, whose real name is Charles, has gone to Persia in an effort to revive the decimated family fortunes. In his absence, 'Rakehell,' the brother with whom you are familiar, is fast gambling away what little capital is left. He is ably assisted in his endeavors by his younger brothers 'Rogering' Ramsay, and 'Rip' Ramsay, who gets very loud when he drinks too much, which is more often than not from all accounts."

Miles felt a twinge of regret that made little real sense given the fact that he had never so much as met his fair Diana. "Bad blood," he suggested.

Coke shrugged and sighed. "Nay, never that! It was no more than the loss of both their parents that sent them all to seed." Tom's voice went soft with affection. He cleared his throat and the air, by saying gruffly, "Great go of a girl. Nothing vaporish, missish or retiring about her." He lowered his voice to confide, "Mark my words. Were I a younger man, and unattached, I would bend knee to her despite the drain her brothers would be on any man's pocketbook. As I am neither, I am pleased she chooses to hang about the place. My girls are completely overawed by her. She stretches the boundaries of femininity, you see."

"And has this overawing Aurora a nickname too?" Miles lowered his glass.

Coke laughed. "As a matter of fact, she does. *L'Amazon,* she is called, by those who pander to the fashion of Frenchifying everything. 'Riding' Ramsay by those who do not. Ride she does, as though she were born in the saddle. Never have I seen a woman with a finer seat."

It was unfortunate that hard on the heels of such a compliment, Miss Aurora Ramsay's partner managed to thoroughly trip her up. As the final chords of the dance were struck, she stumbled into the path of Lord Walsh and Miles's sister, Grace. Walsh was so completely unbalanced by the unexpected interruption to his enthusiastic progress, that with an ungentlemanly grunt, he crashed to the floor, taking Aurora with him in a tumble of pale petticoats and a painful thumping of limbs.

The chamber orchestra sawed to an uneasy halt.

Every couple on the dance floor stopped to observe. Every head in the room, swiveled.

"Oh, my. What have we here?" Coke leapt forward to help the fallen to their feet, but Miles, who had anticipated the tragedy of clumsiness before it occurred, beat him to it.

Aurora Ramsay groaned as she stared up at the exquisitely coffered ceiling and the elegantly gilded chandelier. She took a deep breath, and held the angry exclamation she would have liked to have shouted firmly in check. *Damn* the clumsy twit who had dared ask her to dance when he had no more idea than she how to go about it. *Damn* her own stupidity in accepting his assurances that there was nothing to it. Dancing was not her strong suit. She had never taken the time to master the art. Why had she not acknowledged her ineptitude and clung to the wall and the punch bowl like any other wilting flower, never setting slipper to the polished wood floor where everyone whirled as gracefully as falling leaves? Why did dancing look so simple, effortless, and easy, when it was anything but?

Of all people to drag down in a clumsy heap in the middle of a crowded dance floor, it must be Lord Walsh—Walsh, whom she had decided she must marry—huge, handsome, sandlewood-scented Walsh, who had landed on top of her as they stumbled to the floor, and was crushing the life out of her even as he breathed a spate of oaths into the lace tucker she was sure did not cover enough of the cleavage of her bosom. Dear Lord above! This was, of course, the very position she had hoped to one day share with this man, but the mode and manner of their achieving such a stance exceeded the scope of her imaginings. What a mess! Her face burned. This was not at all the impression she had planned to make.

Lord Walsh got off her quickly enough, but when she put her hand out, expecting his assistance in rising, she was surprised to find it was another gentleman took her hand with alacrity. He was a stranger to her, a vaguely familiar stranger wearing the exaggerated Cossack style pantaloons her brothers were so fond of ridiculing. His shoes were as black as his pantaloons and noteworthy for their glossy shine. The stranger who wore them was struggling manfully not to smile as he raised her to her feet.

He smelled faintly of citrus. They were of a height. He looked her straight in the eyes as she rose. She was struck by the darkness of his hair, by the sharpness of his features, by the deep blue gleam of his eyes.

"Are you badly bruised?" His tone was as formal and polished as the floor she had just risen from. "Do you wish to sit down?" he asked politely. His face, his look, even the question he asked had a sharpness to it, despite the politeness. Cheekbones, chin and nose—he seemed chiseled from the same pale, Italian marble that stared blankly down from the wall behind him.

"Sit? No!" she snapped, rubbing the aching hip on which she had landed. "I do not want to sit. The problem is in having chosen the floor to sit upon, as it is."

The blue eyes sparkled with suppressed glee. His mouth, the only softness in his sharp-edged, clever face, twitched with withheld laughter. She marked him a dandy, first by his pantaloons and further by the wasp-waisted cut of his coat. It was so narrowly tailored to his measurements, she was amazed the seams did not split immediately asunder when he exerted himself in helping her to her feet. He was impeccably accoutered in the Herculean style with padded shoulders, broad, stiff lapels, long coal-black tails, high stock, pristine white gloves, and an unusually fine, figured white-upon-white waistcoat. His sleek black hair spoke of a dandy, too, cut short on the sides, long and curling on the top. Add to this a dazzling, white de Chasse knot stiffly grazing his chin, a heavy gold watch fob, and the mirrored shine of the quizzing glass he raised to regard her, and she felt the perfect country dowd beside him, even in her ball gown.

Her host murmured something comforting and took himself off to encourage the musicians to fill the too-silent room with music again. The guests' attention must be returned to entertainments other than her clumsiness.

The stranger who had offered her his hand, remarked— oh, so smoothly—in a low, cultured voice, "I thought you might be feeling a trifle faint," as if she had gone down in a swoon rather than out of sheer galloping clumsiness!

She darted a piercing look into the stranger's eyes, weighing his intent in remaining by her side and engaging her in conversation. The thought ran through her head that the blue of these eyes as exactly the color of runaway Jack, or hay-maidens as the Gill flower was sometimes called. It was a color she associated with damp, shady places where one might go to be peaceful. It was a color that pleased her. She did not want to be readily pleased with any man while her hip throbbed and her carefully laid plans were laid waste in a moment of clumsiness.

"Do you require smelling salts?" His voice was slick as satinwood and as deep as the shady pools of those eyes. It irritated her. One could not read much through such a polished veneer. Did he jest? Did he dare to make fun of her humiliating predicament? She would pluck the pretty blue eyes out if that was this dandy's game. The endangered orbs, so long and sooty-lashed as to make any female alive positively green with envy, sparkled in a very knowing manner. He was trying valiantly to keep from laughing. There was no misreading the twitch of his lips. How very like a man, she thought. Any one of her brothers would have been slapping his thigh and shouting with laughter by now. This gentleman might be more restrained, but his thoughts ran along the same lines. He found her ridiculous.

"And yet, are you not, in this moment, exactly that?" a part of herself asked. Her predicament was certainly ridiculous. For a moment, her own mouth was in danger of smiling, but she would not openly acknowledge the humor of her situation. Pride stood in her way. She would not be intimidated by this peacock! She challenged his faint smile with a fiercely proud glare and the firm jut of her jaw, searching the depths of his gill-flower-blue eyes. Something inexplicable she saw there unarmed her. For reasons incomprehensible, the peacock liked her. There was no other explanation for the warmth directed her way, unless perhaps he liked all females and was in the habit of smiling at them deep within his eyes.

Aurora lowered her chin, more uneasy with admiration than she might have been with contempt. It was baffling, that this polished prig should find something to admire in a female who danced so poorly as to land in a heap on the floor at his glossy feet. What a picture of fun she must have been, sprawled on her back in the middle of a very formal room, beneath the very gentleman she hoped most to impress. Perhaps she was no more than an object of amusement to this fellow. She bit down on her lower lip. She must not smile. Falling on her fanny in public was not funny! It was horribly humiliating. But, her mouth disagreed as much as the gentleman before her did.

His eyes dared her to laugh. He was most definitely amused.

She lifted her chin, determined to take as much amusement in the peacock as he did in her. "I am quite all right. Really!" Unable to suppress a sudden chuckle, she ducked her head. "How very absurd this is. I do apologize for the disruption."

"Not at all." The stranger's voice was musical in its gliding tones, as if his words waltzed. "Would you care to dance, Miss Ramsay?" He gave a courtly bow and held out his immaculately gloved hand.

She was smoothing her gown when he asked, rearranging the damnable tucker that had come rather dramatically untucked. Her head came up with a snap. "Would I care to dance?" Her eyes narrowed. Had she read him wrong? Was there malice in this prancing peacock after all?

"Have you not just seen me crash to the floor in that very pursuit? Whatever gave you the notion I might *care* to dance?"

"Were you dancing?" he asked in so smoothly satirical a manner that she longed first to laugh, and then to slap him. How dare he stand waiting for an answer to such an insulting question, a faint smile touching both lips and eyes? Lord Walsh did not so humiliate her. He was returned to the dance floor with his partner. Her own former partner, Mr. Potter, had vanished. Her gaze raked over the assembled company. She was no longer an object of interest to anyone other than this stranger.

She addressed the smiling cockscomb with haughty condescension that had more to do with her own bruised pride than any real contempt she felt. "I never dance, sir, with a gentleman to whom I have not been properly introduced."

One of the stranger's narrow black brows rose theatrically. "I see." He made no effort whatsoever to suppress the grin that swept his mouth upward and dug an engaging dimple in his clean-shaven cheek. "We can remedy that. Will you wait here a moment?"

He asked her even as he began to slide sideways through the crowd which revolved around them. He was smiling a contained but confident smile, as though convinced she must agree.

"I shall be no more than a minute."

She did not agree, did not so much as nod, for she had

not truly made her mind up as to whether she was at all inclined to wait. No more than a heartbeat passed, and him
swallowed up in the crowd, when Aurora decided she had
no real desire to wait for any man after the embarrassment
she had just suffered, unless it be Lord Walsh, and he had
not lingered to offer her such a choice. She turned and
began to press her way toward the door, only to come face-
to-face with the very fellow she evaded, on the arm of their
host. For an instant his eyes lit up, as if this smooth, dark-
haired dandy had unfathomable reason to be glad he saw
her again.

"Ah, here she is." Tom Coke patted her shoulder, murmured something appropriate about her unfortunate fall and
graciously gave them formal introduction. She listened with
only half an ear. The dandy, whose name it seemed, was
Miles Fletcher, regarded her with fading joy throughout the
exchange of names. His lively blue eyes, as he briefly took
her hand, seemed overshadowed by disappointment.

Their host quit them once his introductory task was fulfilled, other guests demanding his attention. Aurora
watched him go. She could not look Fletcher in the eye.

"Running away from me, were you?" The young man's
voice was not so smooth as usual. He cleared his throat.
"What a pity. I hoped . . ." He fell silent.

She looked up at him. The charm of his smile was paled
almost to a whisper. He was strangely endearing, even
when he did not smile.

"Hoped what?" she prodded irritably. She was angry
with herself. It had been rude in her to try to lose this harm-
less, cheerful cockscomb in the crowd, as rude as any jesting remark he had made in reference to her dancing.

He shrugged and spread his immaculately gloved hands.
"I hoped we might be friends, Miss Ramsay." He executed
another formal bow. "I am not so pushing as to insist."

She was surprised that he would turn his back on her
and walk away—surprised and frustrated. A growing desire to give chase troubled her. "*Let him go,*" one part of
her urged. "*Explain,*" another voice within her head insisted. She ought to explain. She took two steps toward

that end, and stopped. How did one explain behavior one did not understand? She could not explain her rudeness, could not explain that plans had been made to impress Lord Walsh, painstaking plans, plans gone ridiculously awry, and that it was the failure of those plans that she was angry and impatient with—not him. He might have asked her if she wanted a drink of water as easily as he had asked her to dance. She would have snapped his head off either way. There were those who blamed her short-temperedness on the color of her hair. Aurora had no patience for shirking responsibility. She held herself accountable—the unruly, bad-tempered, tantrum-throwing child part of her that she had never learned to wholly silence.

She set out after Miles Fletcher. She need not explain herself, or her plans to win Walsh, but she must apologize.

Too long had she stood debating the issue. Miles Fletcher stopped to talk with none other than Lord Walsh and the delicate, dark-haired, bone-china female he had been dancing with when she had toppled him to the floor. Lord help her! He knew Walsh! They greeted one another with casual familiarity. She had missed a golden opportunity in accepting Miles Fletcher's invitation to dance. He might have eventually introduced her to Walsh. As it was, he took up the willing hand of the pale-complected beauty Walsh had been parading around the floor and coaxed her to dance with little more than a smile. Dash it all! He looked strangely elegant from across the room in his absurdly fashionable attire. The young woman showed to advantage on Miles Fletcher's arm.

Aurora liked to be right. She wanted to be right in her refusal of Mr. Fletcher's offer of a dance. Perhaps he was clumsy, she reasoned, no more than a prancing, foppish fool, no more graceful than the dreadful Mr. Potter.

But, Aurora had been wrong about every other aspect of the evening. It did not surprise her that she had been wrong in this respect as well.

The music was a waltz. Expecting the worst, Aurora was more than a little jealous to watch Mr. Fletcher and his partner glide across the floor like swans upon the still surface of a lake, his sleek, dark head bent to the young woman's equally dark curls. She smiled in response to his remark. Step, step, glide. The man was a master. There were none who could compare to the fluid, swimming sweep of his movements, none who seemed so much at ease in this new and daring dance step. He looked, in his stark black and white, as elegant and as polished as his words had been.

What a fool she was! Aurora regretted her entire exchange with Miles Fletcher and wondered what it would have been like to count him her admirer. Her future might have been changed had she said yes instead of no to the offer of a young man's arm. Frustrated, Aurora turned her back on the room, wondering if she would have a second chance to prove herself with either Fletcher or Walsh.

"Who is she?" Grace asked of Miles as soon as he led her away from Walsh.

"Who?" Miles replied with mock ignorance. He knew exactly who she meant—the young woman he could not drive from mind or memory—the female who drew him even as she drove him away—whose future he meant to affect. *L'Amazon* stood staring at him, as he and his sister joined the set.

Grace was not about to drop the subject. "You know. The sublimely foolish, falling-down girl with the dreadful dress who blessed your toes by refusing to dance with you."

"Oh, *that* girl." Miles smiled. "Do you not recognize my sublime goddess of this afternoon?"

Grace's eyes widened. "That is never the same creature!"

"Oh, but it is."

"Gad! Whatever was she thinking to pull all of that glorious hair away from her face?"

Miles smiled a tight little smile. "Perhaps she felt her hair too forward for polite company."

Grace laughed. "Fling my words back into my face. Go

ahead. I deserved that. Now, tell me who she is. I am all curiosity and contrition."

"Beyond that she is called Aurora Ramsay, I know very little."

"Not Rakehell's sister?" She laughed. "And what is it they call the other brother? 'Rogering' Ramsay?"

"Watch your tongue, my dear. And your manners. You have neglected to mention 'Rash,' 'Rip,' and 'Rue' Ramsay, also of the same family."

"Have I? What a bother to be the only girl among five such brothers! It's no wonder the poor thing hasn't a clue about her appearance. Tell me, do they all have red hair? It is such a passionate color to carry about on one's head."

"I'm told they do. You may see for yourself as to Rupert Ramsay's passionate head. He is here with his sister."

"Here? Where? Point him out. I must dance with him."

"I do not think, my dear, that even your considerable charms can convince Rupert Ramsay to waltz with you."

"You underestimate me, Miles, unless of course the fellow does not fancy females."

"On that account I am not fully informed, but I have it on good authority that he is not at all fond of dancing. Our host says he frequents the library more often than the ballroom."

"What? A fortnight in the country with a houseful of fascinating company and he closets himself away in the library? What a curious family these Ramsays would seem to be. I am intent on meeting both of them. Perhaps a book before bedtime is in order. Lord Walsh would never dream of looking for me in the library."

"Saucy minx." Miles clucked his tongue. His sister was an incorrigible flirt. "Ramsay had best beware his heart."

"His heart?" She tipped her head to look at him through her lashes with feigned innocence. "Whatever do you mean?"

"You know precisely what I mean," he said. "Men are forever losing their hearts to you, Grace, but I have yet to see yours so much as touched by a fellow."

She tapped her fan reprovingly against his shoulder.

"Are you not immensely relieved it is so, my dear? We are involved in a fortnight where women are outnumbered in attendance by men, four to one. You would be forced to pull me out of no end of scrapes if I easily lost my heart."

Chapter Four

Aurora leaned into the surge of the loping gelding. It had rained in the night. The earth, the greenery, the very sky smelled fresh this morning. Aurora felt as if she might begin anew. When she had a horse beneath her, she could forget the disaster of the evening before. She could forget all of her troubles. On horseback, Aurora was as graceful and sure, as fluid in her movements as Miles Fletcher was on the dance floor. *L'Amazon*, many called her, and she found nothing to object to in the title. The French referred to their serious female equestrians as such. In Greek mythology, the Amazons were a race of female warriors. On horseback she was just that, a warrior—unbeatable, unstoppable, a creature to contend with, as though the power and spirit of the horse joined hers. When she mounted, they became one, a graceful, driven, intelligent entity.

Her knee tucked around the pommel, her legs and hips flowing with the pounding rhythm of the loping animal, she fought wind and gravity and the unevenness of the ground. She fought and won. The trees tried to unseat her without success. Obstacles required surmounting. She and the gelding soared over all of it—walls, gates and hedges—without faltering. For a brief moment, on horseback, as *L'Amazon*, she could outrun the embarrassment of falling clumsily onto her backside in the middle of a roomful of her peers, outrun the awful memory of crashing into Lord Walsh.

There was not much chance of her success in that arena, the way things stood. Walsh had risen from the floor, raked his hair out of his eyes and looked down the length of his distinctly Roman nose at her as though she were an inconvenience one quickly brushed aside.

God, what a painful moment! She nudged her horse to a faster pace, lost in the thunder of hoofbeats, reveling—no, renewing—herself in the energy it took to ride fast and hard. She ignored the muffled beat of hoofs behind her, dismissing a muffled shout. She looked back only when the horse that followed began to close the distance between them. A tall man on a sorrel she did not recognize seemed intent on catching up to her. Well, if it was a race the fellow wanted, she would oblige him. Her fleet, long-legged roan could outrun the best of horses, and she was in need of a flat out gallop. She touched heel to the gelding. They soared over the ground like a low-flying bird. The gentleman on the sorrel, she could tell he was a gentleman by the gruff eloquence of his curses, followed the gelding like a shadow.

He did in fact catch up to her! The sorrel pulled dangerously close to the roan. *Damn!* A hand grabbed at her reins.

"Hands off!" she cried, cracking her quirt across the outstretched knuckles as she drew the gelding to a trot and then a walk. "Whatever do you mean, grabbing at my bridle in such a fashion?" She twisted in the saddle as she fumed, leather creaking beneath her hip, the roan nervously tossing its head. "Do you mean to unseat me, or merely to ruin the horse's mouth?"

It was, *Lord help her,* Lord Walsh who rode the sorrel! His face was crimson. A vein pumped in his temple. His dark brown eyes sparkled with restrained emotion.

"Unseat you? I thought the damnable beast had taken the bit and run away with you! I thought you were sure to land on your backside in the mud." She could not help remembering how she had landed on the same part of her anatomy the night before on the polished wood floor. There was something in the way he icily examined her down the length of his patrician nose that gave her the impression he remembered, too. "I meant to rescue you," he fumed, wrenching off his glove to examine the angry red stripe across his knuckles.

Aurora's chin went up. "I did not require rescuing, thank you. The only moment I was in any danger whatsoever was when you barreled up beside me and tried to ham-fistedly twist the bridle out of my hands."

Lord Walsh glared coldly at her. He was a handsome man when his ire was up, a man of stature and wealth who was accustomed to nothing but respect.

"You may be sure I shall not ride to your rescue again, Miss Ramsay," he said curtly. "I bid you good day." With a sharp nod, he kicked his horse into a trot and rode away without a backward glance.

With a great sigh, Aurora slid from her saddle to walk the roan, cooling him. As they traversed the lane, she beat on the skirt of her riding habit with the same quirt with which she had lashed out at Lord Walsh's hand. "Damn your tongue, Aurora Ramsay!" she hissed.

Whop! Whop! The quirt slapped against the heavy layers of her skirt. "When will you learn to be still? Now the gentleman will never have any desire to further your acquaintance much less propose marriage." She cursed under her breath and kicked a shower of gravel from the lane into the hedge that bordered the road.

"Ow!" came a voice from the other side. "Was that entirely necessary?"

"Who in blazes is there?" Aurora insisted stridently. "Come, skulker, show yourself."

The top of a fashionably clipped head rose above the hedgerow that lined the riding lane she and Lord Walsh had galloped along. It was shining hair, dark and sleek, every lock pomaded in place, so that it feathered back like glossy blackbird wings from either side of a pale, deep forehead. Dark brows, bird's wings again, arched above a pair of amused blue eyes.

Miles Fletcher! The peacock had been there all along!

"I do beg your pardon," he said glibly. "It is Miles Fletcher. Do you perhaps remember refusing to dance with me last night?"

Did she remember him? *Whop! Whop!* Aurora whacked at her skirt. Two days in a row this man had watched her make a fool of herself with Lord Walsh. Two episodes in which she became a source of amusement for a pair of twinkling blue eyes.

Fate was against her.

"How long have you been skulking behind the hedgerow, Mr. Fletcher?" she snapped.

"Skulking?" came the smooth voice again, as amused as the look he bent on her. "I was no such thing. I have been doing something quite productive."

Miles Fletcher was not a peacock at all she decided. He was a mouse, or a vole who stood peering at her over the top of the hedgerow. No, not a vole, his eyes were too large and bright, too blue. His features were too sharply chiseled. Aurora believed all men were animals, it was just a matter of defining which species. Her brothers were animals. She had identified them, every one. Last night she had determined Fletcher to be a peacock. Today she was not so sure. Neither was he a mouse.

Fletcher looked decidedly less mouselike as he leapt over the stile that was placed for the express purpose of crossing the hedge and sat himself down on the top step to wipe the tips of his glossy boots with a lawn handkerchief. He had an agile, sinuousness to his movements, a cleverness about his expression that reminded her more of a ferret or a weasel.

This weasel admired her. She could tell it was true by the amused warmth in his gaze. It was freshly irritating that a gentleman whom she had no desire to attract should like her, no matter the reasons, while the one she wanted to admire her, galloped off in a cloud of dust. Even more confounding, Aurora found herself amused by this weasel, Miles Fletcher. As she had no desire to be amused, she grew even more crotchety.

"Pray tell me what you consider productive, Mr. Fletcher," she said sardonically, sure his productivity amounted to nothing more serious than managing to cross a meadow without ruining the shine on his boots, which were as glossy now as ever his pumps had been in the ballroom the night before.

He bowed gracefully from his perch. He seemed incapable of riling, though all of her exchanges with him bordered on rudeness. His eyes sparkled with suppressed mirth, but he was not at all inclined to allow her to draw him into a quarrel, she could see. That was unusual. She was used to men whose first reaction to the prod of her knifing wit was a competitive desire to best her in verbal sparring. There was power that came with besting an angry man's fuddled wits, and none at all in teasing this clever, unflappable fellow. That he did not fall into a squabble, as she had anticipated, did nothing to improve her mood. She was in need of a row.

His voice was level, vaguely musical in its amusement—almost silken in its smoothness. Aurora felt like a dry-voiced crow in the company of such a voice. "I have been walking about the fields with Ben, a farm laborer, who has been explaining to me how the virtually useless soil here at Holkham has been vastly improved through the use of marl and manure and compost."

"Marl and manure?" She looked at him as though he had sprouted horns. This wasp-waisted exquisite—with walking stick, quizzing glass, and gleaming boots, found something to interest him in marl and manure?

"And what is it intrigues you about something so mundane, Mr. Fletcher?" She tapped the toes of her dusty boots with her quirt.

Miles Fletcher cocked his head like a bird from his perch, examining her expression until she was made nervous by the intensity of his gaze. "I am curious," he said.

"About manure?" she scoffed.

He regarded her with an irritating half-smile, leaning forward, as if to look deep within her soul. So intense was his gaze, she felt compelled to take a step back.

"I am curious about many things, Miss Aurora Ramsay. I am, for instance, curious to know why you so thoroughly distance yourself from any man you so much as come into contact with." Soft and smooth and cool as a brook the devastating words floated around her. "Do you snipe at us, perhaps, in the misguided belief that we would in some way injure you? Do you take a bite out of us before we can sink teeth in your own tender flesh?"

Her mouth fell open.

She would have hated him had he smiled. She would have snapped some cutting remark had he tried to make light of his comment. He did not smile. In fact, his expression was rather more serious than usual, perhaps even a little worried—and the worry was for her. "We would not all eat you, you know, and we do not all conform to your low opinion of us."

She swallowed hard. This man never failed to confuse her. Just when she thought she had some understanding of him, he turned her opinion on its ear. "You *are* curious," she said tersely.

He grinned. It was an engaging grin. "As are you, else you would not be wondering over my interest in marl and manure and land cultivation."

"All right, I am curious," she admitted, feeling bested by this dandy's silver tongue. "You are clearly no farmer. Why should you be interested in marl and manure?"

He watched her with a careful expression from his perch atop the stile, as if he knew, in some part, her thinking. "I have expectations of coming into a patch of land." He sounded as though he found the concept difficult to believe. "I would know how to go about caring for it when I do."

"I see," she said tersely. It seemed unfair to her, that this frippery fellow, who by his own admission had not the vaguest notion how to go about managing it, should have land coming to him. After all, she had none to call her own and surely no one was more deserving than she. She knew all there was to know about managing an estate, and on a pittance at that. Fate was cruel. Yet she would not succumb to it. She meant to marry Walsh. Through marriage she would acquire land—for herself while she lived and for her children when she had ceased caring about earthly matters.

"Would you see what else I have learned today?"

Miles Fletcher's question startled her, for he jumped down off the stile as he spoke, landing lightly in the lane beside her. The roan threw up its head in alarm. Aurora was a trifle alarmed herself. The weasel stood, she thought, too close to her. And yet, she would not back away from him again, not after his provoking remark with regard to distancing herself from men.

"Easy, easy," she crooned to the gelding and then to Miles she said, "We must walk. The horse needs cooling."

"You have a way with horses." He fell into step beside her. "Have you any notion, Miss Aurora Ramsay, how truly magnificent you look on a horse at full gallop?"

The compliment startled her. Aurora was unused to compliments. Why did he persist in them? Why did he take her hand and tuck it in the crook of his arm? Did he think she enjoyed fawning and praise? Did he think he might seduce her?

"You were telling me what else you learned today." She skirted his flattery as a nervous cat skirts a hound.

"Oh, yes!" His face lit up with pleasure. He let go his hold on her to reach into his coat pocket. "I was behind this hedgerow searching out a bit of ribbongrass, so that I might finish the making of this."

He pressed into her palm a love knot, an intricately woven knot made out of cornstalks. Twisted into a double loop, it vaguely resembled a heart.

She blinked when she realized what it was and stopped so abruptly the roan almost trod on her heels. Angry color bloomed in her cheeks.

"Do you know what it is you give me?" she demanded.

"As a matter of fact, I do." He leaned happily over his handiwork, which she held dangling from her palm like a dead rat. "I must admit I have only learned such a pretty thing existed this very afternoon, but it is called a countryman's favor and is woven quite cleverly out of cornstalks. I had to try the thing several times before I managed the knack of it. What do you think of my first completely finished attempt?"

"I think you very rude."

"Rude?"

"Yes, rude, that you would knowingly insult a perfect stranger to you with such nonsense."

"Insult you?" He laughed, his eyes crinkling up in a most appealing fashion. "Nothing could be further from my purpose. I wished to extend an offering of potential friendship. There is a proposal I would make to you—"

She glared at him, indignant. "A proposal? We have only just been introduced, yet you dare to come to me with such a suggestion!" She waved the love knot at him. The roan leaned in over her shoulder with the idea of eating the thing, its head moving back and forth following her movements. She would have allowed the horse to have it, too, had Mr. Fletcher not snatched his creation back from her. "Do not think you can seduce me with your smooth ways and countryman's favors, sir! My brothers may be wild as spring colts, but just because my name is Ramsay, you've no right to assume I am lacking in scruples. A proposal indeed! I am no foolish country lass, ready and willing to engage in a lascivious liaison behind the nearest haystack for no more than a cornstalk love knot."

His blue-eyed gaze fastened on her with fascination. "A love knot?" He blinked and smiled at her in such way as to make it clear to Aurora that the name was a revelation to him. "My dear lady. As appealing a picture as you would paint, a haystack is not at all what I had in mind."

"It is not?" Her heart sank into her boots as she tugged on the roan's bridle and set off at a brisk walk. Lord above! Must she persist in making a fool out of herself before this man? She shot a rueful glance at him.

He was smiling, not the tight, contained little smile she was used to seeing on his lips, but a thoroughly engaged grin that spoke of laughter lurking just beneath its surface.

"I believe haystacks are far more attractive in theory than

in practice. Surely such a bower leaves one both untidy and scratching?" He paused, as if he discussed nothing more provocative than the nuisance of gnats.

"I would not know," she said stiffly.

He nodded. "I suppose the only way to find out would be to test the idea with someone whose acquaintance one does not mind furthering."

"Someone like you, perhaps?" she snapped derisively.

His eyes widened in mock dismay. "You flatter me, Miss Ramsay. I was sure another gentleman's name would pop instantly to mind."

Her gaze slid suddenly down, as though the sheen of his boots was infinitely more interesting than his face. It was a small thing really, her reaction, but Miles was accustomed to reading small gestures—little bits of the language of the body. He had learned to read their significance in negotiating the prices of artifacts and artwork. Bits and pieces of antiquity were hard to place an absolute value on. He had learned to read the signs of agreement or withdrawal. He made a living—a good living—negotiating the ownership of lovely fragments from the past, reading movements such as the one she had just made.

"What has that to do with you?" She lifted her head, her willow green gaze fired with resentment.

Her anger convinced him he was not mistaken. She was interested in furthering Walsh's acquaintance. It had been Walsh she was staring at the first day he saw her, not him. A blow to his pride, but in the earl lay the fulfillment of his promise to Uncle Lester, a quick, neat resolution. Miss Ramsay's future would not be ruined completely by her brother's bad luck. Miles was not altogether happy. His goddess sublime was taken with Walsh before he had a chance to convince her he was much the better man. Mentally shrugging aside his disappointment, Miles proceeded cautiously, keenly observing her every reaction.

"You hope, perhaps, to elicit an offer of marriage from him?"

She flinched. He read the movement without surprise. She answered him, not with words, but with the turn of her head, the tilt of her mouth, the set of her chin. Deep within the willow-green eyes that glared so fiercely, the truth spoke to him as clearly as any voice.

For a moment Miles felt the same tugging regret he had felt the day before when this fiery young woman had so clearly rebuffed his efforts to dance with her. He was baffled then. He was baffled now. What did she see in Lord Walsh that should have this marvelous creature chasing after him? He did not press the matter. She was seeking a proposal from Walsh. He wondered if Gracie would be pleased or peeved by such a turn of events.

"What business is any of this to you?" She was alarmed, perhaps fearful that he might use such knowledge against her, and indeed it was sensitive information he now held. She was like tinder, he thought, dry and brittle and ready to ignite. Perhaps she needed Walsh's money. If so, she might be amenable to a bargain of sorts.

Fingering the precisely braided straw of the love knot he still turned in his hands, he chose his words carefully. "Just as you have—perhaps—come to find a husband, I am here with a number of specific goals in mind. One is that I wish to learn how to go about managing my eventual windfall of acreage."

"What has either to do with the other?" She crossed her arms over her breasts, wholly resistant to his idea before it was even voiced.

He smiled ruefully. "I think we might be in a way to assist one another in reaching those goals. You see, we would each of us appear to have mastered knowledge in which the other needs schooling."

That got her attention! She relinquished her closed posture and reached back to stroke the nose of the roan.

"Go on," she said warily.

Miles could not refuse the question in those pale, willow-green eyes any more than he could resist the idea that the paths of their lives had been destined to cross. Though he found something inherently self-defeating in the arrangement he was about to make, he stepped a little closer to the goddess whose affections he had meant to win for his own sake—with every intention of instructing her in the ways of winning the affections of another.

"My proposal," he went on, "is that I shall teach you the social graces by which you might attract any man of your choosing: the proper walk, talk, gestures, how to dance and flatter and flutter a fan, even how to dress . . . if you will only school me in the arts of which you are clearly my master: riding, agriculture, animal husbandry, archery."

A gleam flickered in her eyes, as if a wind had touched the willow green, turning the leaf in the sun. "You are in earnest?"

"Absolutely." How could she think him otherwise?

"Then I agree." Aurora Ramsay surprised him by holding out her hand to him, as if to seal their bargain with a clasping of palms. "Shall we proceed?"

Aurora was surprised. The arrangement Miles Fletcher suggested was not at all what she had expected. His proposal meant more than he could possibly know and she had no more expected it of him than she had expected he might harness the sun and ride away with her. He held out a lifeline to her as easily as she held out her hand to him.

He took it. Aurora was struck by the odd sensation that their fingers met with the same intimate compatibility she experienced in sliding into the contours of a saddle. There was something insinuating in the manner of Miles Fletcher's hand on hers when he bent to kiss her knuckles, something absorbing in the touch of his lips to her glove. There was a sense of comfort, of rightness, a feeling that with this man the ride would be interesting but not fraught with insurmountable difficulties. Quite irrationally, she did not want him to let go of her. She felt disappointed, one might almost say abandoned, when he relinquished his hold on her.

It was odd. She had been sure she saw some flicker of interest in the sparkling gaze of this polished, prattling popinjay the night he asked her to dance. His proposal to help her win Walsh was so diametrically opposed to her initial interpretation of his intentions that she watched him carefully. Had she completely misread the depth of his interest?

"How shall we begin?" he asked, smoothly businesslike.

She found that it did not really matter to her how they began, only that they should.

Chapter Five

They began straightaway, on familiar territory, with talk of horses and cattle, sheep and pigs, before moving on to a discussion of crop rotation that lasted all the way back to the Hall and engrossed them until dinner was announced. Aurora changed clothes and joined Miles Fletcher in the dining room. He made a polite point of sitting next to her, that he might drop a discreet word or two in her ear about table manners and the topics of light conversation whirling around them that had nothing at all to do with agriculture or animals.

Normally, Aurora would have been lost amid talk of art, music, poetry, and politics, but with Fletcher at her elbow, she began to feel quite comfortable at the table. The conversation always returned to matters of land and animal management in the end, and in these things she spoke with confidence and aplomb. She was pleased to be introduced to a number of guests whose names and titles she was familiar with, but whose company she had formerly been denied because they numbered not among her brothers' acquaintances.

Miles Fletcher appeared to be known to everybody.

"He brought me the most remarkable set of Roman bronzes from Italy," a dapper old gent whispered in her ear.

"No one has a better eye for the value of an oil painting," hinted another.

If she should ever need a rare bit of fabric, or perfume, tapestries or rugs, if she meant to collect snuff boxes or Oriental vases, bronzes or marble, she was assured that Fletcher was the man to consult. He had transported many a delight from other countries. Women especially regarded him with favor, and on Aurora they looked with eyebrows raised, as if her right to sit beside their favorite was questionable.

In the light of so much favorable opinion, Aurora's respect for Miles Fletcher grew by leaps and bounds. So agreeable did she eventually find his company, that she happily settled on plans to meet with him on the following morning, that she might teach him archery. She had, in short, begun to think Miles Fletcher the complete gentleman and just the fellow to teach her what she needed to know in order to charm Lord Walsh, when it became painfully obvious that Fletcher was distracted by yet another female who meant to catch his eye. He did in fact exchange what she could only describe as speaking glances with the dark, swanlike creature he had danced with the night before.

Aurora knew she had no legitimate complaint against such flirtation. She was herself distracted by Lord Walsh. But it was lowering to be abandoned when the fragile, pale-complected, dark-haired beauty at the far end of the table crooked her finger at Miles with an endearing smile.

"Please excuse me. There is someone I must speak to." Fletcher was all politeness. "It will only take a minute."

Even such a mannerly parting was deflating. The dark beauty was well-placed at the table. With Lord Walsh on the one hand and an older gent with stars in his eyes on the other, why must she lure away Miles Fletcher as well?

The swan raised her porcelain perfect cheek for a kiss when Fletcher reached her side. In so doing, she turned her head in Aurora's direction. An enigmatic smile touched her bow-shaped mouth and Aurora could see by the surreptitious glances in her direction, that she was the topic of conversation when the young woman whispered in Fletcher's ready ear.

His gaze strayed her way as well.

To remain the subject of gossip was too insulting to bear! Rather than sit meekly wondering what was said about her, Aurora deserted the table.

*   *   *

"How goes it with your Amazon, little brother?" Grace whispered when Miles bent to salute her cheek. "I expect an introduction before the evening's out. She is a taking thing, though something must be done about her clothes, surely! Your goddess sublime is quite disguised in such an outfit. Gracious, Miles, wherever is she running off to?"

Aurora's place at table was now vacant. Her back was retreating briskly through the door that led into the hallway.

"I've no idea," he said.

Aurora turned her back on a table still laden with half-emptied plates, turning her nose up at the cloying odor of an overabundance of rich foods and the mélange of too many overpowering perfumes. She plunged through the doors that led outside to drink in the cool, damply fresh smell of the grass-lined channel. She walked in the moonlight beside the water, wondering why it should matter to her in the least that Miles Fletcher left her side at the slightest beckoning of another woman. He was not bound to her in any way. Her object was Lord Walsh, not Miles Fletcher. Miles knew she was pursuing Walsh. It should not matter to her in the least whether or not he cared for the dark-haired tabby at the other end of the table. In fact, if the tabby's attentions were diverted from Walsh, she might have more opportunity to win his affections. Yet, if a fellow who fawned over her was so easily distracted from her charms, how could she hope to attach the lasting affections of a gentleman such as Walsh?

The lonely complaint of a grebe carried eerily from the far side of the channel. The acrid tang of tobacco smoke drifted on the breeze.

Aurora shivered and turned from the water toward the sound of footsteps. The dark silhouette of a gentleman descended the steps from the hall. A cigar glowed between his lips. Lord Walsh!

He had spotted her. She would have had to turn in her tracks to avoid facing him. Aurora had never been one to shrink from confrontation. Walsh did not look particularly pleased to see her, but she approached him nonetheless, back straight, chin high.

"Lord Walsh."

He blew a pungent cloud of tobacco smoke and said coolly. "Ah! The very dangerous Miss Ramsay, is it not? I suppose you mean to encourage me not to befoul the air in a lady's presence by tossing me bodily into the channel? No need. I willingly put the thing out."

He was on the verge of flicking his cigar into the moonlit water when she stopped him with "No. Nothing of the kind. I do not mean to discommode you, nor will I bend your ear with mindless commonplaces. I am sure you came here to enjoy your smoke in solitude. I wish only to call a truce between the two of us, and to assure you I regret each of our past encounters. I regret crashing to the floor in the ballroom, and I regret having struck your hand this morning."

He was silent a moment, his expression hard to read behind a cloud of his own making. "A truce it is then." He studied the line of ash on the end of his cigar. "I would not have any young lady regret her encounters with me and I daresay it would be a mistake to continue sparring with *L'Amazon.*"

She shrugged and would have moved past him and up the steps to the hall had he not stopped her, saying stiffly, "I am sorry to have made a grab for your horse. I was unaware, this morning, of your reputation——"

She turned abruptly to face him, ready to do battle. Reputation indeed!

He exhaled smoke, directing it at the moon. "For riding," he went on coolly. "I have since been informed by more than one credible source that you and your horses are not to be trifled with ."

She was amazed. He had been asking people about her!

He went on distantly, his voice, his look, the cloud of smoke between them, keeping her at arm's length, "I am wholly unaccustomed to independent females who ride neck or nothing." His voice held a grudging respect.

She chuckled, for the first time at ease in his presence. "That's quite all right," she said, maintaining their distant posture. "I am equally unaccustomed to anyone catching up to me. Good night, my lord."

A startled bark of laughter, half choked on cigar smoke, followed her up the steps. For the first time since she had literally run into him on the dance floor, Aurora thought with some satisfaction that she might have a chance with Lord Walsh yet.

Miles stood at the window watching with consternation his goddess sublime talking to Walsh in the darkness at the bottom of the steps that led away from the hall and into Coke's pleasure garden beside the channel. It was quite unnatural in him, unmannerly in fact, to stare at people from behind cover of window draperies, but he wondered what these two might be saying. He hoped Aurora did not mean to disappear into the garden with Walsh. That would not do at this stage. Walsh must not consider Miss Ramsay too forward a female. How strange that he should feel a pang of regret when Walsh managed to make her laugh, and she him. It was this young woman's objective to attract the earl. He knew that. He had offered to help her in the pursuit, yet he really had hoped to use his considerable charm to turn her head his way before Walsh could be brought round. Miles backed away from the window. Perhaps it was best this way. Easier.

Had he continued to observe, Miles would have seen Aurora break away from Walsh and head up the steps toward him while Walsh, laughing at something she had said, pressed on in the opposite direction. But Miles did not see. Gracie interfered, arriving breathlessly at his side with a question, her gaze darting nervously from side to side.

"You have not seen Walsh have you?"

"Outside smoking," he informed her.

"Marvelous!" She relaxed. "I have yet to meet the infamous Rupert Ramsay who hides in the library and I mean to beard the bookworm in his den, but I do not want dear Walsh trailing after me, spoiling my—"

"Your what?" Miles raised his brows.

She chuckled shamelessly, her cheeks dimpling. "My

search for a bedtime story. You will hold your tongue as to my whereabouts?"

"If you wish," Miles agreed, his attention diverted as Aurora Ramsay, alone, passed within a few feet of them, with nary a glance in his direction. Anxiously he tracked her progress as she crossed to the stairs. She did not seem at all aware of his presence. That irked him. He knew her to be incredibly sensitive to Walsh's every move. He would have been greatly relieved had he known Aurora was making a concerted effort not to look his way for no other reason than that he stood talking to Grace, with whom she supposed him to be infatuated.

When Gracie headed in the direction of the library, Miles pushed through a press of guests in pursuit of Aurora. Too late. She had already vanished up the stairs.

As he stood considering the idea of charging up the treads after her, he was astonished to observe a gentleman with red hair pulling himself up from a card table in one of the drawing rooms with the aid of a crutch. Rue Ramsay! It could be no other. The young man had a peg leg.

"Oh, dear. Gracie will be in a pet," he murmured.

Crossing to the card table, he made a point of introducing himself, holding his hand out to Aurora Ramsay's brother with as much curiosity as Grace had approached the library. "You are Mr. Ramsay, are you not?"

Rue Ramsay shook a lock of deep auburn hair from eyes that were not green, as Miles had expected, but blue. He acknowledged Miles's introduction in a desultory fashion, as though he suspected some sort of unwanted charity in the exchange of names.

"Are you friend to one of my brothers?" His tone was frosty. He would not be impressed with such a connection.

Miles disabused him of the notion. "I have never had the pleasure of meeting any sibling other than your sister. She impressed me with her riding skills today."

Rue brightened. There was a likeness in the movements of his mouth to those of his sister. "She's at her best on a horse," he agreed. "Few men can match her. Comes from competing with so many rough-riding brothers I suppose."

With the competence of a man grown familiar, if not yet comfortable with his limitations, Ramsay pegged his way to the door and headed in the direction of the library.

Miles followed, and when Aurora's brother had some trouble maneuvering, he resisted the temptation to assist. Ramsay, a former military officer, would not have appreciated the coddling. Instead, his voice never betraying the struggle that went on within, Miles carried on their conversation. "I understand competitive sisters completely. My own competes with me every opportunity fate allows on the subject of Greek and Roman architecture."

Ramsay laughed. Conversing amiably, they were within several paces of the door to the library when Walsh intercepted them. He looked even more ruddy and muscularly robust than usual, juxtaposed to Rupert. "Excuse me for interrupting," he said, "but where has your sister gotten herself off to, Fletcher?" Introductions made all the way around. Miles collected himself enough not to blurt out the truth that leapt so naturally to his tongue.

"Off to bed with a book I believe," he lied, his lips thinning as Grace chose that very moment to prove his lie by sticking her head out of the library door, which was immediately behind Walsh.

Walsh was oblivious to her appearance, but Miles was sure Rupert could not help but see Grace as her mouth dropped open and her head was swiftly ducked behind the library door again.

"I'm off to bed myself then." Walsh yawned. "Anyone care to ride with me at dawn?"

Miles was pleased to turn down such an offer. "Terribly sorry. Prior engagement. Your sister, Ramsay, has promised to school me in archery. Another time, perhaps, Walsh?"

Rupert shrugged. "I appreciate the invitation, my lord, but I am not the best company horseback."

"As you will." Walsh shrugged and pointed to Rupert's peg. "I've a friend in a similar situation. He has had a saddle specially fitted to his peg. Once he is thrown into the thing, he rides almost as well as ever."

"I must have the name of this saddlemaker, sir."

"Done," Walsh said, and with another yawn, headed toward his rooms.

Miles politely bade Rupert good night and wondered what story Gracie might have to tell come morning, when he glanced over his shoulder to observe Ramsay opening the door to the library, and maneuvering his crutch within.

Chapter Six

Aurora found Rupert where she expected to find him on the following morning—in the library.

The library was a golden place. Not golden in a way that spoke only of the guineas that had gone into its construction and the amassing of its numerous calf-bound, gold-leafed books and folios—this room was bathed in the color. It was a long, bright, high-ceilinged space, beautifully coffered—as was most of the Hall—with gold leaf and gilt. Carved doorjambs, windowframes and bookcases were delicately trimmed out in gold leaf as well. One wall boasted a golden, gray-veined, Sienna marble fireplace, in which crackled a fire that added just the right note of warmth to the room's gilt-edged comfort. Above the fireplace hung a particularly fine antique mosaic of a golden lion devouring a gold and black-spotted leopard.

Aurora knew she would find Rue ensconced in this glittering respite most hours of the day, scribbling away at the manuscript he allowed no one to examine. He was a most obliging brother in every other way she had to admit, to come with her all the way to Holkham as her escort, when he had not the slightest interest in sheep, their shearing, cattle or farming implements. He was, he told her, content to explore terrain of quite a different kind, in the gilt-edged pages of the books that the masters of Holkham had collected. He even stayed relatively current on the latest agricultural news by perusing the periodicals Thomas Coke subscribed to, without ever setting foot in field or barn. But, this morning Rupert was not engrossed in a book or scratching feverishly away with his pen. He was standing before one of the windows, leaning on his crutch and staring at the view.

Aurora got the feeling she interrupted a profound state of reflection, so intent was his concentration.

"Rupert?"

He started and in turning to look at her, swung his auburn forelock out of eyes the gray-blue color of Wedgewood. He would bewitch a female some day with those eyes. Aurora was sure of it. Despite his missing leg, Rupert was an engaging fellow.

"Oh, it's you," he said unnecessarily. Of course, it was she. Who else knew to seek him out, here, in Coke's private sanctuary?

Feeling far too green in this golden room, dressed as she was in her Bowman's colors, she plumped herself down on a comfortable gold damask sofa which faced the fireplace and the antique mosaic above it. Aurora found the lion devouring the leopard an intriguing choice of subject for the quiet comfort of a library. It added an edge of violence, of adventure, to the still peace of the place.

"I have come to tell you what I mean to do today."

It was strange she felt compelled to do so. Aurora was not in the habit of informing anyone of her whereabouts now that her mother and father were gone. Her brothers had never required it of her. But today she felt the need to tell Rupert of her intentions.

Rupert looked as baffled as she by this sudden accountability for her whereabouts. With a shrug, he returned his attention to the view. "Yes?"

Aurora gazed at him a moment, as if she gazed at a stranger. Rupert was not the most handsome of her brothers, but there had always been a contained steadiness, a physical self-possession, a level of unruffled intellectual strength about him that she found attractive. These admirable characteristics had served him well in the military. Perhaps too well. They had taken him to Wellington's battlefront at Vitoria and lost him a leg.

Rue had dealt quietly, almost unemotionally, with the loss of his limb. Reserved and studious to begin with, his introverted tendencies were magnified. As for his physical self-confidence, he got around well enough on his peg with a crutch to assist him. His staggered gait was not so distracting as to offend, but Rupert would never be graceful in what was left of his body. He was not yet comfortable with the looks that turned in his direction whenever he limped into a room. Crowds, noise making, and shows of high emotion were an anathema to him. He tucked himself, instead, into still, quiet corners, writing and reading, the lion in the library.

Aurora did not understand such a continuing contentedness with separation. She enjoyed crowds and grew desolate without human companionship in some form every day.

Not Rupert—not since the loss of his leg.

"I don't suppose you mean to sit placidly on the lawn doing watercolors," he drawled.

Aurora laughed. "Whatever gave you that idea?"

He shrugged, his eyes still transfixed by the view. "Some young ladies are content with such pastimes."

"Not my style, Rue, and well you know it." She returned her attention to the wildcats above the mantel. "No, it is just that I mean to spend a great deal of time with a gentleman I have become acquainted with, and I did not want you worrying that he meant to seduce me, or some such nonsense." What was it Miles Fletcher had said? She snapped at men before they had any opportunity to devour her?

Rue's peg creaked as he shifted into a more comfortable stance to look at her. "You are far more capable of defending yourself against rogues who would take advantage than I." His words gave uncanny echo to her thoughts. "Besides, this fellow hasn't a chance in Hades unless you've given up your mad notion to hook Walsh and his land. Who is this poor, misguided fool who wastes time wooing you?"

Aurora frowned at the openmouthed lion. Was she really so single-minded? Was there no one who could stray her course now that she had set out to capture Walsh's attention? She shook her head. "He is an amusing, dandified sort of fellow. Exquisite manners and an odd inclination to teach me the social niceties I have so long ignored. Who knows, he may even teach me watercolors. Miles Fletcher is his name."

"Fletcher?" Rupert perked up. "Yes, the fellow introduced himself to me last night. Mentioned archery. I have met his sister as well. They both seemed nice enough." Rupert was intent in his perusal of the view again. "Does anyone accompany you in these archery lessons, or have you come begging me to suffer that role?"

"No. Fletcher said his sister means to tag along." Aurora stood up from the sofa and crossed to the window. A young woman in an attractively beribboned straw bonnet was set up on the lawn with easel and palette, her head and hand moving in a painter's ballet as her brush dipped from palette to paper and back again. Oh, ho! So it was she who held Rupert's attention fastened to the view. Aurora wondered how long he had been standing at the window. The painter had turned her head. The fetching face beneath the shade of the bonnet brim was none other than the lovely coquette who with no more than a crook of her finger had Miles Fletcher bounding from his chair.

"Do you know Fletcher's sister?" Rue shifted his weight again. "She was in here yesterday, evading Walsh."

"Evading him?" Aurora had no idea Rue was referring to the young woman they observed through the window.

Rue laughed softly. "She said she was looking for a book, but I am certain she was hiding from Walsh, for she ducked behind the door when she saw him. I asked her what title she required, being familiar with the library. She said she had not a particular book in mind. Said she wished to be quiet for a few moments, away from the crush of people. Quiet she was." He sounded as if he might have enjoyed more noise from Miss Fletcher.

The painter on the lawn was packing up her paints.

Aurora directed a piercing look at her brother's profile. Was it disappointment she saw in his eyes? Was he, along with every other gentleman she came into contact with, enamored of the mysterious painter on the lawn?

Aurora closed her eyes against the brightness of the sun,

the beauty of the young woman, and the anguish of know-ing that her brother, who had shown no interest whatsoever in any female since his injury, should be interested now by a pretty, swanlike creature who was sure to break his heart and then glide away.

"Rue . . ." she said, with no idea how to go on.

"Hmmm?" His gaze remained fixed on the watercolorist, a woman who might never so much as realize he existed.

Aurora sighed. "I shall be at the archery range beside the Greek temple, if you should need me."

"Yes," he said absently.

She turned in the doorway to look back at him—the brother she thought of as a three-legged cat. Was her own pursuit of Lord Walsh equally pitiable? Rue still gazed dis-tractedly at the remotest of possibilities, a wounded mouser who dreamed of downing a swan. Aurora wondered how long he would stand, tail twitching, transfixed.

Half an hour later, her manner subdued, Aurora strode into the stableyard of the remarkable barn where Thomas Coke housed his horses and prize cattle. No such magnifi-cent Palladian-style housing for her stock. It took an invest-ment of money, time, and the belief that both were well spent to erect such splendid quarters for livestock. Even the pens for the sheep scheduled for shearing were remarkable for their trim neatness, their roomy, well-planned layout. Aurora had not the money for such extravagant accommo-dations for her livestock. Her brothers saw no value in such things. All save Rupert. What money came into their hands was wasted on women, wine, and cards. Rupert gave her a share of his stipend for the upkeep of the land and livestock that brought in the monies to begin with, but it was not enough, even combined with her own meager share.

So blighted was Aurora's mood by such thoughts, that she did not pay attention to her surroundings as she stepped from the brightness of morning into the twilight of the sta-ble doorway. Her eyes, not yet adjusted to the change, went temporarily blind and so she plowed, quite unaware, into Lord Walsh, who was exiting the door even as she entered.

His hand shot out to catch her by the shoulder. "Miss Ramsay. We meet again."

Aurora laughed, completely flustered by the unexpected encounter. He was a bull, she decided, and she was an indifferent toreador trying to bring him down. "I am sorry," she apologized. "I did not see you."

"No harm done," he said with jovial sarcasm. "This time we did not land in a heap on the ground."

She blushed.

He saved her from the struggle of responding. "A fine morning," he said conversationally. "You mean to ride?"

"Yes." Tongue-tied, she could think of no more response than that."

"I have just been for a gallop myself." He stepped back from the door that she might pass. "Enjoy!"

It was a dismissal. Aurora acknowledged it with a nod and passed him with the thought plaguing her that she would like to have said something more substantive, more scintillating, more self-assured. She could not always answer the man in monosyllables and expect him to fall on his knee to propose to her!

Her already disheartened mood was even more downcast as she made her way to the area within the stables where she was to meet Miles Fletcher.

Fletcher, in direct contradiction to her mood, was whistling a happy tune when she found him. He stopped when she appeared and directed his sparkling Gill-flower-blue gaze in her direction, along with a sunny smile.

"Good morning. My sister has gone on ahead," he fairly chirped. "Everything is arranged. Are you ready to set off?"

Fortunately, their saddled mounts were led out at that moment. Aurora was not required to respond to this all too cheerful greeting.

Her lack of smiles and enthusiasm could not quench Miles Fletcher's sunny mood one jot. He made merry remarks on the beauty of a bird's song and the quality of the morning air. And he demonstrated that he came prepared. Longbows had been obtained from Coke's stores of equipment, and provisions arranged in baskets on each side of his horse.

"Sustenance," he said, when she raised her brows.

She laughed, unexpectedly lifted from the valley of her unhappy thoughts. With so many baskets to accommodate his tastes, this gentleman's queer idea of sustenance far exceeded her own.

Swinging onto the horse that stood saddled and waiting for her, she put heels to the animal. "Come then," she called out as the gelding bolted into action. A good gallop would restore her spirits. "We must work up an appetite."

They proceeded apace to the temple, Aurora tearing along in the lead, Miles more sedately bringing up the rear, his baskets full of booty clanking with what sounded like glass and cutlery.

How amusing, Aurora thought as she and the gelding flew with gratifying haste across the turf, that a man should feel a picnic required such accoutrements. Walsh would never have burdened his horse with such a rattling compliment of condiments. A hunk of cheese and a heel of bread would have contented his needs, just as it would have hers.

Miles's excess struck her not so much as satisfying her requirements as his own. He was, she decided as the horse stretched out beneath her, a finicky sort of fellow, a man who knew not how to feel comfortable in mud-caked boots and wind-blown hair, a man who might ride all afternoon and still not smell of horse. He was wearing chalk-white breeches this morning! Such a gentleman was a mystery to her, a pitiable creature. He had no comfortable place in her world.

Her brothers were the sort of fellows Aurora was accustomed to: rough, brash, loud, and reeking of the outdoors or an overindulgence of spirit. Aurora tried to imagine Miles Fletcher drunk as a wheelbarrow, and could not. He would probably reel quite gracefully, she decided, if he allowed himself to imbibe too freely. He did not strike her as the type to allow such a loss of control, and in that realization, came a strong clue to the essence of this man's difference from all the men she was acquainted with. Miles Fletcher had himself under tighter rein than the galloping horde to which she was used to dealing. Control governed his every move. Such control baffled her. She was not used to thinking of men as more than green-broke creatures. Rupert, the only exception in her experience, was governed by the limitations of his leg and the memory of military order. There was a difference.

She found this difference, this contradiction to her assumptions with regard to the wildness of the male gender, amusing to the point of the ridiculous. She could not have dreamed up a fellow more different from her brothers, more removed from Lord Walsh. Cutlery on a picnic! The very idea had her grinning like an idiot during the whole pleasant gallop to their destination. The weather was fine, the light good, and the targets still conveniently at their disposal. There was much to keep her smiling, the least of which was not the cutlery-bearing exquisite, whose horse trailed hers by several noisy furlongs.

Aurora slid laughing from her horse to wait for Fletcher to catch up to her. An attractive bay was tethered in the clearing before the temple, evidence of the Grace who had gone ahead. Of the horse's rider, there was neither sight nor sound. The clearing was still. Light poured like golden syrup through the trees onto the pale, dun-colored brick of the temple. The birds had stopped singing, disturbed by her noisy approach. The setting held an otherworldly aura. Aurora felt she had stepped out of her normal time and place into some other, more interesting reality. An uneasy quiet settled around her like a Norwich shawl. All she could hear was the thudding of her own heartbeat and the echoing thud of hoofbeats as Fletcher's jingling mount approached. Silverware and white breeches on a picnic! He was an amusing part of the strangeness of this setting.

Aurora was reminded of the library. There was, inherent in this coming together of two unchaperoned strangers, an unsettling air of danger mindful of the mosaic lion eating a mosaic leopard in the golden peace of the library. Who in this instance was the lion and who the unlucky leopard?

As Fletcher's horse clanked into the clearing and he swung from the saddle, Aurora decided there was an awkward tension in being left alone with a man who was not a relative, or in any way known to her or her family, for the purpose of teaching him what came so naturally to her. With five brothers, she was used to men telling her what to do, not the other way around. This strange fellow with whom she had struck a bargain of shared knowledge, this exquisite gentleman who watched her with as much amusement in his gaze as she must possess in watching him, turned her life strangely upside-down. There was amusement to be enjoyed in such a topsy-turvy state of affairs, but beneath her amusement ran a thread of uncertainty and fascination that made her every moment alone with Miles Fletcher an adventure.

Fletcher, unaware of the effect he had on her peace of mind, relieved his horse of its burden. Handing her one of the bows and taking up the other, along with a quiver of arrows, he asked expectantly, "How do we begin, Miss Ramsay? I await your wisdom."

Aurora liked the ring of his words. She liked, too, the look of anticipation he concentrated on her.

"We begin with the stringing of the bow," she said with a show of confidence as she lifted the string. Miles made her nervous and self-conscious. He was too attentive a pupil, watching and listening with lively curiosity, head cocked to one side, eyes twinkling, mouth curved in an unshakable half smile.

Surely the silly flutter in her ribcage would go away, given enough time and a moment's relief from the unsettling focus of the man's gaze. Aurora's hands betrayed her as she showed him the method of stringing, which involved stepping through the bow to use one's leg as leverage in bending it to meet the string. So intently did his eyes follow her, she could not even begin to hope he did not notice the shaking of her every finger.

"Will you be so good as to repeat that last bit?" He raised his quizzing glass and bent to more closely observe the movements of her leg.

She obliged him, but was struck by the notion as she did so, that his glass remained focused on her nether regions far too long. Aurora bent her head, bringing them eye to eye.

"Did you get it that time, Mr. Fletcher?"

He blinked at her. His quizzing glass dropped to the end of its ribbon. "Actually"—his eyes met her glare with an unabashed gleam—"I got it the first time, but could not resist the opportunity to examine a noteworthy pair of ankles, Miss Ramsay."

She gasped. Here was evidence of the rough grain of crass masculinity lurking beneath his polished veneer after all. She was almost relieved to find it.

He went on, unperturbed. "I am, you see, an insatiable observer of beauty."

She glared at him, unable to come up with a clever rejoinder. Her customary responses for this sort of male behavior simply would not do for this peacock. "Where is your sister, Mr. Fletcher?" was all she could manage. "Does she mean to join us?"

He neatly stepped one glossy boot into his bow and precisely followed her example in stringing it, smiling contritely when he was done. "My sister is a painter, and like most who are artistically gifted, she tends to lose herself in her work. She will not have wandered far." To prove his point, he whistled a bit of a tune. When he paused, from a distance a whistled refrain picked up where he left off.

Another painter. Aurora almost sighed. Was she the only woman in the world who took no joy in watercolors?

"If I promise to refrain from further impertinences, will you continue your instruction?" The weasel was rather handsome when he smiled.

Aurora bit back a retort. Could she win in a battle of words with this erudite young man? With businesslike firmness she took up her bow again. "The next step is to understand why there is a cock feather on your arrow and how to go about nocking it in a smooth and consistent manner."

She paused, daring him to provoke her a second time with some predictably craven double entendre in connection with the suggestive terminology. Miles no more than raised an eyebrow, his eyes sparkling. Aurora thought he showed admirable restraint in refraining from any cruder reaction. Her brothers would have never allowed such an opportunity to slip by.

"You are an unusual gentleman, Mr. Fletcher," she said.

"Unusual?" His interest in what she said deepened. She had not thought that possible, yet his focus on her intensified. His eyes had never looked so cool, his expression so serious. "In what way do you find me unusual?"

"It is just . . ." She frowned and nervously fingered the arrow in her hand. She was far more comfortable aiming at targets than in trying to pin truth. How did one go about saying such things without giving a false impression of undue flattery? She shrugged and blurted out exactly what had run through her mind. "It is just . . . I've so many brothers I thought I understood well the ways of men. Yet you are wholly unlike any of them."

His brows rose. He splayed his hands. "I do not know whether to be flattered or confused. What is it you find so different in me?"

She tried to make light of what she said. Despite the effort, there was too much importance, she thought, in the way the words tumbled out. "It is just . . . I have never had a gentleman pay such favorable attention to my every word. I suppose"—she licked her lips and laughed—"the men I know have never so patiently allowed me to point out their ignorance."

His laughter joined hers. She thought, perhaps, from the sound of it, that she surprised him as much as he surprised her. The thought pleased her. His amused understanding made her feel as if she might tell him anything and not worry over the words.

"If one cannot acknowledge one's ignorance, one cannot move beyond it," he said, as lightly as she. "You've a wealth of knowledge and skill worthy of anyone's undivided attention."

Again that focused look. Again a compliment! She blushed, but he was not yet finished paying court to her.

He paused, his eyes unfocused, as though he saw through her to some far horizon. "Man is to woman what a bow is to its cord, bending one to the other, inexorably drawn to one another with a tension of sufficient power to loft arrows."

His words stirred Aurora in a way that words never had before. There was something suggestive in their flow—in the use of such imagery—far more subtly suggestive than the crude connection most men made between cock feathers and notching arrows, but suggestive nonetheless. How did one respond to such subtleties? She had no experience with word play. Flustered, she ducked his gaze, focusing on the topic of how to arm one's bow.

He watched keenly, his expression openly appreciative of all she had to teach him about determining one's dominant eye, the importance of a loose grip on the bow, a squared stance in facing the target, and a smooth draw. The lesson proceeded with no more talk of men and women to unnerve her. Miles Fletcher's first shots found their way to the target.

"Excellent," she said. "Once the target is met, the rest is no more than finessing."

He carefully positioned another arrow and took aim.

She reached out to adjust the positioning of his arm.

He started violently, unnerved by her touch. Inadvertently his fingers slipped from the bowstring. Ill-launched, his arrow arced right over the top of the target and disappeared from view.

"I am sorry," she said, trying very hard not to smile, for if she smiled, she must laugh, and to laugh now would surely be hard on Fletcher's self-esteem.

He had no such qualms about amusement. "I do hope my sister was not endangered by that preposterous misfire," he said with a droll expression. He looked pleased when a chuckle exploded from her lips, and said, "Tell me, Miss Ramsay. Did you mean to test me in the art of grace under pressure?"

"I do apologize—" she began.

He stopped her. "Never, Miss Ramsay, never must you

apologize for catching a gentleman off guard with no more than a touch. 'Tis a gift my dear, a genuine gift."

"I meant only to tell you that if you flex your arm too much in this manner"—she demonstrated the position by paralleling her arm with his on the same bow—"the string will strike you. Here." She touched his arm again, but he was ready for her this time. There would be no second instance of a loss of control.

"Let the string slide off of your fingers. Like so," she said. Her fingers plucked at the string just above his. In flexing, her arm slid against his. In following her direction, his shoulder grazed against her breast.

It was Aurora's turn to flinch. She could not be sure Miles Fletcher realized in what manner the fabric of his jacket had touched her, but every cell in her body hummed with awareness. There was something disturbingly pleasant about the feeling.

She had only to turn, to brush her lips against the flat plane of his smoothly shaven cheek, had only to dip her chin to nestle it in the hollow of his neck, so that she might more fully inhale the enticing lemony spice of his cologne. With but a slight shift in her stance, her breast would graze against his back again. She wondered why she should have such an inclination. There was no denying it. She wanted to repeat the sensation.

Frightened that this man aroused such yearnings, Aurora stepped back from such thoughts and away from Mr. Fletcher.

"You must keep your eyes locked on the center of your target," she said briskly. "Your arrow should be slightly below center on the bow and the bowstring pulled to the corner of your eye in a smooth, controlled movement. Where you look is where the arrow will go."

"Eyes locked on the target," he echoed, his gaze shifting to look, not at the targets, but at her. She could feel the change, could see the shift in the periphery of her vision. Warmth rose uncomfortably along her neck. Did Miles Fletcher mean to infer by the lingering intensity of his gaze that she was in some way his target? Could it be he had begun a lesson of his own—a lesson in the art of flirtation? Was he testing her? She turned to look at him, to search for the answer in his eyes, but simultaneously he returned his attention to the cloth target, frustrating her intent. Smoothly drawing back the bowstring, he let the string roll off his fingers as she had suggested. *Thwap!* His arrow quivered in the center ring of the target.

"Excellent, Mr. Fletcher."

He turned to look at her. His eyes gave away nothing. He hid his true thoughts, his true feelings, she realized, behind the smoothly polished veneer of an urbane smile. "I receive excellent instruction."

Aurora was growing accustomed to flattery from Miles Fletcher. There was something as smooth and slick, as polished as his smile, in the delivery of such praise. She assumed he was as generous in pandering to everyone. It was probably no more than commonplace to receive his compliments. Commonplace or not, it was pleasant to be praised. In this manner too, he was wholly opposite to her brothers. She wondered briefly whether she might expect such flattery from Walsh.

"Try to hit the center again, Mr. Fletcher," she said. "One arrow in the center may be no more than luck. Two arrows shows promise. Put all of your arrows consistently in the gold ring, and I will call you master."

"Master?" He smiled elusively, his manner vaguely suggestive. "Will you indeed? I aspire to the gold with renewed vigor. I should like you to call me master."

Again he played with her words and won. Again, she found his expression difficult to read. The thought crossed Aurora's mind that Fletcher was a marksman after all. He hit dead center every time when it came to targeting her with his pointed remarks.

Chapter Seven

Very good concentration, Mr. Fletcher. You have admirably bracketed and clustered your shots."

"Shall we call a halt?"

"Yes. I am anxious to see what provisions you have packed into so many baskets for our enjoyment. Perhaps you will be so kind as to lay out your feast while I collect the arrows and dismantle the bows?"

Miles seemed only too pleased to oblige her, digging into the baskets in a lively fashion.

"Where shall we consume our feast?" he enquired of Aurora, when she joined him. "Indoors or out?"

There was, Aurora decided, an unusual stillness about Mr. Fletcher as he asked the question.

Sensing that his question was of more importance than at first it might appear, she prevaricated. "Will your sister be joining us?" Without waiting for an answer, she wandered through the shaded doorway of the temple.

It was quiet inside, but for a faintly alarming buzzing noise. Aurora's footsteps echoed hollowly. The buzzing came from a colony of bees which had built a nest in the heights of the domed central chamber. Honey dripping from their hive left a sticky, golden pool on the floor. The incessant buzzing added to Aurora's uneasiness as she studied the nude statues that graced four alcoves. Their nakedness, combined with the heady drone of the bees, gave her gooseflesh.

Aurora peeped into the two smaller rooms off the domed chamber. Long windows let in sunshine and allowed an excellent view of the channel, yet one seemed cut off from the bustling crowd that had overrun Coke's estate for the shear-ing. Aurora's pulse quickened. She knew now why Fletcher's question was more important than at first it sounded. This lovely temple was the perfect setting for an illicit tryst! She returned to the main room.

Miles Fletcher had followed her in and was leaning non-chalantly against the doorframe. The humming of the bees signaled danger above them. The intensity of his look sig-naled a different danger.

Her conviction that Miles Fletcher was no more than a source of amusement was seriously jeopardized by that look. She shivered with something other than the chill.

He filled the doorframe, swinging the basket, looking very handsome in his tight-fitted blue coat and carefully tied cravat, looking, despite his polish, quite capable of se-ducing her. The thought of seduction from his quarter sur-prised Aurora. Her mind had been so firmly fixed on Lord Walsh as a potential suitor, that it had never occurred to her she might find herself drawn to another man. Certainly not this man, with whom she had so little in common! She shook her head, rearranging her thoughts. The sound of the bees rubbed her nerves raw. She was not drawn to him. She must not be drawn to him. He was drawn to her. That was what this was all about. Nothing more.

His deep blue gaze pulled her. She found herself unable to look at anything else and the intensity of his gaze left her uncertain and unsettled. She had to get out of here to escape the bees. She had to clear her head. She had to pass him, to regain the outdoors.

He did not move, just watched her, the basket no longer swinging. For a heart-stopping moment she wondered if he meant to block her escape.

"Indoors or out?" he asked. His voice, low and husky, in-truded on the space where she stood trapped, as much as the scent of his cologne. The room seemed smaller than be-fore.

"Out," she said thinly, the word sticking in her throat.

*   *   *

The warm balm of the sun and the normality inherent in spreading out their provisions on the steps eased the strangeness that the intimacy of the temple had aroused between them. The tension between them was as palpable as the food they consumed with an almost fierce relish, as heady as the wine they sipped from the telescoping silver cups he had brought. He had been convinced for the briefest of moments that his fair Diana was contemplating the idea of a private tête-à-tête, perhaps a moment of unbridled passion within the walls of the temple behind them. He knew he had anticipated such a scenario with eagerness.

The look he had seen in her cool green eyes as she studied his face, fired that hope. Perhaps it was no more than wishful thinking, no more than the power of his own desire for her. God knew he desired her, but there had been an elusive moment, a flicker of interest, that Miles could not ignore.

He thought about it now as they leaned against the columns, munching companionably on pork pasties, a wedge of cheese, and fresh berries washed down by a bottle of wine, all the while chatting inanely about nothing of substance—the beauty of the view, the perfection of the weather, the charm of the setting, and the delectability of the cheese.

"Your sister is not hungry?" she observed with studied nonchalance.

"She forgets food when she gets caught up in her painting."

With that, there came a lull in the conversation.

Aurora Ramsay shifted her position against the column as much as she shifted the tone of her voice when she inquired carefully, "What is it you mean to teach me today?"

There was an uncertainty in her voice that made Miles think immediately of all that he longed to teach this fair young woman if only she would agree. She had only to rise and walk through the shaded door of the temple. He had only to follow and take her into his arms . . .

But, she would not rise. She would offer him no encouragement. The very carefulness of her questions about Grace convinced him of that. Miles erased the image of an afternoon of unbridled passion from his thoughts and smiled evenly at her. There were more subtle methods of seduction. He reached over her for one of the baskets. She drew back with a look of alarm. *Slow down*, he thought. No good rushing things. Beautiful things should not be hurried, and surely the winning of a woman's trust was a beautiful thing.

"Can you handle a fan?" he asked, therefore, in the most mundane of tones as he pulled a narrow, sharkskin box from a pocket in the basket and held it out to her.

She took the box. "Of course I can handle a fan." She slid the lid off of the box and unfurled the fan within. "This is a pretty thing. It looks old. Is it yours?"

"No. It is only temporarily in my possession, one of a set of fans I have gathered together for an old roué who is willing to pay me handsomely for troubling to find this particular type of breeze stirrer. He means to come for the sheepshearing this weekend for no other reason than to fetch them."

"There is something unusual in this fan then?" She turned it over in her hand and studied the painted silk and the pierced tortoiseshell sticks, which were not so terribly unusual in and of themselves.

"It is an old fan, as you suggest, but while this one dates from at least a hundred years ago, that is not why it is unusual. It is a French *double-entente* fan."

"Whatever do you mean?"

"Here, let me demonstrate." He held out his hand. She returned the fan to him and for a brief instant their fingers brushed. Their eyes met as briefly as their fingers. She looked away, blushing. Smiling, he unfurled the fan, as she had, to reveal a pattern of painted flowers on one side, and the painted image of shepherd and shepherdess on the other. The characters faced opposite directions as they looked out over their flocks, one of white sheep, one of black. Their view of one another was obstructed across the middle of the pleated silk by a copse of trees, in which a fat Cupid lurked with bow and arrows.

"When opened from one direction, one picture is seen." He closed the fan, snapped it open again from the opposite direction, and revealed a different picture. The shepherd and shepherdess were now come together in a passionate embrace in the copse of trees, while their flocks mingled. Cupid hung laughing above the scene.

"Oh my!" Aurora gasped.

"A trifle tawdry, I will admit, but please do not tell me you are offended. I took care to bring the least suggestive of the lot. Most *double-entente* fans are far more lewd in nature."

"You did not bring this with you to inure me to the lascivious nature of mankind then?"

He sat staring at her a moment, surprised that she should be so innocent of worldliness, endowed as she was with so many worldly-wise brothers. "Not at all." He frowned. Perhaps it had been wrong of him to bring the silly fan.

"Why did you bring it?" she asked, as if she read his mind.

He flicked the fan open and moved it gracefully about. "I brought it so that I might teach you the language of romance."

She sat up a little straighter against the column on which she leaned. Had she been a hedgehog, she would have bristled.

"The language of the fan," he said.

"This romantic language you would teach me, is it as scandalous as the behavior of your silly shepherd and shepherdess?"

He stilled the fan and considered her expression. "If you are offended by the language of love, then you may deem it so. But you are attempting to capture the love of a man who is virtually a stranger to you, are you not?"

The indelicate question hung between them like an insult. Her chin went up.

He flicked the fan from one graceful position to another, his long, tapering fingers eloquent and elegant in the movements. The imagery on the fan flicked back and forth from tasteful to tasteless with the changing position. "Flirtation is a skill," he said evenly. "I thought you would appreciate the practice."

Warily she watched him.

Miles hid his face behind the fan, as if he were shy, and peeped only his eyes up over the edge. Time to take it slow again. Her back went up whenever the subject of their conversations turned to love and Lord Walsh. Their relationship, he thought, was rather like the fan in his hands. Turn it one way and one picture was seen. Turn it another and the picture changed.

"Any fan speaks this language I would teach you. It began in Spain, where it was necessary to create such a form of communication because young ladies there are so carefully guarded against lovers' exchanges by their duennas. So lovely was the mystery of this graceful language, that all of Europe began to follow the fashion."

"What do you say now with this rare and provoking fan?" She could not disguise her curiosity.

He slowed his movements, placing the fan near his heart. "You have won my love," he said, and wondered if she had any idea how appropriate he found the words. Some level of his earnestness must have been conveyed to her. She blushed, the hue of her freckled cheek assuming a particularly rare shade he had never witnessed before. She darted uncertain looks in his direction.

He was pleased with her reaction. Teaching her the language of the fan offered him the opportunity to voice his feelings for her. He lifted the shut fan to his right eye. "When may I be allowed to see you?" he said, and then unfolded a corner of the fan, so that three sticks were shown. "Three?" He spread the fan wider. "Seven?" He opened the fan wide. "Wait for me." He covered his left ear with the open fan. "Do not betray our secret," he whispered, and waving the fan, touched it with his other hand. "I long to be near you." He touched the tip of the fan. "I wish to speak to you." He drew the fan across his cheek. "I love you." He smiled at her, closed the fan and presented it to her with formal grace, as though the two of them were dancers in a hand ballet. "Do you love me?"

She took the fan, her face still glowing with heightened color, her eyes avoiding his. "One can say all of that?" She turned the painted silk and tortoiseshell as though seeing it for the first time and fanned the heat in her cheeks.

"That, and more." He nodded. "If you touch the handle of the fan to your lips . . ." She followed his direction even as he spoke and he smiled, his voice dropping, "Yes, just so." Leaning forward, he very deliberately raised her chin with the light touch of the tips of two fingers and kissed her. Her lips tasted of berries. "You have just asked me to kiss you," he said lightly, pulling back to see how she would react.

She snapped shut the fan and waved it menacingly in his face. "That was both impudent and uncalled for! You take unfair advantage, sir."

He did not respond immediately, merely sat in the dappled sunlight, studying her. A dove cooed, asking with muted persistence, *What? Who? Who? Who?*

Yes, he took unfair advantage—in more ways than she realized. He had set out with the intention of righting an unfairness for her, as Uncle Lester had requested. Stolen kisses were not part of the plan. He meant to help her capture Walsh, didn't he? He had promised as much. And yet, in this moment, in the golden, sun-kissed, dove-interrupted stillness beneath the trees, he was moved by a desire to do anything to the contrary, anything that might serve to make her forget Walsh and look on him with favor instead.

"You wish to seduce Lord Walsh, do you not? Seduction is an art like any other. Surely you must allow yourself to be seduced a little if you are to fully comprehend that art." The negotiator within him sprang to the fore, finagling the truth in a way that made him wince and yet in a strange way serving both of his intentions, fine and base.

She gave the matter due thought. "There is a perverted sort of logic to your suggestion. Seeds are not as likely to grow in unbroken ground as in that which is cultivated." She tilted her face toward his, her eyes open, observant, and very serious. "Kiss me, then. If I should know how it is done," she instructed. "I will not resist."

He blinked, unable to believe his good fortune.

What? Who? Who? Who? sounded the dove.

Should he take advantage of the opportunity now that it was his? Miles leaned forward, eyelids drooping. Aurora, on the other hand, kept her eyes open. There was something very disconcerting in her wide-eyed attention to his advance—so disconcerting he drew back again, their lips untouched.

"Do you mean to keep your eyes open?"

She looked confused. "How can I see what you are about if I do not?"

He shrugged. There was sense to what she said, but only sense, no emotion other than that. "As you will," he sighed. Unnerved by her owllike observation of his every move, he placed a hand on each of her shoulders and drew her toward him, his mood for kissing spoiled by such an absence of sensibilities.

It was an anticlimactic endeavor. When he touched his lips to hers and pulled away, she was still watching him with wide-eyed curiosity.

"That's it?" Her tone was mildly derisive.

He gazed at her in disbelief. His prowess had never been questioned.

"No," he said huskily, pulling her into his arms again. "Now shut your eyes. *This* is it." His lips closed on hers differently this time, hungry for response. This was no polite peck that she might question with mild derision. This kiss welled from deep within him and poured over the two of them like honey.

Still she resisted the power of the kiss, her lips pressed together in unresponsive resistance.

Miles was not about to admit defeat to an obvious novice who clamped her lips together like a trap while her eyes remained wide open to examine him with unbiased objectivity. She held herself as rigid in his arms as a block of wood.

"Part your lips," he whispered thickly into her hair, his fingers trailing seductively along her jawline. "And, pretend I am Walsh."

It was demeaning to say such a thing, yet it triggered the

desired response. She gasped at his suggestion. He took advantage of her surprise, kissing her half-opened mouth with increasing warmth and fervor, determined to keep her mind and senses occupied with anything but Walsh. She gasped again, this time with pleasure. He pushed the kissing lesson a step further. "You should know that the French have some interesting variations on this theme," he whispered in her ear before demonstrating in the French fashion how adroit a tongue might be involved in the art they explored.

She succumbed to his expertise, succumbed to the power of a mercurial energy that coursed between them. Her limbs seemed to melt into his. Her lips became as active in the search for what it was that lay between them as his.

Miles was shaken by her passionate response. This lesson he meant to teach her had turned on him. He was the one who learned the most in her sensual abandon, for in that moment it became very clear to Miles Fletcher that contrary to his plan, he was become completely infatuated with Miss Aurora Ramsay. He wanted these lips, wanted to explore them minutely. He wanted to make love with this young woman with complete abandon right here, beneath the whispering leaves and the cooing of the dove. He wanted to strip away her Bowman's colors and let down the fiery waterfall of her hair, despite the fact that Grace might walk onto the scene at any moment. He wanted Miss Aurora Ramsay as he had never wanted anything before. His need shook him. It made his knees feel weak.

What? Who? Who? Who? asked the dove. What was he doing here? Whose needs did he meet with the passion of these kisses? Alarmed, Miles pulled his lips from Aurora's.

She swayed, fiery lashes still brushing her cheeks, her lips damp, parted and ripe with color.

He resisted temptation. He restored control. He dropped his hands from her shoulders.

Her eyes flew open, a hungry light firing in them, but before she could say a word to threaten his newly regained sense of equilibrium, he clasped his hands over hers beneath the fan. "One can also beg forgiveness with the fan." He slid the fan from her grasp and drew it across his eyes.

"I do beg your forgiveness, Miss Ramsay, for having taken unfair advantage not once but several times." He opened and shut the fan several times. "You can tell me I have been cruel."

She looked, for the moment, more confused than ready to accuse him of anything. He drew the fan theatrically across his forehead. "Tell me that I have changed," he instructed.

What? Who? Who? asked the dove. He was changed. The yearning for her mouth would not leave him. He twirled the fan in his right hand and thought of Walsh. "Tell me that you love another."

She bit down on her lip.

He held the fan out to her, but she was too distracted to realize he meant her to take hold of it. It dropped into the grass between them.

"Oh dear!" she exclaimed.

"Oh dear, indeed." He bent to pick it up again and stood to find her eyes wide, her tongue passing uneasily over her lips, as if they were in some way foreign to her. He wondered if she could still taste him there.

"Is the fan broken?" she asked uneasily.

"No"—he shook his head—"but a dropped fan means we shall be friends." The seriousness of his tone brought a pucker to her forehead.

"I would think, after what has passed between us this afternoon that we were fast becoming just that, Mr. Fletcher."

He allowed the hint of a smile to tilt lips still warmed by their contact with hers. "I had hoped for more, Miss Ramsay. Far more."

Chapter Eight

Aurora spread the naughty fan before her face and wafted a cooling breeze across flaming cheeks. She did not know what to make of Miles Fletcher or his remarks. The popinjay had become a swooping falcon. He hoped for *far more!* And yet, it was he who had stopped the soft wonder—the tender heaven of their kisses! Dear God, what did he mean? He hoped *for more* lovemaking perhaps? Such a thought made her very ears burn. *More, far more,* he had said.

She brushed a curl away from her eyes with the end of the fan.

"Have I changed?" he asked.

His voice, cool, calm, and collected in the asking of such a question, startled her. "What?"

He pointed to the fan. "The language of the fan," he said. "Did you mean to tell me I have changed?"

Oh my! The mere touch of the fan to her forehead carried a message. How provoking! And yet, this moment of misunderstanding offered unexpected opportunity to return their conversation to more comfortable footing.

"Have I remembered it rightly?" She touched the fan to her forehead again.

He nodded, studying her expression. "I do apologize . . ."

The movements of her hands with the fan mimicked his words.

He stopped in the middle of his apology, studying her. "Do not betray our secret," he hazarded.

She held the fan out to him. "I do not remember that one. Will you show me?"

You have won my love; I long to be near you; kiss me; do not betray our secret; over and over the words and movements were uttered between the two of them, strangers who would never have voiced such thoughts under different circumstances. These were expressions of such intimacy she had never imagined voicing them to a man, much less voicing them over and over, with both fan and voice until she had them down by rote. How odd, to be comfortable with such words, to have said them so often they became commonplace.

"Kiss me," she repeated the gesture and watched him warily, in case he should take her literally, as he had once before. She could not say the words, or repeat the gesture of the fan, its handle pointing the way, without reliving the unexpected silky warmth that had so insistently descended on her lips. How nice it would be to experience such a sensation again. How nice if life were simple enough that she might say "kiss me" and suffer no consequence other than a lovely feeling. But, life was not simple.

He hoped for more. Still she pondered Miles Fletcher's meaning as they packed up the picnic remains.

"Your sister. Does she mean to return with us? Surely she is hungry?"

Fletcher was loading his horse with baskets. "I shall go and ask her."

As before he whistled and received an answering noise. He made a move to set off in the direction from which the answer came and then turned to ask Aurora, "You do not mean to ride away while I am gone, do you?"

She shook her head, chastened by this mild reminder of her former rudeness to him in the ballroom.

"I shall only be a moment." He set off with one of the baskets.

She watched him go. The phrases they had practiced would not stop running through her head, like the unending chorus of the dove whose voice came softly from the trees above. *You have changed; kiss me; do you love me; kiss me; do not betray our secret; kiss me.* The memory of his kiss touched upon her lips like the breeze that lifted hair from her brow. She closed her eyes and reminded herself it was Walsh she meant to have. Surely an earl's kisses would taste as sweet, surely his touch would make her knees buckle just as much as Miles Fletcher's did.

Fletcher returned empty-handed. "My sister has been joined by three young men, your brother among them."

"My brother?" She was surprised.

"Yes." He laughed. "Her lure is strong."

If it was half as strong as her brother's, Rupert was in trouble. The blue eyes watching her seemed to probe her thoughts. Aurora found it difficult to meet that knowing gaze. "I should very much like to meet this alluring sister of yours," she said.

"And so you shall, but for the moment she is in the midst of a watercolor, and will not be budged."

Aurora was pleased he did not expect her to make her introductions immediately. How did one converse intelligently with a stranger when one had just been kissing her brother?

They set off toward the Hall at a leisurely pace. This time she did not dash ahead of her companion, but rode at a companionable pace beside him. As they progressed, Aurora stopped on occasion and slid from the saddle, to break off a branch of shrubbery or pluck up a plant in order to stop the phrases that ran through her head like the chorus of a song just sung: *You have changed; kiss me; do you love me; kiss me; do not betray our secret; kiss me.*

"See this?" She handed the first specimen to him. "It is Enchanter's Nightshade."

"Do you mean to enchant me?" His tone was polite, almost jesting, but his words reminded her of the kisses that still burned hotly in her memory.

No, she thought, *you have enchanted me.* Miles Fletcher managed to make everything a matter of flirtation, even when she would push such stuff completely from her thoughts. She refused to blush or answer in kind.

"There is nothing enchanting about nightshade when one is raising sheep," she said briskly. "The fruits get bristly and catch on the bellies and tails of livestock. Consider them a pest plant, along with goose grass, thistles, burdock, and hound's tongue. Such stuff tangled in a fleece reduces its value."

They rode on, Miles studying the plant, until she found another that was worthy of his attention.

"What do you think of this?" She handed a lacy green leaf on a long stalk up to him.

"Is it parsley?" he ventured.

"Fool's parsley. Now, crush one of the leaves."

Miles did as she requested and recoiled from the odor. "It smells very unpleasant." He dropped the plant to the ground in disgust.

"A stench it does one well to be acquainted with," she agreed even as she was wondering if she were the fool today to let a man kiss her whom she barely knew, and to be affected by that kiss. "Fool's parsley is poisonous in all its parts. Hemlock, dog's Mercury, and nightshade, all poisonous, have foul odors as well. I make it a practice to hold suspicious any plant that stinks." She must hold her feelings for this practiced lover as suspicious as any smelly plant. She had seen him charming other women in both the ballroom and dining hall. He must not be allowed again to charm her defenseless, to close her eyes to her goals with no more than a kiss or two.

"Are there many poisonous plants?" Miles asked, looking out over the land on either side of them as if he were suddenly plunged into a place as dangerous as she considered his arms.

She felt settled only if they stuck to matters of plant life and livestock. "Parts of many plants are poisonous. Sometimes it is the root or tuber; sometimes the leaves or fruit. Some are always poisonous; some only when fresh. Some kill immediately; some only over time. Fortunately, sheep, cattle and horses tend to avoid the noxious-smelling varieties if provided with a more pleasant alternative, but it pays to be familiar with the worst culprits in case a flock starts dropping dead on you right and left."

"And have you had entire flocks affected in this manner by no more than a weed?"

His deep blue eyes seemed more open than she remembered. His curiosity was genuine. She swallowed hard and would not look at him.

"Yes, on occasion. Last year I hired a Scotsman as shepherd—superb with both sheep and dogs, but unfamiliar with a plant that does not grow in the north: white bryony. A dozen sheep had miscarried premature lambs before the man's ignorance was recognized. I was afraid I might lose an entire flock."

"How unfortunate." Miles Fletcher's voice was so gentled by empathy she could not stop her mouth from twisting with the pain of remembering.

She nodded, bit her lower lip, and bent to pluck up another weed, hoping her expression did not give away the sorrow that had welled up inside of her. This polished fellow, no matter how sympathetic his manner, could not truly understand the depth of her feelings for her stock, could he? She willed her voice not to shake.

"Ragwort is another nasty weed. It is very widespread. You are sure to see it in your pasturage." She tipped back her head to hand him the ragged-leaved yellow flower, unaware that the tears she had stopped from falling, glistened brightly in her eyes. "Ragwort's effect is not immediate, but it is quite dangerous to your cattle if they eat it on a regular basis."

Ragwort was as dangerous to cattle as she was become to him, Miles thought as he watched the emotions that played across the freckled face of the female before him. He was feeling a trifle inadequate. Here was a woman who nurtured flocks of sheep and was moved almost to tears by the state of their health. Here was a woman who rode like the wind, kissed like a temptress, shot arrows like a man, and knew all there was to know about breeding cattle and fertilizing the land. She was a storehouse of useful information, deeds, and knowledge. Whenever she spoke, he could not help but wonder just what it was he had so long wasted his time doing with himself.

Could the buying and selling of antiquities and the mastering of drawing room etiquette even begin to measure up to her accomplishments? He thought not. And then, defensively, and because he had always considered himself a worthy fellow, he convinced himself that he was trying to compare Kent's genius with architecture to Constable's eye for scenery. The world was surely big enough and varied enough for both he and Aurora Ramsay to co-exist. In the process they stood to learn from one another. He certainly hoped they might eventually learn more of one another's lips.

So valuable were the lessons he felt she offered him in more serious matters, that he was more determined than ever to offer her equal measure. He meant to set things right. He would see to her wardrobe, if she would allow it. He would teach her to dance if she so desired. He would, by God, polish the rough edges that kept this gem from being recognized by one such as Walsh. He would . . .

"Whoa! Stop right there!" he insisted. They had clattered into the stableyard and Aurora was preparing to dismount in the very competent fashion with which she had climbed up and down from her mount all afternoon.

"What?" She turned to look at him.

"Stay right where you are," Miles insisted, sliding from the saddle and moving swiftly to her side. With a smile, for he enjoyed his every exchange with her and could never predict her reaction, he gently touched her arm.

"Another lesson, Miss Ramsay. You must not even begin to think of dismounting from a horse unaided when there is a gentleman nearby to assist you."

Aurora, who had unhooked her knee from the sidesaddle in preparation of jumping down, cocked her head to stare at him skeptically. "I am perfectly capable of an unassisted dismount, sir, and well you know it. I have been on and off this saddle at least six times this afternoon in fetching plants to you." Her tone and expression were meant to be quelling.

"Yes, and each time I was struck by the feeling I proved a most inattentive riding companion in allowing you to do so." Miles held out his arm in assistance, though she had just as plainly told him she did not require it. "You would be wise to display your competence judiciously," he murmured, as he stepped closer to her horse. "You will meet many a fellow who neglects to offer you such courtesy, but when a man would be gentlemanly and help you down, especially any man whom you respect and trust, or simply find interesting, you must honor his courtesy."

"As I suppose I must indulge yours now?"

"Precisely!" He held both arms up to her in invitation.

With a sigh of resignation, Aurora placed her hands on Miles Fletcher's perfectly tailored shoulders and slid down from the roan. Miles caught her around the waist as if she were a child who required assistance from the back of a pony, but when her heels hit the ground and she dropped her grasp on his shoulders, she realized he was not at all interested in treating her like a child. His hands remained familiarly on her waist!

"There are advantages to allowing oneself to be assisted in such a manner," he said suggestively, his eyes meeting hers with unmistakable intent as she realized herself neatly trapped between horse and man, and both too close for comfort.

She was tempted to box his ears. "You may take your hands off of me now, Mr. Fletcher. I am safely come to ground."

"Ah!" He complied. "I thought you were yet a trifle unsteady."

Oddly enough, she did sway a little when he let go his warm, bracing hold of her. She wondered why she felt unaccountably dizzy. Perhaps it was the memory of the last time he had held her.

He tucked her hand in the crook of his arm as the horses were led away, and leaned close, to say in an undertone, "As you can see, the dismount is a deliciously unremarkable mode in which a male and female may for an instant come into contact with one another."

She flinched away from him, away from the warm, tickling sensation of his voice in her ear. "And why should that be of the slightest interest to me, Mr. Fletcher?" she inquired tartly.

His blue eyes twinkled. "Oh, but you must learn to take advantage of what few opportunities lie open to a female if you truly mean to pursue the attentions and affections of a gentleman such as Lord Walsh." He neatly dismissed her offended air.

Aurora glared at him, her pride completely undone. She could not think of a word with which to respond. She was used to using sarcasm as a shield against any man who rattled her feeling of control, and Miles Fletcher had unexpectedly done just that throughout the course of this afternoon. It was galling that not one single witty or biting remark occurred to her.

He patted her hand, and as if it were no more than commonplace, said, "It has occurred to me that our next lesson might best be conducted after dinner—in your room."

She wrenched her arm from his clasp. "In my room? What mischief is this, sir?"

"Tut, tut." He smoothed his sleeve, deftly recaptured her hand, and placed it in the crook of his arm again. "You miss another opportunity, Miss Ramsay. There are any number of ways to respond to such a provocative statement, and indignation, while an admirable reflection of your character, is perhaps not the wisest in this case."

"Sir, you insult me," she snapped.

"Shame." He nodded. "Yes, that is another possibility, though much in the same vein, really."

"I am going to pummel you if you do not make an attempt to explain yourself at once," she promised, her voice low and angry as they crossed the channel and approached the Hall.

"Threat. Hmmm!" He considered. "That is certainly another stab at it."

He dodged a kick in the shin and winked at her. "Violence, my dear, is quite out."

She stopped, unable to control a laugh. "You are become unbearably irritating, sir. Do tell me why you dare to suggest a tête-à-tête in my chambers before I go mad and jump into the channel."

"Bravo!" He squeezed her arm, his face a collected picture of approval. "You come at last to the more productive means of dealing with most any situation. Humor. It is a priceless commodity. Nurture it, and discard all mad thoughts of throwing yourself into the channel. I will now explain my somewhat forward suggestion that I invade your privacy—in a single word: wardrobe."

"Wardrobe?"

He smiled his contained little smile, neither lip fully engaged. "Indeed, Miss Ramsay. I would see to the dressing and undressing of you."

She gasped and opened her mouth to voice again her indignation.

The lifting of one sleek dark eyebrow silenced her. "Humor me with humor, Miss Ramsay."

She closed her mouth on the acid retort she had been about to utter, thought a moment, and then tipped her head to say, "I have a proposition, Mr. Fletcher."

"A most promising beginning," he said with approval. "Pray, tell me, what is this proposition?"

"I will allow you the dressing and undressing of me, sir, if you allow me equal favor."

His eyebrows rose. "My dear, you are a quick study. I am intrigued. Please go on."

She could not suppress a smile. "Well, the next time we ride together, I would see some more practical color on your person than white. You are your valet's nightmare, sir. A gentleman should not be required to sit upon a napkin rather than soil his breeches on a picnic, sir."

He smiled. "If you indeed mean to dress and undress me, Miss Ramsay, I will follow you about with nothing but bells on if you think it suits me."

She maintained her composure. "Bells? A clanker, sir, if ever I heard one."

Her remark won a laugh.

*   *   *

Aurora took her leave of Miles Fletcher with a smile. Pleased with the way her time had been spent and imbued with the same galloping rush of energy she was used to experiencing after a cross-country race, she spent several hours in and about Tom Coke's remarkable barn, examining the condition and conformation of his stock. Aurora could not have planned a more pleasant day.

Informed by one of the grooms that her brother was returned, she fairly skipped into the library, her heart as buoyant as her step.

"Rupert, I have passed a most delightful day!" she blurted, before she had even laid eyes on her sibling.

He was there, and from the looks of his attire only recently returned from outdoors himself, but Aurora was brought up short halfway across the room, amazed by the changed atmosphere of her brother's sanctuary. The fire had gone out, no candles or lamps had been lit, and Rupert sat without any signs of animation, in one of the darker corners of the room. His face was obscured in the shadow.

"Aurora," he said huskily, "a letter is come!"

Four words, no more, and yet she knew from the way they were uttered that the letter brought bad news.

"Who writes?" She could see the letter in the shadow of his lap, a white square against dark kerseymere breeches.

"Roger."

"Roger?" She stared at the folded bit of paper as if it were a viper, ready to strike her hand should she reach for it. Her gaze sought Rupert's. Roger was not much given to letter writing. "What does he say? Has his illness taken a turn for the worse?"

Rupert closed his eyes and lolled his head back against the chair. His voice was as lacking in energy as his body. He lifted the letter as if it were a thing of weight and held it out to her. "It's Jack. He suffers reverses."

Aurora's fingers leapt to unfold the letter. Rupert did not stir to see her reaction as she crossed to the window, the only place bright enough to read. With deep foreboding she scanned the crossed and recrossed lines. "No!" she gasped. "Oh God, Rue! How could he?" Her hand flew to her throat. The truth danced before her eyes. She dropped the letter, sank into the nearest chair, and stared blankly out of the window.

"He has lost the land?" she said unsteadily.

"The hall as well."

Aurora clapped a hand over her mouth least she cry out. "Dear God, Rue! He has paupered us all. How could he?"

"How could he?" His voice was acid with sarcasm. "Exactly the same way he has done away with everything else of any value he ever owned."

"We must leave at once," she said uncertainly.

"Why?" Rupert's tone was flat. "We've nothing to return to. What's the hurry?"

As all light faded from the rosy sky, so too all light and color faded from Aurora's face.

Chapter Nine

Aurora's haze of euphoria over a day spent pleasantly in Miles Fletcher's company, a day in which she had learned flirting and flattery and the pleasure of two minds well met, a day in which her plans to marry Lord Walsh seemed a distant and unnecessary objective—had dissipated. With the arrival of a folded and franked piece of paper, a great weight had been yoked about her neck. Her heart was squeezed by an unfriendly fist. Her brother, Jack, her foolish, wastrel of a brother, whom all of London referred to as Rakehell Ramsay, had lived up to his name once again. The Ramsay lands, all that were left of a once respectable fortune, were lost to a superior hand of cards. The only way to save Jack's disreputable hide from a debtor's prison would be to sell everything—house, land, cattle, sheep—the lot. The silver, the family portraits, the furniture, the coach and four, all had gone to pay off Jack's obsession with betting—dice, cards, horses, it did not matter to Jack as long as there were odds to wager. There had been nothing left to lose but that which mattered to Aurora most: the land, the cattle, and her flocks.

It was Roger who wrote—Roger, who had his own cross to bear in the form of the wasting illness he had brought upon himself by frequenting too many brothels. He offered little comfort and even less assistance. Roger was more often out of the family picture than in it of late. Damn the letter!

Damn Jack! How could he? The child within her wept and screamed and wanted to throw things. How could her own flesh and blood so carelessly lose those last few things into which she had poured the very essence of her soul? Her happiness was squashed, the sunlight dimmed, all laughter made hollow. Choice, and the luxury of time were swept from Aurora's grasp—all choice but Walsh. He was her only hope.

She thought of nothing but winning his attention as she and Rupert went quietly in to dinner and pushed food about Tom Coke's exquisite bone china plates. Walsh was her last hope, her best hope—the answer to all of her ills. Odd, how she had passed the whole morning with scarcely a thought entering her head with regard to him. Now she could think of nothing and no one else. Miles Fletcher tried to catch her eye as the soup was served, and again when the main course was delivered, but she paid him no mind. Her eyes, her attention, her very soul's intent were fixed on Walsh. He sat at the far end of the table, on the opposite side. They were not at all in good position to exchange glances. And yet, she was determined to share, if not conversation, at least a passing glance with the man who, all unknowing, held her Fate in his pocket.

The letter from Roger—poor pox-ridden Roger, who could not save himself much less his debt-burdened brother—had redirected her thinking, reminding her how precarious her very survival might be without success where Walsh was concerned. The urgency of marrying, and marrying well, was increased a hundredfold.

It was over dessert that her objective was finally met. Walsh looked absently along the line of diners across the table from him. Their eyes met briefly. His gaze traveled past her and then returned. He inclined his head ever so slightly. She inclined hers. That was all, but it was enough to give Aurora hope, and fire her with enthusiasm to get on with the transformation that Miles Fletcher had promised to wreak on her wardrobe that evening. Miles, she realized, had watched her exchange with Walsh. She could tell, because he inclined his head exactly as Walsh had and then raised his glass in ironic salute.

He approached her when the table was cleared and

leaned down to whisper provocatively, "I shall join you in your room in a quarter of an hour."

For a moment, the heat of his breath on her neck closed both Aurora's eyes and her mind to the troubles of the day. For an instant her heart was light again. "I shall listen for your bells," she quipped.

He pulled back to smile his tight little smile at her, offered a courtly bow, and left her to explain to Rupert. "What bells?"

"No bells at all," she replied, her smile fading. As Miles was swallowed by the crowd, her spirits sank.

"Come," she tugged at Rupert's arm, "you must accompany me, though it means mounting the stairs."

Rupert was exhausted and surly by the time the flight of stairs had been navigated.

"Damn!" He sank into a chair in her room and flung aside his crutch. "I do not understand this wardrobe business in the least! What is wrong with your wardrobe? I think you have always presented yourself quite nicely. As to the business with Walsh . . . You know I am dead set against the idea of putting on airs to attract the eye of a man who cannot recognize quality unless you dress it up for him. Love surely does not require such studied pursuit."

"Love? I suffer no illusions of love. It is security and survival I seek, not love."

"Yes, but why must your avenue of survival be determined by *Jack's* foolhardy antics?" He spat the name. "I do not see why you feel it your responsibility to rescue the scoundrel from his financial woes, when it is his own folly landed him under hatches. Charles should be here, looking after this business, not galavanting around the Far East."

She sighed. "Charles is doing his best to rebuild the family's fortune. As for me, I have little choice but to marry, and marry well. The money lenders will take everything without Charles here to stop them, even my sheep. I cannot halt the inevitable liquidation of all that is left of Father's estate, of all that is dear to me. . . ." Her voice faltered. She took a sobering breath and squared her jaw. "I cannot stop it any more than I could stop Jack's gambling, or Gordon's drinking, or Roger's whoring." She blinked angry tears from her lashes. "All I can see to do is to arrange my own life as wisely and as swiftly as I am able. If that arrangement requires Mr. Fletcher's assistance in refurbishing my wardrobe in such a fashion as to catch Lord Walsh's eye, then I will do what I can. *I must*."

Rue sank back in the chair and dropped his head into his hands. "But at what price, Aurora? Your happiness? Your future? I beg you, do not sell short what must be dearer than land or cattle or flocks of sheep." He pulled at his hair. "Would that I might sell some of my scribblings . . . or that I had two legs to stand upon so that I might go to Jack and uncork his nose . . ."

She sank down beside him and ran a soothing hand through his hair. "Your stories will sell, Rue. Do not throw yourself into a pet, my dear. You are the best of brothers, in every way. You need not try to make up for the rest of our wayward siblings."

"As you do?" His voice was hoarse, his face haggard when he lifted it to look at her.

She frowned. As she did? Whatever did he mean? Did she try to make up for her siblings?

A knock on the door saved Aurora from troubling with an answer. She smiled half-heartedly. "Cheer up! Things will work out."

Expecting to find Miles Fletcher, she opened the door. It was not Miles, but Rue's watercolorist from the lawn who stood waiting, the swanlike female who seemed capable of enchanting every young man who laid eyes on her. She was, Aurora discovered, even more beautiful up close than she had seemed from a distance.

"Good evening. Is Miles here?" she had the effrontery to ask.

Aurora blinked at her. "No. Shall I inform Mr. Fletcher you seek him out?"

It was their visitor's turn to blink. "Did he not tell you to expect me, then? I do beg your pardon. He asked me to come along this evening. I hope you do not mind."

Of course Aurora minded. She did not want this pretty thing observing this evening's work, but she could not say so to her face. She opened the door wider and waved the young woman in. "Not at all," she lied.

"Oh!" The girl stopped short when she spotted Rupert, who had done a manly job of recovering himself in rising to greet their guest. "I'd no idea you were to be here."

"I would introduce you," Aurora said with forced mildness, "but we have, ourselves, never been introduced."

Rupert looked dumbfounded, but had enough presence of mind to extend his hand, his eyes never straying from their visitor's face. "We have met."

The swanlike creature smiled prettily and dipped a graceful curtsey as she placed her hand in his. "We have."

Aurora had no more opportunity to pry from the stranger her name, for in that instant Miles Fletcher arrived and walked boldly through the open doorway with yet another woman in tow.

"Mrs. Hall, the local seamstress." He presented the lantern-jawed woman as though she were a duchess. "I see you have already met Gracie."

Aurora was given no opportunity to contradict him. Like an admiral commandeering his fleet, Miles swept across the room, made his greeting to Rupert, and flung open the wardrobe where Aurora's clothes were neatly hung. His mission required immediate attention.

"Gracie!" He emerged from the wardrobe, his arms full. "You will arrange these for me on the bed, please, according to color."

Without the slightest hint of demur, Aurora's unexpected female guest did as she was bid while Mrs. Hall also answered Fletcher's beck and call, pulling from a basket he had carried into the room for her a number of fabric swatches in varying hues.

"You!" Miles Fletcher rounded on Aurora. "Sit here!"

He arranged a chair in front of the long mirror that hung from one wall. Frowning, Aurora sat. There was no question who was in charge of these proceedings. Miles Fletcher filled the room with his coolly controlled presence.

He made it his, studying Aurora, once she was seated, from all angles, as if she were no more than an object to him, a chair, perhaps, that required a change in upholstery. Such remote objectivity in Mr. Fletcher's regard was disturbing. There was a judgmental assessment in his searching perusal of her now, that made her feel like a prize cow. For a brief but alarming moment, she was a child again, with Nanny peering down and directing her to "Turn about, miss, that I might see what damage you have done your poor tattered skirts out climbing trees."

"Here we have the possibilities." The woman Aurora knew only as Gracie began to hand Miles garments one by one, her gaze searching the mirror with a frown as they were held up in front of their mistress.

Aurora's favorite muslin gown was eyed with disapproval. Its critic spoke to the intrusive Grace over the top of Aurora's head, as if this stranger had more role in this discussion than the owner of the dress.

"Hopelessly outdated," Fletcher dismissed the garment and would have flung it across the bed, had not his Gracie stopped him.

"No, no, Miles." She had leave to call him Miles! "All of these white things may be salvaged. I am sure of it. This one requires only fresh trimmings on the bodice, which must be cut a trifle lower as has become all the vogue. And here, do you not think a velvet spencer in willow green, to match her eyes, will smarten this quite nicely? Blond lace, no—bands of narrow satin ribbon at neck, cuffs, and hem, and matched satin rouleaux several times around the skirt are all that is required to freshen up this hailstone muslin, with perhaps a sash and bonnet trimmings to match."

She fingered several fabric swatches in greens, gold, and a vibrant burnt umber that matched the darker tones in Aurora's hair. "What do you think of these?"

Miles squinted at the swatches, held each to Aurora's cheek, and nodded. "Excellent choices, my pet. I knew your taste would prove infallible."

His pet, Gracie, whom Aurora was beginning to detest for her very worthiness, pulled a blush-pink garment from the bed and bit her lip in consternation. "This one may be beyond helping with her complexion, unless perhaps it can be dyed a darker rose shade."

She pressed it to Aurora's shoulder.

Miles stood back to examine its effect, his eyebrows shooting up in dismay. "You actually wear this color?" For the first time he addressed Aurora directly.

She nodded firmly, prepared to defend herself, despite the fact that she did not really care for the dress. "It is a very fashionable color," she insisted mulishly.

He squinted at it, his lip curling. "Fashionable on a blonde perhaps, but not at all attractive to a young woman with your coloring."

Aurora had had about enough of these two deciding her fate without so much as a word to see if she agreed. She had had enough of everyone deciding her future so summarily. With a long, drawn-out *Oooh!* of frustration, she whirled out from under the pink dress and flung it and herself across the room.

Gracie's despised, lilting voice assailed her before she could make the door. "Whatever is the matter, Miss Ramsay? Are you feeling ill?"

Her concern was so sickeningly sweet, so provokingly genuine, that Aurora whipped around to face them all, her lips tight with displeasure, her breast heaving in agitation. The day, and all of its disappointments pressed in on her. "I am feeling sick. Sick of people deciding what is best for me without ever asking my opinion. Sick, too, of the snide remarks and veiled insults that go on behind my back with regard to my quite unavoidable coloring. I will not stand for further insults. Good night to you. All of you!"

With that she swept out of the door in high dudgeon . . . and catapulted into none other than Lord Walsh, who caught her by the arm to keep her from falling.

"Ready to bowl me over again, Miss Ramsay?" he said, without smiling, in a deep, unruffled voice. "We really must make an effort to encounter one another without violence one of these days."

Aurora, already humiliated by what she took to be Miles

Fletcher's intentional slight to her in bringing along so many females and in taking over her room, her wardrobe, and the assessment of her coloring, was struck by how appropriate Lord Walsh's inquiry was under the circumstances of her pursuit of him. Speechless, she ducked her head, mumbled an insufficient apology and wrenched herself free of his hold. She ran, seeking in this house full of people, some place where she might vent her frustration alone. The anonymity of darkness beckoned to her from the doors that led outside. She answered its call by ducking into the night.

Gracie held up her hand in the uneasy silence that descended in the wake of Aurora's outburst. "Oh, dear!" She turned a stricken look on her brother. "Miles, you must go after her."

He was already on his way. "Wait here," he said as he swept through the door. He would not be stopped by Lord Walsh who promenaded in the hallway just without, though the earl raised his hand and cried out. "Is aught amiss?"

"No time to explain," Miles said, waving his walking stick like a pointer, "only tell me, which way did she go?"

Walsh helpfully grabbed the end of the ebony stick and jabbed it in the direction of the stairs, saying, "Flapped the unflappable Amazon, have you?"

Down the stairs Miles plunged, following the flash of Aurora's skirts as persistently as Walsh's aroused curiosity followed him. "Guilty, as charged," he admitted tersely.

Walsh leaned over the stair rail. "Whatever did you do or say, old man? I would have thought you might as soon squeeze tears from a stone."

Miles frowned. The earl's attitude did not bode well if Miss Ramsay's objective was to win his affections enough to wrench a proposal from him. Without responding, without pausing, he lunged through a doorway into the night. Miles Fletcher, a gentleman who was not at all wont to discommode himself by hurrying after anyone, male or female, charged along the walkway to the bridge, slowing only when he realized that the pale figure stopped in the middle was Aurora. His eyes adjusted to the darkness. She stood leaning over the wooden railing, staring down into the water, a moonlit picture of dejection.

Miles stopped to lean upon his walking stick, catch his breath, and plan what he would say to her. His sublime Diana peered into the water as though it was a looking glass. Her defeated posture would seem to indicate she was not happy with what she saw. Miles felt himself responsible for her dissatisfaction.

His pulse returned to a more even tempo, Miles walked up beside her, his reflection joining hers, caught in ripples that made their boundaries indistinct, so that in the water, they became one.

"I should like to tell you a story." His voice was as gentle as the wind rustling in distant trees. He meant to lull her with it.

"What story?" She shifted uncomfortably away from him—still angry. "Perhaps it were better told to another female, like that Gracie creature you brought along without so much as asking me if I minded."

"Did you mind her presence? I do apologize." He studied the water. "It is just that you had said you might like to meet my sister, and she has such an eye for color, I assumed her opinion would please you as much as it pleases me."

"Your sister?"

She was startled. He heard shock in the high pitch of her voice. He turned to study her profile. Good Lord! She had not known Gracie was his sister! Could it be jealousy that had lit the tinder of her impatience with his lack of consideration? Was it jealousy made her fly from the room? The idea pleased him.

"As to telling Gracie this story . . . I have told my sister all of my tales at one time or another. I am certain she would only yawn at me."

She sighed. He could not tell if the noise was a sign of relief or exasperation. "Tell me your story."

He held out his walking stick. The pale, marble-fisted top with its silver fitting caught the moonlight so that it seemed to float above the white of his glove, suspended by magic instead of an ebony stick so dark it disappeared in the darkness. "The tale is that of my walking stick's creation."

"This fist?" She ran her fingers lightly across the knuckled knob. "Does it remind you of me?"

He ignored the jibe. "It was in Greece, at a temple, I found this handful of marble—another crumbling bit of marble in a city filled with crumbling bits of little or no value—refuse to the inhabitants, who used such fallen dross to fill in walls, or as kick balls for young boys.

"The guide who led me about, when shown this marvelous misplaced hand, would have tossed it back down in the courtyard had I not stopped him." He dared move a little closer to her, studying her shadowed features. Moonlight washed the brilliant fire from her hair and paled the freckling of her complexion and still she was beautiful. Softly he said, "My gift, dear Miss Ramsay, is in recognizing beauty where no one else will acknowledge it—beauty in ruins, beauty locked away in cupboards and attics, beauty that requires but the right setting, the perfect frame for all the world to open up their eyes and acknowledge that yes, here stands a masterpiece."

He stared intently at her. Perhaps it was time to tell Aurora why the display of her beauty was so important to him. Perhaps not. The truth, in this fragile moment, seemed too harsh. He settled for a piece of it.

"I perceive a rare treasure in you, my dear. Do you have any idea how beautiful you are?"

Aurora Ramsay shivered, though the night was warm. A tear, he thought it was a tear, glistened in the corner of her eye. She leaned over the bridge. He realized she did so, that it might fall unnoticed, a single drop lost among many in the water below. Yet Miles was watching her so intently he saw it fall. He had not meant to provoke tears, but perhaps such evidence of emotion was a good thing. He tried once more to convince her of his proper motivation.

"I would frame you to advantage, Miss Ramsay. It is my gift, my most singular talent. I offer it to you with good intentions. I would set you off, you see, like a fist set in chased silver."

Aurora said nothing, but a breath shuddered from her lips that made Miles believe his cause was won. She was convinced. He read the language of her body unerringly.

"Come, we have much to do." He held out his hand to her.

She turned her gaze from the water, turned so the moonlight gleamed in her eyes. She fixed him with that moonlit stare for what seemed an eternity. Without a word, she took his hand.

Chapter Ten

M iles would never insult a lady. He is all compliments when it comes to women, you see. A dangerous fellow where hearts are concerned because of it." Grace Fletcher—viewed with far less jaundiced eye now that her relationship to Miles was established—was helping Aurora with the buttons at the back of her dress. Miles had left the women to conduct the measuring and changing of garments in private. He had taken Rupert with him. Even so, Aurora, unused to the company of other women her own age, found it strangely discomfitting to discuss Grace's brother as she was being stripped of her gown. It was as though she stripped herself of defenses along with the muslin.

"Take heed, Miss Ramsay." Grace found nothing unusual in their circumstance. She rattled on without pause. "As one who knows," she confided, "I would warn you to guard your heart jealously. You must not take anything Miles says, pretty words or plain, too much to heart—else you will suffer as much as any other female who has mistakenly believed my brother might love her for more than a moment."

That Miles Fletcher was a ladies' man came as no surprise to Aurora, but she had been very moved by Miles Fletcher's eloquence in the moonlight, as moved as ever she had been by his kisses. It made her stomach tighten to think his words might be no more than the efforts of a rake to charm her.

"Arms up, miss."

Aurora held up her arms and turned this way and that as she was bid. The seamstress efficiently snaked her measuring tape over Aurora's shoulder, then encompassed her arm, her waist, the fullness of her breasts. Mrs. Hall's gentle, unintrusive ministrations wove a mesmerizing sort of spell, just as Miles Fletcher's gentle, unintrusive compliments had woven a mesmerizing spell under the moonlight. Had she not been so determined to marry Walsh, Aurora was sure her head would have been turned by those words. Never before had a man told her to her face she was rare and beautiful. Never before had a man gone to such lengths to ensure she believed him.

Grace's voice interrupted her thoughts. "My brother's nature made thus perfectly clear to you, I do not hesitate to confide that he has become quite tiresome in filling my ear with nothing but praise for your honey-gold skin and hair the color of fox fur."

Aurora shivered. In discussing Miles with his sister thus, she felt as if she allowed him to get too close to her bared flesh.

"I've done with my measurements, miss," Mrs. Hall said in a businesslike manner. "If you will be so good as to pull this dress over your head, we will mark the bodice."

Aurora nodded and raised her arms for the cascade of parchment-colored silk that slid over her head.

The flow of Grace's conversation washed over her as smoothly as the silk. "What was the word he used to describe you on the first occasion we saw you?" She asked without expecting any answer. "I remember being quite struck by it at the time."

Grace's fingers were as busy as her tongue as she tugged at the string closures on the back of the evening gown. Aurora felt as if she were being tugged at from all directions. Mrs. Hall was tugging in front as much as Grace tugged in back, her fingers delving into the low neckline of the evening gown, deftly turning it under and pinning it in place because the Fletchers had unanimously determined Aurora's decolletage was not low enough to be considered fashionable. Aurora blushed to be handled in such a manner, no matter how impersonally it was done.

"What was it he called you?" Grace asked herself again.

So distracted was she, that Aurora had not heard a word of what Grace was saying until the babbling brook that was her tongue ceased running. Had she been asked a question? Did Grace expect some sort of reply?

She frowned uncertainly down at the lowered bodice. There was a great deal more cleavage to be seen than she was accustomed to. "Surely that is too low?"

Grace peered over her shoulder, then turned Aurora on her heel to peer absently at the objectionable neckline. "Sublime!" she crowed, her eyes brightening.

Aurora flushed. "You find this embarrassing display sublime?"

"Have I pinned it too low, miss?" Mrs. Hall was concerned.

Grace blinked and then burst into peals of contagious laughter. "No, no," she gasped. "The neckline is fine, but not at all what I was referring to. 'Sublime' is the word that my brother used to describe her in the first instance he saw Miss Ramsay."

Aurora was laughing too. "That would have been the occasion in which I had fallen in the middle of the dance floor with Lord Walsh flailing about on top of me?"

Grace was weeping, so deep was her amusement. As she finished pinning the bodice, Mrs. Hall regarded them as if they had both gone mad.

"By no means," Grace, her composure regained, hastened to set Aurora straight. "The remark was not sarcasm. It was made in complete earnestness at the archery competition you were in the midst of winning. Come, turn around and we shall have you out of that dress and into another."

Aurora struggled to remember the day of the archery display as the gown was undone and dropped about her ankles. Another was pulled over her head. As if in pulling her head through the cloud of muslin, she burst through the cloud of the past, and remembered. The coach! Miles and Grace Fletcher had been in the coach that had pulled into the clearing, that its occupants might observe the competition. Her attention had been momentarily distracted from the targets because she had been watching Walsh and he had gone to speak to someone in the vehicle just when she thought most to impress him. Instead, she had impressed a complete stranger, Miles Fletcher. What an odd turn of Fate.

"Step out and mind the pins," Mrs. Hall instructed. Obediently, almost blindly, Aurora stepped out of the dress pooled around her feet.

"Strange, how Fate does twist and turn on us at times," she whispered.

Grace nodded as she helped to settle the newly donned dress along Aurora's shoulders. "My mother always said, 'Life's a tangle and we must go about bravely unknotting it.' "

Aurora pondered the words as Mrs. Hall familiarly pinned away at her bodice again. What a knot she had herself just untangled. Miles Fletcher found her sublime and yet meant to help her win Walsh! There was something disturbingly perverse in such contradiction. His gift, he had said, was framing beauty that others might recognize it— and take it off his hands, he should have added.

She understood now, with far more clarity than before. She was art to him, a bit of marble, no more than a fist to be set in silver, a form to be measured and pinned and set in beribboned muslin and lace so that someone else might hang her on his arm.

With an indefinable sadness, she asked, "Does your brother keep any of the fine bits of art he collects for other people?"

Grace looked puzzled by this strange non sequitur of a question. She shrugged. "Very little. The art is, after all, his living. He must make a profit."

"And those pieces he keeps . . ."

"Yes?"

"Do you know why he holds on to them?"

Grace looked at her as if she asked something remarkable. "How strange that you should ask. I have pondered this very matter many times, myself. It is not value, in terms of pounds and pence, that Miles will hold on to. His tastes are eclectic and do not follow any one recognizable theme. I have decided, as a result, that those possessions he prizes most, have so struck a chord in his heart or his soul, that he cannot let them slip from his fingers and so he does his best to go about convincing collectors who might have bought the thing off him, that they did not really want the item after all."

Aurora smiled, remembering Miles Fletcher's performance on the bridge. "Well, if anyone might change someone's mind, it is your brother. He is a very convincing fellow."

Grace's affection for her brother was evident in her expression. "He is, isn't he?" She wrapped her arm around Aurora's waist as if they were longtime acquaintances. "I am pleased you like my brother, for I have had a lovely chat with yours this evening about artistic aspirations, of which I have a few of my own." She gave Aurora a squeeze. "I am sure we are all meant to be the dearest of friends."

Aurora smiled, but she could not so easily fall into demonstrating care-free affection for Grace Fletcher as the engaging young woman did for her and Rupert. She still feared for Rupert's heart with regard to this swanlike creature. "I should like that," she said carefully. "I am sure Rupert would agree."

And indeed, Rupert did agree, quite vociferously, once Grace and Mrs. Hall had packed up measuring tape and fabric swatches and left them in peace. The hour was much advanced, and Aurora yawned with fatigue. It was strangely wearing to have been the center of judgmental attention for hours on end.

Rupert was not worn so thin. His face was alight with the happy memory of Grace Fletcher. He seemed in a mood for conversation. "They are a most delightful brother and sister, don't you agree?" He spoke with unusual enthusiasm. "They are as compatible—as cheerful together—as ever I have seen two siblings."

"Too cheerful," Aurora said wryly, her nerves frazzled by that incessant good cheer. She had felt inadequate in the presence of such spritely conversation and tasteful observation as the Fletchers effortlessly generated. They had unintentionally pointed out to her how woefully inadequate her relationships with her own brothers were. Other than Rupert, she exchanged pleasant conversation with not a one of them, certainly not such agreeable chatter as Miles and Grace had demonstrated. Beyond that, their remarks made her realize how out of touch her life in the country left her, not only about fashion, but about the world as well. These two had traveled to many and varied faraway places. The broadening of their horizons evidenced itself in familiar references to the very countries from whence the fabrics they meant to wrap her in originated. Draped in samples of French muslin, Indian gauze, Chinese crepe, Italian silk, English wool, many decorated in designs inspired by Greece and Rome, Egypt and Persia, Aurora yearned to expand the boundaries of her experience.

"It is a pity he cannot marry her," she said in jest. "They would make a pretty couple."

"Aurora!" Rupert was not used to such humor from her, though it was the very sort of playful, biting remark that had passed between the Fletchers all evening.

"Did you not think they sounded just like husband and wife at times, finishing one another's sentences the way they did, and wrangling in as agreeable a fashion as might be expected over color and cut and cost?"

"Would that I might one day wrangle so agreeably with a wife over such things," Rupert said wistfully.

"You will," Aurora promised stoutly, devoid of the strength required for defending his future any more energetically. "You'll see. All will be well." Something that Grace Fletcher had said wandered through her consciousness. She sat up briskly. "Come! Tomorrow's sheepshearing is soon enough for unknotting life's tangle. I will help you down the stairs so that we might both get ourselves to bed."

At the top of the stairs they were hailed.

"Hallo!" Miles Fletcher called.

"I thought we were rid of you," Rupert said lightly.

Miles smiled. Aurora had never before noticed how attractively the corners of his eyes crinkled when he smiled. "I'll gladly go away again if you wish," he said, his remark, indeed, his entire attention focused on Rupert. "It occurred to me you might appreciate a stout shoulder to lean upon, Ramsay. I came back to offer mine."

Rupert accepted. Aurora was impressed. It was unusual for her brother to entrust himself so readily to a stranger's care.

As the two made their slow progress down the steps, she half expected Miles Fletcher to glance up at her, to ascertain her reaction to his offer of assistance to her brother. She was even more impressed when he did not.

"Thank you," Rupert said a trifle awkwardly when he and Miles reached the foot of the stairs.

Miles thought Aurora's brother looked exhausted by the effort of taking the stairs by peg and crutch, as exhausted as the fabric that made up his coat and waistcoat. Both had seen better days. Miles had noted the same worn condition on the hems of several of Aurora's dresses. The Ramsays were not particularly flush in the pocket, it would seem. He motioned to a nearby bench. "Will you sit here a moment and talk? I am ashamed to admit I have not assisted you for purely altruistic reasons."

Rupert readily sank onto the bench, curious. "Your motivation is a selfish one?"

"Absolutely!" Miles made light of what he would ask. "I am hoping you now feel so indebted to me that you will reveal the mystery of why your sister"—he looked around to be sure they were not overheard—"is bent on receiving an offer from Walsh." His manner was that of a man in jest, but his question was in earnest.

Rupert shrugged. "That is a question best asked of Aurora," he equivocated. "I do not even begin to pretend to understand the motivations of my siblings."

Miles frowned. Rupert sounded annoyed. "Perhaps I approach the topic too bluntly," he apologized. "You must know that I have promised to help your sister in her quest for Walsh's affections?"

Rupert nodded, but would not meet his eye. "Hence the wardrobe business upstairs," he said.

"Exactly." Miles studied Rupert. "It is not commonly my role to play matchmaker with anything other than antiquities. I would not meddle in such a matter if I felt such a course ran contrary to good sense. You have but to say the word and I will cease dabbling in your sister's affairs. I would not continue down any road if you feel it runs contrary to that which will in the longterm make Aurora happy."

Rupert studiously avoided his eyes, staring instead at the top of his crutch, which he held before him like a cross. "My sister must decide upon her own happiness," he said at last. "Her reasons . . . are her own. If you come to me, seeking endorsement of your assistance to her, I must send you away unsatisfied."

"Let me ask you plainly then, have you any objection to Walsh as a brother-in-law?"

"No, nor of my sister's marrying him if he will make her happy." He frowned. "Circumstances I am not at liberty to divulge factor heavily into this course she has chosen. Due to said circumstances, I am quite certain my own definition of marital bliss would not coincide with Aurora's."

Miles thought he was rather more informed as to the mysterious circumstances Rupert mentioned than either Ramsay would have appreciated. He did not disclose as much to Rupert.

With the aid of his crutch, the young man had risen.

"I wish you a pleasant evening." His politeness had a frosty edge that put an end to further questions.

"Good night." Miles remained where he sat, puzzling the matter as he watched Rupert's slow progress across the gleaming marble floor.

"Blast!" he said forcefully under his breath, setting off after him. The promise he had made to his uncle was proving far more difficult to honor than he might have imagined.

Rupert seemed to expect him. He paused in his progress as Miles's strident footsteps rang in his wake.

"One question and I will pester you no more."

Rupert looked him in the eye, waiting.

Miles passed a hand across his lips. "Are these circumstances you referred to financial?" he asked bluntly. "Perhaps I may assist you?"

Rupert regarded him keenly. "You are very kind, Mr. Fletcher. But I cannot accept your kind offer. The circumstances I mentioned run far deeper than mere money. A river of gold has already run through Ramsay hands. I would not have you casting good money after bad."

Chapter Eleven

The following morning the sheepshearing began. From a very early hour the level of noise and bustling activity around Holkham Hall increased tenfold, but the Hall itself could not begin to compare to the noisy concentration of carriages, people, and livestock that writhed in masses around the barns.

Aurora was in her element. The crowd was enough to daunt most females. Not Aurora. With a smile she wound her way through the press. Barns had always been a safe haven for her. All of Thomas William Coke's guests were on hand, as were most of his laborers and a great majority of the local neighborhood. In looking at the vast crowds here, Aurora felt she shared a special kinship with the men and women gathered. These were the folk, common and noble, who would rather sit horseback than on a drawing room couch. The love of the outdoors was written all over their sun-touched faces.

There was an air of a country fair to the proceedings. There was not just the shearing to observe. The Hall's prize bulls were paraded around the grounds, along with a number of fine horses and a pig or two. The latest of farming equipment and machinery had been arranged in one area for all to see and discuss. A group of aproned and bonneted women were clustered some distance from the shearing, cleaning, carding, spinning, and dying some of the freshly sheared wool.

Closer to the barns, in a clipped, grassy space, makeshift willow-branch pens had been put together to hold the sheep. The gentle sound of their babylike blatting was a constant reminder of the reason for this gathering.

Dressed sensibly in boots and riding gear, her skirt buttoned high, Aurora made her way among the spectators, sheep, shepherds, dogs, and shearers. Large squares of oiled canvas had been spread by the shearers. One by one the sheep were led to these mats by their shepherds, easily identified by their long, pale smocks, woolen hose, and tall staffs. At their bidding clever, sharp-eared dogs moved with concise, concentrated precision among the press of men and beasts. The shearers, also smocked, were bent to their task, as they would be all of this day and for many more to come. This was no entertainment for them, but a long, backbreaking day's work amid a gaggle of onlookers. Wielding wicked-looking, long-bladed shears as casually as butter knives, their object was clear. They meant to trim away the thick fleece on every sheep that came within arm's reach.

Aurora had no real notion when it was that Miles Fletcher came up beside her. She found the shearing of sheep a fascinating spectacle and watched it with narrowly focused concentration until Walsh joined the group of spectators a few feet to her right.

Walsh, she noticed. Grace hung on his arm and Aurora hoped she would notice her, perhaps call to her to join them. But Miss Fletcher did not so much as glance in Aurora's direction, no matter how deliberately Aurora stared.

Miles watched Aurora with the same concentration that his sister avoided looking at her, just as he had instructed her to. Aurora did not notice. She had eyes only for sheep and Lord Walsh.

"Tell me exactly what goes on here, Miss Ramsay." He made a point of speaking just loud enough that Walsh must hear him.

Aurora, startled, jumped a little as Walsh turned toward them, just as Miles had hoped he would, to say, "Good morning, Miles, Miss Ramsay."

"Your Grace." He politely tipped his hat in return, returning the focus of his attention to Aurora, whose gaze flickered over his shoulder and back again, as though she anticipated a move toward Walsh and his sister. Miles could read the expectation in her eyes. But he was far more subtle than that. He wanted Walsh to join them of his own volition, not the other way around.

"Tell me," he said gently, distracting her, "what is it that the shearer uses to cut away the sheep's hooves?"

Any disappointment she might have harbored at his failure to approach Walsh disappeared as her focus shifted to the activities of the man who bent over the prostrate ewe, his hand moving swiftly from hoof to hoof.

"Those are clippers," she said, comfortable in her knowledge. "The hooves must be clipped every once in a while."

"And is the shearing done with the wicked garden shears?" he asked with deliberate ignorance.

"They are called blades and you are right in calling them wicked. You can see the shearer has bound the palms of his hands in gauze—protection against accidental slicing should the sheep decide to move about unexpectedly." She fell silent.

"Go on," Miles encouraged. "Tell me, step-by-step, what he is doing and why. I would understand it all."

Aurora obliged him without demure, the information flowing readily from her tongue without any trace of superiority. This world of sheep and shepherds and shearing fit her comfortably, like an old pair of gloves.

"The first 'blow,' for so each stroke of the blades is called, is the brisket blow, there between the front legs. It is followed by the belly wool blow, which is generally clipped and set aside. The rest of the wool will be sheared away in one large piece, so down each leg he goes, and around the dock."

"Why is a sheep's tail docked? Is it the fashion, like docking a horse's tail?"

"Not exactly. Many shepherds believe docking keeps their sheep cleaner and healthier, as there is no tail to catch dirt and manure and burrs." As she answered, Miles slid a glance in Gracie's direction. Her attention was on Miss

Ramsay—as was Lord Walsh's. Everything was according to plan.

"Do you dock your sheep?"

Both Lord Walsh and the shepherd whose ewe was being sheared tilted their heads in her direction. Miles could tell their interest was keen by their arrested stance.

Without noticing the attention she received, Aurora nodded decisively. The shepherd nodded his approval. "I recommend my shepherds dock lambs if they are not already in the practice."

Miles nodded.

She went on in her description of the shearer's movements. "Now, he has done the neck blow from brisket to cheek, and the topknot," she pointed to the ewe's head. "He is finishing out the shoulder blow, where the wool is best, and is moving along the side."

Zzzt, zzt, zzzt. The blades snicked faster now through the wool, which fell away from the ewe's sides, pale and clean, almost buttery next to the animal's skin.

"As he works across the back, the shearer takes what are called long blows." Aurora was in her element, her eyes focused on the swinging movement of the shearer's arm, her words flowing as effortlessly as the wool seemed to slide from the sheep's back. Faster now, the blade sang through the wool as the ewe, passive as a rag doll beneath the hypnotic movement of hand and blade was gently rolled so that the other side might be worked. Faster still the blade sang through the creamy wool, and faster still Aurora described the final bladework on this, the whipping side of the sheep.

Aurora's voice had drawn a crowd of attentive listeners. Most of them focused on the sheep and shearer with occasional glances in Aurora's direction as she spoke. Lord Walsh was among them, but the focus of his attention differed from that of the onlookers around him. He was as mesmerized by Aurora as the glassy-eyed sheep was by its own shearing. There was an amazed sort of wonder in his gaze, as if he were vastly impressed by something he had not expected to affect him at all.

Miles felt a jealous pang of connection. Did *he* look like

that when he gazed at Aurora? Like a smitten schoolboy? Was his own chance of securing the young lady's affections being clipped along with the wool? Would she now fall into the arms of the man she had so long and arduously pursued as readily as wool fell from the back of the ewe?

"Wool away!" the shearer called out, as the ewe sprang from the pale mound of its shorn fleece and shook itself, a dazed look on its face.

Lord Walsh blinked, as dazed as the sheep.

Two women stepped in to bundle up the wool. Another creature was led to the mat.

"Come!" Aurora beckoned Miles, oblivious to the change in Lord Walsh. "If you would understand the full process of shearing, we should follow the fleece. There is much yet to be done with it."

Miles was cheered by her excitement, cheered immensely. He held out his arm to her. "I am yours to command," he said and away they would have sailed, out of Lord Walsh's field of influence, had not the man blocked their path, Grace disposed upon his arm.

"Would you mind our accompanying you?" he asked with a courtly bow to Aurora. "Your knowledge of the shearing process is considerable, Miss Ramsay. I am sure Miss Fletcher would be greatly entertained to hear more."

"Greatly entertained," Grace agreed. "Tell me, does your brother intend to join in the festivities today?"

Miles was forced to smile and respond to Walsh's small talk politely, when in truth he would have liked to tell both Walsh and Gracie to go to blazes. He had grown used to having Aurora Ramsay to himself. He realized how much he would like to continue that state of affairs.

But his wishes were not to be fulfilled. Hers were. His Uncle Lester's were. Walsh clung to them like a thistle burr, exactly as Miles had originally planned.

Chapter Twelve

On the following day it rained. The shearing continued in the crowded confines of the barn.

Many of Coke's guests declined to brave the weather.

Under ordinary circumstances Aurora would have donned her boots without hesitation and slogged through the mud. Today she found the turn in the weather an irritation and a nuisance. For the first time in a long time, she had an aversion to getting either wet or dirty. Mrs. Hall had sent over two of her redone gowns, as promised, as quickly as they were finished. Aurora had torn into the parcel with great expectation. She had made such a positive impression on Lord Walsh the previous day that she hoped to impress him again, this time with her appearance. She had donned the prettiest of the two dresses.

The changes were tasteful and understated. Nothing looked added on or out of place. Feeling girlish and pretty, as if she had been handed an entirely new dress, Aurora paraded in front of the mirror, wondering how to pay for her indulgence, and concentrating again on the advantages of marrying a man of means.

A French modiste would be at her disposal if she could wring a proposal out of Walsh. She whirled before the mirror at the prospect. Miles had been right. His sister had an unerring eye for color. To a simple round-necked, ecru-colored gown, boasting no more original detail than Frenchwork across the bodice and around the hem and cuffs, color had been judiciously added. Satin piping in a green to match her eyes ran in tiers along the base of the skirt and around the cuffs, disguising any worn spots. In addition, green corded lace epaulets had been fashioned for the shoulders. When the epaulets had been suggested, Aurora had balked at such an addition.

"I do not care for fussy bits hanging off my dresses."

Grace had shrugged. "As you wish, but epaulets are all the rage, and as they are worn by all manner of gentlemen in the military, I cannot agree with your assessment in labeling them fussy. Quite to the contrary," she had exclaimed, "they lend a military trimness to one's shoulders."

Aurora was glad she had relied on Grace Fletcher's expertise. The epaulets, indeed, everything about the dress, suited her admirably.

She descended to the breakfast parlor, where one fended for oneself by partaking what one would from a well-stocked sideboard. There, over slices of ham and poached eggs, she received several pretty compliments on her appearance, the most valued of which came from Lord Walsh, whom she encountered coming into the room as she was taking herself out of it.

"Miss Ramsay!" He stepped back out of her way. "We seem to be in the habit of running into one another in doorways."

"*Au contraire,* sir," she said pertly, favoring him with a dazzling smile, "we have almost got the knack of *not* running into one another. I would say, instead, that we have the unusual good fortune to *encounter* one another in doorways."

He smiled, as much in a mood for banter as she. "With good fortune, the next time we encounter one another, we shall both be headed in the same direction. I have noticed that you spend your mornings on horseback when weather permits. Perhaps, if it does not rain again tomorrow, we might turn our horses' heads in the same direction?"

He asked her to ride with him!

"At what hour would I encounter you in the doorway to the stables?" Her voice sounded surprisingly calm.

He seemed pleased with her response. "Seven would find me there. Does that suit you?"

She inclined her head. "I shall make an effort not to bowl you over, sir."

He allowed himself a smile. He was very handsome when he smiled. "I do not mind in the least being bowled over by a beautiful woman, Miss Ramsay."

Aurora parted from him, her hopes very high. But faced with a day indoors and rain lacing all the windows in busy Holkham Hall, Aurora's euphoria did not last. She did not want to wait. Tomorrow promised too much. Today, she was certain, must be a complete waste of her time.

Miles found her pacing from window to window in the drawing room a quarter of an hour later, a caged wildcat in refurbished muslin. She was wearing one of the dresses that Mrs. Hall had transformed. He recognized the willow-green trim. He would make a point of seeing to it that Mrs. Hall was handsomely recompensed. The change in Aurora Ramsay's appearance was charming.

"You look lovely." He joined Aurora in her pacing and nodded his head toward the trim that enlivened her shoulders.

Aurora fingered her sleeve. "Do you like it? Two dresses were delivered to me this morning with a promise of two more this afternoon."

He smiled, his approval undisguised. "More important than what I like—do *you* care for the change?"

She could not disguise her pleasure. Her eyes lit up like stars and a self-conscious smile tugged her lips. "Who would have thought such a small change could make such a difference?" She tucked her hand into the crook of his arm.

He might have taken pleasure in that telling evidence of her growing affection for him, had she not imparted in that very moment how effectively the dress had caught Lord Walsh's eye.

"He has asked me to ride with him tomorrow morning! Isn't it wonderful!" She gave his arm a squeeze.

He was pleased she had prospects for the future, but he could not be pleased they were with Lord Walsh, whom he was convinced, now more than ever, after having traipsed all around the sheepshearing grounds yesterday in his company, was not at all the best man for Aurora Ramsay.

Aurora was staring out of the rain-drenched windows. Imagining her ride tomorrow with Walsh, Miles suspected.

She sighed and followed a raindrop down the pane with the tip of her finger. "This is my least favorite sort of day. We are trapped indoors by such weather. In lieu of studying livestock or cultivating tools, what do you suggest we do?"

Miles regarded the mist-shrouded landscape. "I realize there are many who would agree with you, but I beg to differ. Rainy days are my favorite. The familiar world beyond ones window is lent mystery by such weather. It never fails to make me feel fortunate to be indoors—warm and dry, with a good book in hand and an extra log on the grate."

She no longer stared bleakly out at the sodden landscape. She stared instead at him. "My brother would agree with you. However it would seem that on every matter, you and I are at odds, sir."

"Indeed," he smiled. "As a result, our conversations are never dull. Come! This weather offers us the opportunity to spend an entire day exploring my favorite subjects." He led the way out of the drawing room. It was becoming far too crowded for his taste.

"Is dancing one of them?" she suggested hopefully.

"You would dance with me, Miss Ramsay?" He was genuinely surprised, and touched. Too much proof of his pleasure must have evidenced itself in his expression. Too swiftly she relinquished his hand, too quickly did her gaze drop.

She placed herself in a defensive posture, as though she must in some form recant her enthusiasm. "I have observed how skilled you are," she said gruffly.

He wanted to preen, so pleased was he by her compliment. He restrained himself, bowing instead, and taking her hand with the promise that they would dance before the day was out. "Before such exertion, I would explore other arts: painting and sculpture and music, all of which you should be familiar with in order to attract the attention of a peer of the realm. The arts, you see, speak to us in such a manner that we need never feel completely alone or cut off from the world, no matter how confining the weather."

She shrugged and swept a hand toward the painting adorned walls of the room they passed. "Dazzle me. I am listening."

He stepped into the room. Empty at the moment, it was a sparsely furnished reception area for the Green State Bedroom, striking for its red damask-covered walls, that were hung, as were most of the rooms in the house, with fine paintings. Turning a slow circle, Miles said, "All right. Would you have a story of politics, mythology, history or romance?"

Her gaze roved the paintings. "All of that looks down on us from these walls?"

"That and more."

"Tell me of romance, then," she said.

Beckoning her to a chair, he leaned over the arm of it, and lowered his voice, deliberately heightening the intrigue. "The portrait of our host is the painting I shall tell you about. Not the Gainsborough over the fireplace, but the one before you, of Coke in all his finery."

She fixed her eyes on the painting in question.

Marveling a moment at the beauty of her face as each feature set itself in concentration, Miles turned his attention to the portrait. A younger, trimmer Thomas Coke was nonchalantly posed against the base of a marble statue—a reclining female who gazed wistfully from her stone perch at the handsome young man. Coke was worthy of wistful feminine glances, exquisitely garbed as he was in a pale silver-gray coat and pantaloons, finished out with a heavy silver-lace collar, silver buttons, silver trim, and salmon-red ribbons. A tailed ermine cloak was thrown negligently across one shoulder. Its salmon-red lining accentuated the identically hued feather that curled over the brim of a hat dangling from his right hand. Matching ribbons graced his throat, tied just below the knee, and laced his silvery gray shoes, the heels of which were also salmon red.

At his feet, on one side was depicted an odd collection of what looked like broken marble bits fallen from the columned temple in which he stood. On his left, a white spaniel with dark brown ears and a patch of brown at the base of his tail, nosed the feather in his hat, staring up at Coke with adoration. Coke seemed unaffected by either the dog or the wistful, bare-breasted marble female behind him. He gazed in the opposite direction, his eyes clear, his expression mild, his complexion as pale and smooth and unblemished as a girl's.

"The artist is Batoni," Miles began. "He was specially commissioned to do Coke's likeness by a countess who was soon to become a princess."

"A princess?" Aurora expressed interest with a reluctance that made Miles smile. She had set her mind toward having a miserable day, and Miss Ramsay's mind, once it was made up, was not easily swayed. He knew all too well that she was interested in spite of herself.

"Yes, a princess. No more than twenty years old at the time, she fell instantly in love with the handsome young man in the painting, despite her betrothal to another."

Aurora turned her arresting green gaze to regard him intently a moment.

"Go on," she said, her tone slightly cynical.

"This painting depicts our host, the object of her affection, in the wedding finery he wore on her wedding day to another man. It was offered to our host as a token of the young woman's deepest affection and esteem."

She was quiet a moment, frowning with concentration at the painting. "This romance of yours is a tragedy it would seem."

"Yes, I suppose it is. But then, marriages of convenience do often tend to tragedy. Do you not agree?"

He meant to prod her conscience with such a remark despite all promises to his uncle. She seemed aware of his intent. Her eyes narrowed, though she uttered not a word. He went on. "The princess certainly thought her marriage, and thus her happiness, was doomed from the start. The statue of the lovelorn Ariadne there in the background, a young woman trapped forever in stone, is meant to represent her feelings. The fragments of frieze work and broken column at Coke's feet, are her broken dreams."

Aurora's eyes were narrowed, her lip caught between her teeth. Miles gave her a moment to study the image. The dream, the longed-for future he meant to fulfill for Miss Ramsay in the form of Lord Walsh—surely it was only proper that it be questioned.

"Who was this princess? Whom did she marry?"

He leaned closer to whisper theatrically, "Countess Louise of Stolburg. Her prince was Charles Edward Stuart."

"The Pretender?" She turned to stare at him in awe. "The child bride of Bonnie Charlie himself was enamored of Tom Coke?"

For an instant it occurred to Miles that he would like to commission a painting of Aurora as she appeared to him now, her eyes sparkling with interest, her vibrant hair backlit by the mellow candlelight of a rain-dimmed room. Better yet, as he had first seen her in the woods, before the Doric temple, bow in hand. Instead of broken stone, a rejected love knot belonged at her feet.

"What became of them?" Her question shattered his thoughts.

He sighed, reluctant to relinquish the picture in his mind. "Well, the bonnie prince was fifty-two at the time and considerably less bonnie than he had been at his bride's tender age. He was, I believe, prone to public drunkenness in the years preceding his wedding."

"And the countess?" She was gazing again at the beautiful maiden trapped in stone.

"I am told the prince hoped to beget an heir to his claim to the throne." He frowned, imagining Aurora swollen with Walsh's child. Would such a future truly make her happy?

Aurora's eyebrows rose in mute question.

He blinked away the disturbing image. "Charles was disappointed," he said. "And the young countess—having borne no sons—endured his disappointment for eight years, then found herself a younger man and ran off with him."

"Did she really?" Aurora gazed with new interest at the painting before her.

Miles had positioned himself that he might gaze at Aurora while appearing to fix his interest on the Batoni. Would Aurora end up disappointed in a marriage to Walsh? He thought she might.

"Well, Mr. Fletcher"—she turned to him with a sheepish smile that made him long to kiss her upturned mouth—"I must admit you have the right of it."

"Have I?" He smiled. Such an admission was hard won. "Can it be arranged marriages you refer to, or the fact that paintings are far more entertaining than you first assumed?"

"You are most persuasive with regard to both." She seemed almost shy in her compliment. "Will you tell me more? The morning has proven far more entertaining than I ever might have anticipated. I have not once considered the gloominess of the day."

High praise indeed!

"I should be pleased if it brings you pleasure. There is a particularly fine marble of Diana in the statue gallery that you might find interesting."

In their progress to the statue gallery, however, they were accosted by Grace, who was followed by a footman bearing a handful of oil lamps that looked better suited to the stables than the luxurious interior of Holkham Hall.

"I have found you at last!" she crowed. "Only guess Miles, what I have arranged as entertainment?" She waved at the lamp-bearing footman as though he must give away said entertainment immediately.

Miles directed his gaze at the ceiling. "A trip to the attic?" He had a very good idea what it was Gracie had in mind.

Grace nodded enthusiastically. "Am I not a clever girl?" Without awaiting his agreement she reached out to clasp Aurora's hands in her own. "You must come with us, Miss Ramsay. We are in for such a treat!"

"But what is in the attic that can so excite you both?" Aurora asked.

Intentionally mysterious, Miles whispered provocatively

in her ear. "Hidden treasures, Miss Ramsay, that few have the honor of witnessing! Do you mean to come?"

As he had hoped, Aurora was far too intrigued to resist such an invitation.

Chapter Thirteen

The treasure hunt was a chillier affair than Aurora had anticipated. The attic was dark and cobwebby. It smelled musty. The rain drummed loudly on the slates above their heads. Their swinging lanterns sent light and shadows moving and shifting on all sides of them, illuminating heaps of cast-off furniture of an earlier day and stacks of boxes, trunks, and storage crates. Aurora hated closed-off spaces, places without breeze or sunshine. She hated the attic. Most of all, she hated the dark. Whatever was she doing in this dusty place in her newly refurbished dress? Why had she agreed to this stupid jaunt? What treasures were to be found here?

In her heart, Aurora knew the answer even as she asked it of herself. Her curiosity had brought her here, curiosity about hidden treasure and curiosity with regard to the man whose lantern held the darkness from her heels—the man in whose every mood, every movement, every word she found fascination. These were the reasons she braved dust and darkness. There had been something so compelling in Miles Fletcher's expression as he spoke of the treasures locked here that a scramble in an attic had begun to sound like an adventure.

"Here we are." The footman who led them held high his lamp to indicate a wooden rack that held several enormous, canvas-draped rectangles. "Please stand back. There is sure to be dust."

Aurora looked at Grace. Unmoved by the threat of dust, she remained where she was, her eyes fixed on the paintings. Aurora was not so inclined to suffer. She stepped back the way they had come, testing the shadows, shivering as Miles Fletcher passed her, taking the light of his lamp with him.

Aurora would have preferred that no one had noticed her shivering. She considered such a loss of bodily control embarrassing evidence of weakness, a weakness that her brothers would have leapt on immediately had any of them been there. They would have chided her fears, chided, too, her foolishness in wearing no more than muslin against the damp and cold.

Miles turned and held his lamp high. The light shone full on her face.

"Are you cold, Miss Ramsay? I am prepared to swear that I have just heard your teeth chattering." His liquid voice reminded her of the rain on the roof. It was a persistent, penetrating sound. Before she could stop him, he had put down his lamp and was slipping off his exquisitely tailored jacket, holding it out as though he expected her to wear it.

She would have accepted it with alacrity had it not entailed putting down her lantern. Darkness would fairly swallow them if she put down her light. She did not think she could stand such an encroachment, even temporarily.

"Are you not cold, then?" He leaned closer to her. "But of course you are. My ears do not deceive me. Your teeth are chattering." His breath was warm on her face. His very presence was a warmth, so close to her.

"I am afraid of the dark," she whispered.

He did not laugh at her, nor did he repeat what she had said in disbelief as she had feared he might. He was only quiet a moment before taking up his lamp again, to prop it on top of a stack of crates. "Better?" he asked, holding his coat open, that she might easily slip into it.

She reached up to set her lamp beside his and turned to accept the garment. "Much better," she had to agree, as the warm weight of his jacket enfolded her. "What a kind and thoughtful fellow you are. I have never known a gentleman so solicitous of my comfort, so willing to help fulfill my desires."

A strange look passed over his features, a troubled look, but perhaps it was only the flickering light of the lamps. She could not be sure.

"You are very kind, Mr. Fletcher. Will you not now be chilly?"

The teasing, flirtatious half-smile she had become quite fond of seeing in his expression reappeared. "How can I be cold, when I think of you wrapped up in my jacket? Such thoughts are marvelously warming."

She laughed. Everything he said was in some way suggestive and yet she did not think he meant a word of any of it. Flattery was a game to him, an exhibition of his talents. Aurora was amused and touched by her exchanges with Miles Fletcher. Long after he had left her side to return to the paintings, she stood cocooned in his warm, citrus-scented coat and pondered his affect on her. She was used to being ridiculed for her fears. That Fletcher should so nonchalantly do the opposite of what she expected, amazed her. She was deeply touched by his kindnesses, his every indication of concern for her comfort and well-being. As a result, she was struck, in a way she had never before noticed, by how attractive Mr. Fletcher was. The man's attention to detail, the very polish of his appearance, seemed such a reflection of his character, that she found it appealing where once she would have declared it absurd.

The paintings were unveiled one by one.

" 'Jupiter Caressing Juno,' " Miles said reverently. "A Hamilton."

The second dustcloth fell, and the third. Miles identified them with ease, sounding very much the expert he was reputed to be. " 'Perseus Delivering Andromeda,' Chiari. 'Tarquin and Lucretia' by Procaccini."

The names meant little to Aurora, but the paintings themselves took her breath away! There was no mistaking the reason why these massive canvases, rendered in rich color, had been removed from the walls downstairs. They were done in the Classical style, most depicting gods and goddesses, scantily clad, muscles rippling, breasts bared. Each might be described with the same two words, passion and seduction. Desire was captured on canvas, raw and urgent, the pursuit of woman by man.

The treasure hunting party stood silent a moment—overwhelmed by the treasure in the attic—frozen by the power of the work, by its size, scope, and subject matter. The emotions these canvases laid bare were too big a thing to be experienced in the dark, chill closeness of an attic. Aurora felt swallowed up, as if figures and forces and feelings she had never before encountered reached out to her from the glowing paint, entreating her to cross the threshold of reality into some other world—a place that flooded her ribcage with too much air, or not enough, she could not be certain—a place that lit a fire deep within her being. Her blood seemed to simmer, her cheeks flamed. Unmentionable parts of her anatomy burned with the heat.

She could not take her eyes away from the paintings for fear they would disappear like a dream too beautiful to forget and too perfect to remember. Breathlessly, she looked until she was filled with looking. She thought private thoughts and listened to the others breathe, and knew they could not be as affected as she.

Grace reached out and touched one of the paintings. "Marvelous musculature."

Aurora could not look at Miles.

"Hard to believe they are close to a hundred years old." He turned to her. He meant to ask her what she thought of them. She could feel the question hovering between them and yet had no ready answer when the question came.

"What do you think of them?"

What could she say? How could she explain the way these expanses of canvas and paint affected her? Aurora didn't know how to begin. She was unused to seeing passion depicted, given life and form and color. She was even more unused to discussing how such passion affected her. She did not want to say she was shocked and titillated and convinced, as nothing before had convinced her, of the power of art. What could she safely say? How was she to express her feelings? Most of what passed through her mind and heart was too personal to discuss.

He stood looking at her, awaiting her answer. An answer she must provide.

"They are provocative," she said, the words wholly inadequate.

"Yes." He was watching her closely—too closely, she thought. "They cry freedom, don't they?"

He required no answer and so she gave him none. Something in his expression made her feel he found answer enough in her silence.

"Such passion should not be shut away in the attic—ignored." His tone made Aurora wonder if Miles Fletcher meant to pass judgment not just on these paintings and their place in the attic, but also on the state of her own bundled-away passion. The gentle nudge of such a remark gave her pause. Was she locking away something beautiful and vibrant within herself, something as urgent and naked, as warmly stirring as this collection of living, breathing canvas and paint?

Miles seemed content to let her stew in the broth of her thoughts and feelings. He questioned her no more.

Aurora's gaze slid uneasily from one painted scene to the next. They gave life to the part of her impending relationship with a husband that she liked to think of least—this naked grasping of hand and limb. If she put herself in the role of the women in these paintings, her heart began to race, her temperature rose, her pulse pounded. Could she picture Lord Walsh as a near-naked Jupiter, caressing her as Juno?

The thought unnerved her. She found no joy in such a picture. In fact, her eyes turned time and time again to regard Miles Fletcher and the passionate manner in which he stared at the paintings—eyes glowing, lips parted, his breath accelerated. She was far more apt to consider him in the role, far more likely to wonder how he might go about rousing his Juno. There was far more of the requisite level of fire and heat and ardor in this man's little finger than in Lord Walsh's entire being. She had been warmed by it on more than one occasion.

Such a realization served no purpose other than to frus-

trate and give rise to feelings of discontent with her chosen
lot. Aurora turned from the display of painted flesh with a
shiver. It would serve her purpose far better to be downstairs chatting with Lord Walsh this very moment, than
standing here beside Miles Fletcher, staring at these
provocative paintings.

"I'm cold," she said abruptly. "If you've no objection to
my taking away one of the lights, I mean to go downstairs."
Without waiting to see if anyone meant to go with her, or if
indeed they objected to the loss of the lamp, she plunged
into the darkness of the attic, searching the route by which
they had come in.

Miles had watched Aurora's reaction to the paintings. He
had seen the rise and fall of her breast, the parting of her
lips, the way her cool green eyes drank in the powerful imagery. She did not stare so, as his sister did, to analyze a
brushstroke or the use of shadow or background to better il-
luminate the rendering. She was struck by the passion depicted. Her blushing told him as much. He was himself
moved, not so much by the paintings as by Aurora Ramsay's reaction to them.

When she plunged away from them, he knew it was the
feelings these paintings had awakened that she could no
longer examine. That she would face darkness rather than
stay and face her own aroused passions, made it imperative
that he should be the one who followed her, the one who
found her in the dark. There was a feeling not to be denied
in the closed-off, rain-scented depths of the attic, a premonition of potential passion as wild and moving as that he
had witnessed in the paintings so carefully hidden away
here.

He took no light himself, only struck out in the shadowed space as fast as he could without knocking things
over, following the bobbing passage of her lamp.

She was lost and breathing hard when he caught up to
her. Turning toward his footsteps, she held high the lamp,
her eyes wide, as if she expected him to be one of the fear-
fully passionate gods stepped down from the canvas in pur-

suit of her. He had never seen her so vulnerable, this Amazon of a female who was so completely fearless in so many other ways.

"Aurora!" he dared call her by her given name, his voice gentle. He would not further threaten her. He approached slowly, his manner as unthreatening as his voice. "You have taken a wrong turn," he said softly. "Shall I take the light and show you the way?"

He reached for the lamp. Her hands were shaking. In her agitation, she tipped the lamp too far. The wick was doused. Their light was extinguished.

Just as they were plunged into absolute darkness, so too did she plunge—in his direction—flying into his chest, grabbing at his shirt, fearing the dark more than she feared her proximity to him.

"It's all right, Aurora," he soothed her, his voice low, his desire close to the surface. "I shall have the lamp lit again in no time." He could feel the pounding of her heart against his chest. His arms came about her, seeking out matches, and in opening up the lamp and relighting it. She offered no resistance to his embrace, clinging to him like a child. Even with the light renewed and the soft glow of it revealing how close they were to one another, she did not step away. Her trembling was not yet entirely abated. To warm her chill, to still her trembling, he pulled her deeper into his arms and continued to whisper to her. "I am here, my dear. There is nothing to fear. Nothing at all."

Her face was too close to his for him not to think of kissing it.

She nestled in his arms, her lips turned not away but toward his. He kissed her chin, he kissed her cheek. With a sigh that washed his face with the desire she unveiled to him here in the attic, she turned her mouth to meet his and their lips became one with the darkness: mysterious, musky, and as drenching as the rain that peppered the roof above their heads. Nature herself seemed in tune with the deepening of their kisses. Wind-driven, the rain grew heavier on the slates, as if determined to penetrate the rooftop barrier that separated them.

So eagerly anticipated was Miles Fletcher's embrace, so meltingly perfect the placement of his lips, that it crossed Aurora's passion-fogged brain that she was in need of rescuing after all—rescuing from herself and the feeling of completeness, of rightness, the feeling that she was exactly where she was supposed to be—in Fletcher's warm embrace.

That Miles Fletcher's lips should blot out the chill, darkness of the attic so completely, replacing it with a warm, citrus-scented haven in his arms, did not surprise her in the least. She had fled the possibility of passion from this man, but now that their lips were met, she could not imagine their ever being pulled asunder again. This hot, caressing pressure of his mouth against hers offered blessed release from the passion that had built within her as she gazed at the paintings. So in tune with the emotions that had coursed through her was this urgent embrace, she would have lain down in the dust of the attic, if only to perpetuate its satisfying intimacy.

His kisses, his hands, his straining need for the barriers between them to be gone, seemed matched by her own ardent desire to bend herself to him. Her lips, her hands, the little moans of pleasure she breathed as he rained kisses on her face and neck and breast, all spoke of a pleasure that equalled his, or a desire roused to fever pitch, a desire and passion that rivaled that depicted by the paintings too wild to be displayed downstairs.

Miles wanted her desperately. He wanted to take her, right here, right now, in the rain-racked darkness of the attic. Thunder rumbled, Nature echoing the power of his need.

The thunder was so loud it rattled the floorboards of the attic.

"No," she murmured as his lips trailed hotly from her throat to the cleavage of her breast. Even as she said no, her back arched, her body pressed more provocatively against his. He traced a line down the center of her neck. She shivered.

"Do not deny yourself, Aurora." His voice was husky.

His lips closed on hers again.

She kissed him, but her mind was at war with her body. She broke away from the embrace, pushed away from his chest and again the word "No!" came between them. Her head was winning the battle with her heart. This "no" was stronger, more decisive. This "no" was nonnegotiable.

"Stop," she insisted. "We must stop this. Why do you kiss me, when you know I have set my heart on winning another man's affections?"

"Are you certain you did not wish to be kissed as much as I have longed to kiss you?" Breathing hard, Miles let her go. The rain lashing the slates above them seemed to protest this uncomfortable conclusion to such promising beginnings. She was right, of course. He had yet to tell her the reasons he had first sought her out, had yet to explain his uncle's involvement. Without the truth between them, such an unleashing of their passions would be wrong. "Are you sure it is Walsh you would offer these honeyed lips to, the next time you offer them to a man?" he demanded.

Uncertainty wrinkled her brow. Uneasily her hand rose to gently touch her lips as if to ascertain they were indeed her own. "At this moment," she said, "I am certain of nothing." She took up the light, as if to defend herself from him with it and began to back away.

"I will not press the lesson," he said softly.

"Lesson?" She snatched her hand away from her mouth. "Did you mean no more than to teach me the art of love-making, sir?"

His voice, cool and dispassionate gave no clue to his true feelings. "Passion is not to be taught to the unwilling," he said.

Her own voice was as unsteady as the light in her hand. "You are a strange professor, Mr. Fletcher. How many pupils have been so schooled by your hand?"

Before he could utter a word in response she said, "No matter. I grow wiser for your every lecture."

She backed farther from him. With her went the light. "I would have you teach me the way to the drawing room below where I might further my education in the company of—"

"Lord Walsh," he finished the thought flatly. He had been prepared to bare all truths to her until this mention of Walsh. How could another man enter her head when they were both still warm from such an embrace?

She pursed her lips and drew herself to indignant height as if to declare him impertinent. "Do you mean to lead me, sir, or do you mean to lead me astray?"

"I, my dear lady," Miles said with forced politeness, his needs at war with his words, "will take you whence you will. Your wish is my command. You have but to ask."

Chapter Fourteen

Aurora required Miles to return her from the attic to the hall below. The noisy, crowded brilliance was a marked transition from the dark, musty silence above. Driven in by the rain, the house was milling with people. Among them, where he had not the privacy required to argue his case, Aurora spoke to him in a politely lowered voice so that their conversation was lost in the babble that flowed around them.

"Will you now leave me unmolested by your presence for the remainder of my time at Holkhan Hall? I've no desire to be troubled further by lessons in lovemaking, sir."

She made her request stiff-backed and proud, her cheeks suffused in embarrassed color, her eyes never remaining in contact with his for more than a moment. Gathering pride about her like a cloak, she slipped his coat from her shoulders and returned it to him.

Miles knew better than to challenge her edict. He knew, from long experience, not to press a point when it served only to irritate.

"Your wish is my command." He bowed. "You have but to ask and it is done." Without any more argument than that he turned and walked away, the smell of her, the very heat from her body gathered up in his arms in the folds of the coat she had been wearing. As he walked away, he could feel her gaze follow him.

His heart, his very soul cried out to him to stop, to turn, to fall at her feet and beg her forgiveness, but intellect saved him from the error of responding in such a foolish, lovelorn manner—intellect and experience. He would make his peace with Aurora when both of their emotions were more settled. He knew she was as affected by their kisses as he was. He had awakened passion, perhaps for the first time within her, which must be allowed time to grow and mature. He would wait for another time to press his suit with Miss Aurora Ramsay. He had pressed it too far today, perhaps irrevocably so.

Aurora spent a restless evening playing cards in a room jammed with people. She was never alone, either with Miles Fletcher or with her own thoughts, but she could not remember a time when she had felt more lonely. In the darkness of her bedroom, she spent an even more restless night, tossing and turning, reliving the dark moment of her weakness in the attic. She had surprised and unsettled herself. She had been kissed by a man, passionately kissed. Her lips still burned when she thought of such kisses! Who was to blame? No one but herself. She had wantonly rushed into Miles Fletcher's arms! Her fear of the dark was not excuse enough for such free behavior.

Admittedly, Miles had taken advantage of her mad dash in the dark, but it was she who had allowed him, even encouraged him to do so! Aurora was mortified. Whatever had taken possession of her better senses?

Feelings she had never before encountered had been unleashed today, feelings intimately connected with the brilliant, passionate, larger-than-life canvases hidden away in the darkness above her head. The imagery of those paintings would not release their hold on her consciousness any more than the tactile warmth of her comforter could be disassociated from her warm memories of Miles Fletcher's comforting arms when she had admitted her fear of the dark.

As a result, Aurora woke the following morning with a sense of unrest—of dissatisfaction and of hunger. Breakfast did not satisfy the emptiness within. She could not wait to be in the saddle. She yearned for the familiar pounding rhythm of a horse beneath her at full gallop. That she must first put herself in the company of Lord Walsh and concentrate on pleasantries so that he might be drawn to her in the very manner Miles Fletcher had been drawn to her, seemed an almost unbearable irony. Aurora was thus sorely out of sorts when she met Lord Walsh in the teaming doorway to the stables, as planned.

"Good morning." He shouted to be heard above the noise of the sheep and those gathered for the shearing, which continued today, as it had the day before, inside the barn. The skies were clear but the grounds were muddy. "Are you ready to ride?"

"Never more so!" said she with a level of vehemence, almost a passion, that exceeded even the noise their conversation must overcome. Her tone gave him a moment's pause before he threw her into the saddle with an accommodating "Let's be off, then."

To Aurora's profound relief, Walsh, unlike Fletcher, was not especially cheerful or talkative of a morning. He focused instead on his mount and the heavy ground and the route they would take. Aurora gladly followed suit. Happily, as she had expected, in the surging, heart-racing, mind-numbing exertion of a flat-out, mud-flinging gallop, she found exhilarating release from all that troubled her.

It occurred to her later, as she relived every moment of the morning, that her ride with Walsh had been like a dash across the countryside with a shadow of herself. They were superbly matched riders. Like a team of horses they never fell out of step or questioned one another's direction. Their skills, their knowledge, the very subject matter they discussed—for they did at last begin to talk when the horses were exhausted and their own breath came in identical clouds of chill morning steam—was of a gratifying equality.

They talked about the ground they had ridden over, the condition of the horses, the suitability of one bit over another. They both evidenced appreciation for the abundance of trees Coke was in the habit of planting, heartily approved his plans to reclaim land along the seafront and the layout of the model village he proposed to erect. The superiority of the stock to be seen grazing on his land was discussed at length. Neither of them was surprised to discover that their philosophies of breeding technique ran in tandem.

Conversation became a source of amusement to Aurora, so nearly did they agree on every issue raised. The only surprise in their conversation was the very compatibility of their ideas. Aurora could not have scripted a more amiable exchange.

Humor was the only area in which they would seem to be at odds. Several times Aurora turned a particularly clever phrase, twice she interjected the perfect pun into the midst of serious discussion in hopes of lightening the mood, but each time her jest flew right over Lord Walsh's head. Miles Fletcher would have rolled his eyes with delight in each circumstance, but, she reminded herself she did not come on this agreeable jaunt to think of Miles. She came to forget him.

She made a concerted effort to forget Miles Fletcher's smiles, Miles Fletcher's eyes, and most of all, Miles Fletcher's mouth. She convinced herself that Miles Fletcher's kisses had not shaken her any more than another man's kisses might. She did in fact study rather intently the curve of Walsh's lips in the midst of something he was saying. Surely these lips would rouse within her the same restlessness that had kept her tossing through the night.

"Would you care to be on hand, Miss Ramsay?" her riding companion inquired in that instant. "I know some females find such an event not at all to their taste."

Oh dear! She had not been attending. On hand for what? She could not tell him she had been woolgathering with regard to his lips in the midst of one of his most animated soliloquies. The man she meant to have as husband would surely judge her distraction harshly.

"And when is this to take place?" she asked, wondering if she might formulate her response based on related information.

"The day after tomorrow. The mare is to be brought to Coke's stable from a neighboring farm where I have put her to graze."

Breeding. They had been talking about the breeding of

colts. Of course! He was asking her if she wished to be on hand for the covering of one of his mares. "I'd be honored," she said, winning a nod of approval.

With that nod, the morning might be deemed a complete success. Lord Walsh asked if she cared to take breakfast with him when they had stabled their mounts. Over ham, toast, and tea, they arranged to meet again, to tour a display of farm implements.

The morning was seamless perfection, an unruffling *fait accompli*. When at last she and Walsh parted, Aurora could not for the life of her decide why she was so completely miserable.

She halfway convinced herself that lack of sleep was to blame and nothing more. She went to her room to lie down. There the answer to her dissatisfaction stared at her from the mantelpiece. A bouquet of fresh wildflowers had been arranged there, every one of them a bloom she had identified for Miles Fletcher. Tucked among them was the love knot Fletcher had once handed to her, along with a proposition. This time it came with a note.

The love knot made Aurora frown. She pulled it from the midst of the flowers as if it were a snake, ready to bite her. This braided bit of grass and all it stood for made her realize exactly what stood between her and her happiness with Walsh. It was Miles Fletcher. Miles Fletcher and the kisses in the attic, those surprising, baffling, overwhelmingly satisfying kisses she had exchanged with a man who in no way matched her temperament or purpose as well as Walsh did.

Her mouth! Her treacherous, traitorous mouth. Why must her lips tingle every time she so much as thought of Miles Fletcher?

She ran a hand across her lips and opened the note.

Aurora Ramsay,
I have not forgotten the bargain we made, nor the reason it was agreed upon in the first place. I would still deliver on my promises. If you can find it in your heart to forgive my recent lapse of both manners and judgment, meet me in the

marble hall at two. I would like very much to dance with you.

On my word, I will be a gentleman.

Miles Fletcher

Chapter Fifteen

Miles pulled his watch, like a plump, gold turnip, from his pocket and flicked open the ornately chased casing. It was ten minutes until two. He came early to the entry hall he had chosen as meeting place. What better place to decide Fate than in a hall modeled after Fortuna Virilis, the Roman temple of Justice?

This marble-walled entry was a cool relief after the heat outdoors. An imposing work of artistry, the space was meant for little more than walking through. But what a walk! From the flowing, marble stairway that led to the sunken center of the hall, to the vaulted heights of the intricately coffered ceiling with its bands of cherubs, fruit, and flowers, every inch of it, top to bottom, had been planned with the idea of making an impression. First impressions were important, after all. Miles remembered distinctly his first impression of Aurora. He wondered what her first impression of him had been. As he wondered, he took a seat on the wooden bench at the foot of the steps and stared at the cherubs above.

Perhaps a Cupid lurked here. He hoped so. Miles felt as if he and Aurora entered into a new stage in their relationship if this meeting took place. They had come to an entry hall of their own, a place where each must choose between any number of doors leading either deeper into what lay between them, or out of it altogether. He flicked open the face of his watch again. He could not look at the beautiful tangled chasing on his watch without thinking of the love knot he had left in Aurora's room. Would she come? It was almost two, the designated time of their assignation.

The sound of wheels and hoofbeats, a flurry of footsteps outside and the entry hall was suddenly loud with the noise of guests arriving. A retinue of servants flew to meet them. Like a summer shower the cloud of visitors moved through the entry hall into the main body of the house, shedding hats, cloaks, canes, and gloves like rain. The noise of them faded away. Miles consulted his watch again. Two exactly.

Was that the sound of footsteps? He closed his eyes, the better to concentrate. Footfalls loomed and then faded away—false hope. He opened his eyes, and snapped shut the watch. He would wait until two-fifteen.

The salesman within Miles knew that sometimes the best way to sell a client on what they wanted was to demonstrate its superior qualities, then deny any desire to sell. Miles meant to do just that in this dancing lesson. His goal was clearly lodged in his mind. He would teach Aurora Ramsay to dance as promised. He would teach her so that she might dance away from his arms and into Walsh's, but he meant to teach her in such a way that every step she took would have her thinking of him, just as he'd had thoughts of nothing and no one else since that amazing moment of darkness in the attic when she had thrown herself against his chest and willingly submitted to his kisses.

Another group of people swept through the doors. Absentmindedly Miles greeted an acquaintance who called out his name in passing.

He had known his heart was lost from the moment he had kissed Aurora Ramsay over an *entende* fan, but he had not known her heart was equally engaged until she had kissed him in the rain-scented attic. She was, he was certain, as affected as he.

Miss Ramsay was not destined to become Lady Walsh. No, he was here to change all that. He was here to win her in any way he could. He was here, too, at his uncle's request, "to be certain that Lester Fletcher's last act on this earth did not leave a poor girl penniless because of her brother's bad luck over a hand of cards." Miles had first thought to honor that wish by winning Walsh for Miss Ramsay. He knew now that would not be right. He knew, too, that he must inform Miss Ramsay of his role in the loss of her land. What a tangle! How to unknot it without destroying all chance of happiness?

Once again, the doors opened to admit someone who was not Aurora Ramsay. Surely Fate was not so cruel as to point out his love to him in the very instant another man snatched her away? Miles flicked open the watch casing and blinked at the hands of time. A quarter past. Perhaps she was not coming.

He would wait five minutes longer, no more.

"Mr. Fletcher?"

Her voice was so soft Miles thought at first he had imagined it. But no, it came again, a little stronger this time.

"Mr. Fletcher?"

He rose from the bench.

She stood, uncertainly, at the head of the waterfall flight of marble that led down to him. She had been unable to see him until he stood because the columns blocked her view. He had not heard her approach in the flurry of arrivals. How long had she been standing there, like a fawn that meant to fade away into the forest at too loud a noise or too abrupt a movement?

"Miss Ramsay. You have come!" He must not allow her a chance to reconsider. Slowly he approached her, as one approaches a kitten that would skitter away from beneath one's hand. As he drew closer, he said, "I am pleased."

Her chin rose. Her shoulders straightened. She looked him bravely in the eye. "Do not mistake my reason for being here, Mr. Fletcher. I wish to dance, and dance well— nothing more. I would not land on the floor with Lord Walsh on top of me—"

The door swung wide again, halting her in midsentence by throwing light and noise and the smell of the outdoors between them. Before the talking, laughing tide of gentlemen could descend on them, he held out his arm, unsmiling and serious, though he could not but be amused at her ironic reluctance to roll about with her chosen one. It seemed such a contradiction of intent. "Shall we proceed to the South Tribune? We will not be bothered by so many interruptions there and the flooring is ideal."

She took his arm warily, her manner so stiff it did not bode well for the intimacy that dancing required.

"Proceed," she said.

Aurora blushed when they arrived at last at the South Tribune, a book-lined chamber separated by way of an arch from the statue gallery. He was right. This place was empty but for a footman who was restocking the grate in the fireplace that warmed the long, open gallery when the evenings got too cool. The gallery reminded her of her first meeting with Miles. He had pulled her from the floor, a host of stone faces looking down their noses at her, when she had fallen in a heap with Lord Walsh. She was on the point of saying something in connection with that awkward moment when Fletcher took up her hand and whirled her in a lively fashion around the room.

For a moment, Aurora felt as if she were dancing—as if, in an instant, all of her limbs coordinated perfectly with the movements of her partner. His hands, firm and expressive, told her exactly where it was she should be, so that they did not run into one another, or crush toes. Just as suddenly, her mind rebelled against the notion that learning to dance could come so easily to her in this man's arms. As if her doubts affected reality, she missed a step and trod firmly on his foot.

"Oh, dear," she whispered.

Without any indication through word or gesture that he regretted her recent overbearing contact with his foot, Miles Fletcher stopped dancing and began instead a running monologue, describing his every move and how he expected her to interact with him.

"You would do well at first," he suggested briskly, his manner that of a schoolmaster, "to accept the hand of none other than the young men of your acquaintance whom you are convinced have a proper grasp of both the form and steps of any dance in which you wish to participate."

She thought of Walsh as Miles held out his hand to her.

She must think of Walsh or forget him entirely in this gentleman's company. She placed her hand in Fletcher's, and again, as before, when they came together, he had her whirling like gossamer in a summer's breeze. He stopped their progress before she chanced to mangle his toes a second time, saying, "An informed partner can help your form immensely. The pressure of his hands, the tilt of his head, even the direction of his gaze will hint at your direction." As he said this, he moved toward her.

She took a step back. She had been expecting this sort of move. He meant to take advantage of her.

"An informed gentleman," he assured her coolly, stepping once again too close for comfort, "will place himself a little to the right, and the proper distance in front of you."

She edged away from him, determined not to fall prey to his smooth maneuvering. She must remember her purpose here. She must remember Walsh. Fletcher did not smile, but his eyes twinkled for a moment in a most audacious fashion, as if he read her very thoughts and was amused. Deliberately, he closed the distance between them again.

"The proper distance," he repeated.

Aurora felt a flush of heat rush from the base of her neck to the roots of her hair. She swayed a bit, but she did not back away this time. She must not allow him to see how much he rattled her. She meant to remain resolute.

"We begin with the waltz." His voice was so gentle, she looked him in the eye, only to find he was gazing somewhere over her shoulder. "Your partner will encircle your waist with his right arm." His actions followed his words.

Remembering the last time this arm had crept around her waist, Aurora tensed. He was far too close to her. She could not ignore such proximity. Like a block of wood, she stood rigidly before him, wondering what might happen if their eyes met, if his lips sank to brush the lobe of her ear, if the hand at her waist drew her nearer still.

But, his focus was complete, almost studied in its propriety. His every move was governed by the dance, nothing more, just the dance. Walsh stood between them, not physically, but certainly in her mind.

He took her right hand in his left. "Your right hand, in mine, fingers laced," he instructed. "The arm should bend at the elbow, but in a relaxed fashion."

Everything he described he demonstrated, every element was double-checked. His gloved hand laced warmly with hers, but not too warmly. The hand at her waist darted up to check the positioning of her elbow. She blinked in consternation, far more moved than he would appear to be, to find their limbs in intimate contact.

"You should, in fact, try to be as relaxed as possible. Your left hand . . ." she knew instinctively that it was meant to rest on his shoulder. "Very good," he said, and as he said it, he looked her in the eye for a brief but telling moment, and her heart and stomach were strangely aflutter.

"Relax," he pleaded softly, his gaze moving on to touch fleetingly the hand that rested stiff as cordwood on his shoulder. The solid touch of his fingers was anything but fleeting as, like a puppeteer pulling strings on a marionette, he gently flexed her wrist.

"Relax, relax," he crooned. "You cannot dance well if you do not relax."

She was anything but relaxed. Her chest rose and fell, a sign of her agitation. Her pulse pounded in her temples. Her gaze met his a moment as he flexed her wrist.

Miles Fletcher was completely unrattled, as cool as a cucumber. He was not trying to seduce her at all! He seemed, to the contrary, to be holding her aloof, if not with his arms, then with his attitude. Aurora was confused. She didn't know what to make of such a complete change in his approach.

"We shall begin with six steps and then repeat. We shall start slowly and build speed as we get along. Right?"

"Right," she agreed dubiously, glancing uncertainly at her feet, which seemed too close to a very glossy pair of boots.

His voice was warm, but not too warm. When the footman rose from his task and quietly abandoned them, Aurora was not at all embarrassed. Miles sounded like a governess dictating form. "Right. As my left foot glides back, your right foot glides forward." He pulled her with him as he moved. She stiffened. "Relax." He drew her irresistibly toward him with the movements of the steps. "Keep your knees loose. There is no need to stiffen. Now the left foot advances in front of the right as you rise onto your toes and turn halfway round."

"Oh!" She froze. Her movements, none too accurate, had brought her in physical contact with his chest.

"Perhaps we move too slowly," he said, unperturbed, leaning in close to her ear. His breath disturbed the curls that hung from her temples. There was, Aurora decided, something almost as alarming about his lack of any attempt to take advantage of their nearness as the alternative.

"May we begin again?" she suggested, wondering if he felt nothing for her, and had merely taken advantage of what was so freely offered in the attic. "I shall do my best not to run you down this time," she said, and waited for some flirtatious retort.

"I leave that privilege to Lord Walsh," was what he said, as if to acknowledge Walsh's precedence over any claim he had on her.

She frowned. This was not at all the response she had expected. They began again and again, and again and again, until she had mastered all six of the steps—their bodies moving in uneasy unison. Their thoughts, their very hearts, she could not judge so well. She could not begin to guess what he was thinking or feeling. His remark with regard to Walsh may have been meant to calm her, but instead she was perturbed by his ready capitulation.

"Shall we put them together?"

For a moment so deep were her ruminations that she did not grasp his meaning. "Together?"

His eyebrows rose. "The steps you have learned. I think you are ready now to put them all together."

She stared at his boots and wondered how much damage she might do to the perfect sheen of their polish in stepping on his feet. "I suppose," she agreed.

He lifted her chin with a gloved knuckle so she would look at his face rather than his boots. For a wild moment her heart would not be still. She thought he meant to confound her again by kissing her.

Such was not his purpose.

"If you promise not to laugh at my whistling I shall do my best to provide us with music." His smile reminded her of the happiness of his lips on hers. His eyes seemed deep enough to drown in.

"Whistle away," she whispered, the words sticking in her throat.

He puckered his lips and whistled, his breath stirring tendrils of her hair, occasionally raising a cool chill along her neck and across the exquisitely sensitive recesses of her ear. She closed her eyes with his every breath, remembering the perfect harmony of their movements, of their very need when he had taken her in his arms in the attic. With that memory they moved in harmony again, their steps mirrored, her arms no longer wooden in his, her waist at home with the heat of his hand.

She could feel the difference in their dancing. Every step, every sway was in perfect time. Having done well, she was pleased enough to look up at him. They whirled quite magically together for a moment, face-to-face, he with his lips provocatively puckered, she with her eyes fastened for an instant on his mouth.

His whistling ceased.

She stumbled a little, and he quite naturally drew her closer to keep her from falling. Their lips were suddenly almost on top of one another. The blue of his eyes had swallowed her up. She stiffened. Now, what she had been waiting for, what she had feared, must come to pass. Surely, he meant to kiss her again, to take advantage of the moment!

Again she mistook his intentions. He did no more than steady her, his hands firmly grounding her, so that she neither staggered nor fell into him or away. He stared for a moment into her eyes, his own dancing merrily, his mouth amused as though it bit back something suggestive, either in word or deed. His tongue passed once over his lips. He took a deep breath and said lightly, "Perhaps you will hum a little with me. We shall soon have you dancing fit to sweep any man off his feet."

She could not resist the quip that must naturally follow such a remark. "A man has already been swept off his feet by my dancing," she said wryly. "It is to leave him standing that I endeavor."

He smiled. The smile didn't meet the blue of his eyes.

"I am mistaken then in assuming you wished the fellow brought to his knees?" Deftly, his humor topped hers, at the same time reminding her of Walsh, whom she had vowed not to forget.

Miles Fletcher, Aurora decided, was changed. He was more restrained. Thankful as she had at first been to see such a transformation, in the end, when the dancing lesson was pronounced a success and they parted, she went away wishing—she had to admit it to herself, if no one else— wishing he had kissed her.

Chapter Sixteen

To be reminded that tension is to be desired between a man and a woman, Aurora had only to come into the company of a Fletcher. She had begun to feel herself completely at ease in Walsh's company, perhaps too much at ease. They rode again on the following morning, a successful, if uneventful, coming together.

In the course of that ride, Aurora encountered her first Fletcher at the Doric temple in the woods. A jovial group of ladies and gentlemen gathered in the clearing before it. Aurora approached the spot with reluctance. This place had become too endowed with meaning, too intimately connected with her feelings for Miles Fletcher. Here, she had been taught many things. Fearing Lord Walsh would insist they take part in the conversation and laughter, she skirted the temple widely.

Grace Fletcher and her easel were set up under the trees along the track Aurora chose. It was not Walsh, after all, but Aurora who insisted, "We must pause a moment! I would wish Grace a good morning."

Walsh hesitated, his eyes dwelling heavily on the young woman who chose to capture forever this place in paint. He did not seem in the least inclined to step down from his saddle.

"I would not interrupt an artist in the midst of a burst of creativity," he said.

Grace turned her head in that moment to stare at them, no, to stare at Lord Walsh, who appeared more comfortable approaching those who gathered under the trees, than in lingering to discuss art.

Rue was one of those sitting comfortably in the shade and he waved a greeting to Aurora. She waved back and dismounted to quietly approach the spot where Grace and her easel commanded a small rise. Grace was daubing paint on paper with dextrous authority.

"Will I disturb you in wishing you good morning?" Aurora ventured.

"Not at all, Miss Ramsay!" Grace claimed, her focus fixed first on her painting and then on the gathering beneath the trees. "I must, after all, boast to you of my success in first coaxing your brother out of the library and then in introducing him to a local writer who has come to watch the shearing. He is, I am very pleased to recount, as taken with Rupert's scribblings as I am." She waved her paintbrush at one of the gentlemen Rue spoke to. "They will talk of nothing now but the ins and outs of publishing."

"You have read Rue's writing?" Aurora was astounded.

"I was up half the night reading what he has with him," she said, as if such a thing were not at all unusual. "I am sure my complexion will be ruined if I make a habit of such nocturnal excess."

"How very kind you are!" Aurora exclaimed. "Rue seems very animated in his discussion. He is actually smiling and laughing. I can recall only one other occasion in this visit to Holkham when I have seen him so happy." That moment, too, had everything to do with Miss Grace Fletcher, but Aurora forbore mentioning as much. Perhaps she had been hasty in judging Grace a trifling female who meant to break Rue's heart.

Grace was cleaning her brush on a much-daubed rag that hung from the corner of the easel. "Come have a look," she said. "And tell me what you think of my watercolor. I would much rather be remembered for my artistic endeavors than for my kindness."

Aurora was only too happy to view the work in progress. She had been quite consumed with curiosity as to what Grace did, but considered it a rudeness to peer without an invitation.

"How lovely," she said. Her first impression was just that.

The watercolor, shimmering and light—ephemeral in its half-finished state as only a watercolor can be—was of the clearing. The temple figured large, just off center in the middle of the page. Before it a party was gathered, as there was a party gathered now, with the difference that there were two extra characters painted into the scene, a man and a woman.

"Oh my!" Aurora breathed. The woman had red hair and was wielding a fan as she bent her head coquettishly close to that of the gentleman, whose face and hair had yet to be painted in completely.

"Do you like it?" Grace asked. "I am striving for the feeling of a Watteau. He captured the romance of the outdoors so well. Do you not agree?"

Aurora paid little attention to her words, much less what painter she might have modeled her watercolor after. She was lost in the memory of the picnic brought to life again with this dabbling.

She could not tear her eyes from this evidence, trapped forever on paper, of her indiscretion with Miles Fletcher. It would not do for Walsh, or anyone else, for that matter, to view this display.

"I am immensely taken with it," she managed to say without choking. "Do you mean to keep it?"

"Why do you ask?"

Aurora wondered if Grace meant to tease her. Her expression looked bland enough, but surely she must be conscious of the consternation the working of her hand did wreak.

"I was wondering if I might coax you into letting me have it," Aurora said, panicked, and yet truly taken with the painting for all the embarrassment it might cause her. It promised to be above the average in its rendering.

Grace dipped her brush in a dark green color and set to work adding depth to the treetops in her painting. "I am very flattered," she said sweetly, "but the painting is already promised to another."

Aurora felt her panic rise. "Oh? Who is the fortunate recipient? I must do my best to persuade them to part with it."

"You are welcome to try such persuasion, but I do not foresee any success in such an endeavor. Miles can be quite mule headed when he latches on to something. He assured me he had never been more taken with any of my earlier watercolors. The setting struck him most particularly."

Aurora was caught completely off guard by such a revelation. She might have argued more vehemently for the painting had not Walsh called out to her that she must come and meet his friends. With the feeling that she and Grace left their discussion unfinished, she obliged him.

It was as she smiled and traded meaningless niceties about the weather with Lord Walsh's acquaintances that she looked again in Grace Fletcher's direction. Rupert stood now beside the casel, his posture a trifle awkward in leaning upon his crutch, as if he were unsure of his reception. Grace, too, was changed. She seemed less focused on her watercolor. Her face was luminescent when she smiled. There was, Aurora thought, a tension between the two. Rupert stared at Miss Fletcher too intently, too earnestly, while she shot Rupert only an occasional glace from beneath lowered lashes. Those darting glances increased the tension that hung between them. Aurora felt another twinge of concern for Rupert's tender heart.

Walsh, who had witnessed the same exchange between Grace and Rupert, was in a sudden hurry to ride on.

"Shall we take them for a gallop?" He set heel to his mount with a pent-up energy Aurora was unused to sensing in his demeanor. She was left to follow, and there was a strangeness to this chasing after Walsh that Aurora could not like.

It was in skirting one of the cultivated fields of which Thomas Coke was so proud, that the riders encountered the second Fletcher to put Aurora in mind of the tension between men and women. Miles Fletcher and Tom Coke were bent over in a row of swaying wheat, examining the soil.

They were engaged in earnest conversation, interrupted only when the horses came almost abreast of them.

"Well met, sir," Coke cried, holding up his hand to stop their passing as he rose from the wheat field like a dolphin rising from the sea. "Well met, indeed! I have news for both of you."

Miles Fletcher rose from the swell of unripened grain as well, but he made no move toward them as Coke waded through the knee-deep crop, patting his pockets with a look of concentration. His expression was troubled. He could not seem to locate what he was searching for, and so he opened up his coat and began to dip into the pockets within.

"Your mare, I am sorry to report, my lord, has jumped the fence at Farmer Pelham's," he said as he searched.

"Jumped the fence?" Walsh was alarmed.

"Yes." Coke was unperturbed. "Naughty girl to go gallivanting. But never fear, the farmer and his lads have been dashing about the countryside after her. She is safely home again and tucked away in the barn. There is only a scratch on her foreleg I thought you might like to take a look at. Ah!" Coke discovered what he sought in his pockets and drew it forth. It was a letter. Aurora recognized the scrawl that addressed it.

"For you, Miss Ramsay." Coke held it up to her.

Aurora took the letter, but she took no pleasure in its having come. Her brother's handwriting marked the outside, and no good news was to be expected from that quarter. She tucked the letter in her breast pocket after a cursory glance, and looked up from doing so to find Miles Fletcher watching her, as though he found it odd she should not open it on the spot.

It was strange how this gentleman could reach out to touch her from the middle of a wheat field with no more than a look, while the man she meant to marry, the man who sat horse beside her, spoke outright to her and raised no feeling at all other than a concern for his mare.

"She was not exposed to a stallion at any time during this mad midnight dash, was she?" Walsh was saying. "Blast the beast. This cut is not serious is it?"

Coke was eager to soothe. "If Miles has no objection, I will be happy to ride with you now to take a look at the beast."

Walsh turned to Aurora. "Do you mind if we cut short our ride? It would seem I've a mare needs attending."

Aurora had opened her mouth to say that she would like to see this precious mare, but before she could stick her foot quite firmly between her teeth, Miles Fletcher interrupted.

"I should be pleased to escort Miss Ramsay back to the stables, if she has no objection to the scheme."

For the first time that morning, Aurora felt a surge of anticipation. "Yes. Yes." She waved a dismissive hand at Walsh. "Do go on. See to the horse. I shall be quite content to remain in Mr. Fletcher's care."

"You will not forget to join me at the barns for her covering?"

"I will not forget."

Thus it was arranged, and as Lord Walsh and Tom Coke rode away, Aurora pondered her choice of the word "content" to describe her feeling at being left alone in Miles Fletcher's care. Content was not really an accurate description. She would feel more alive if left in Miles's care. She would feel more vibrant, clever, and amusing. She would feel the tension she had seen humming uneasily between Grace Fletcher and her brother this morning.

That same uneasy awareness made her start nervously when Miles approached her through the swaying stalks of grain, saying, "Would you care to read your letter, Miss Ramsay? I do not mind waiting. I have myself received news today and would not keep you from yours."

Aurora bit her lip. "Thank you," she said, "but, as this missive brings me nothing but bad news, I am in no hurry to read it." She wondered why she felt free to tell him as much.

He stopped when he reached the edge of the field, a frown troubling the smoothness of his brow. "Has this aught to do with your brother's recently incurred gambling debts?" he asked gently.

Her head rose so abruptly, her mount shied. "How do you know of that?" she demanded, sliding nimbly from the saddle.

He guessed her intention and moved to help her dismount, but she had no need of his assistance and landed almost on top of him. For an instant they stood toe to toe, almost nose to nose. His gaze, she thought, lingered far too long on her lips.

Life was short, Miles thought, far too short to continue denying his desire for Aurora Ramsay. He must tell her, and tell her now of his discussion with her brother, of his uncle's part in Jack Ramsay's latest reason for the nickname "Rakehell," and what it meant now that Uncle Lester was dead. And yet, the words did not come easy. Lester's demise, relayed to him by the same post that brought her word from her brother, was too fresh to be mentioned with composure. And Miles was a man who prided himself on his collectedness.

She was impatient with his silence and struck at the weeds that grew along the perimeter of the field with her riding crop. "Has the latest gossip arrived then, along with the latest guests from London?" she snapped.

Miles frowned. "I have bad news from London, news I would share with you," he suggested gently.

"Oh? What news?" She continued to thrash the weeds, unhappy in the receipt of her letter or unhappy with his suggestion, he could not tell.

He watched her intently, offering no clarification.

Slap. Slap. The weeds were decapitated. The green of her eyes had streaks of gold in them when she was angry. How could it be he had never noticed before?

"As you seem unwilling to tell me," she said, turning away from his scrutiny, "shall we talk about weeds again, or perhaps dirt?" She stabbed her quirt into the ground.

"Depends on the type of dirt to which you refer," he said agreeably. How was he to go about telling her of his involvement in the current state of her affairs? It would be best if he explained before she read her letter. It likely brought her news that hinted of his involvement. Yet, how did one explain the knotted situation he had come to unravel? "I will gladly discuss dirt with you, or any other subject for that matter, if you will but tell me one thing."

"What might that be?"

"Does your brother's recent folly at cards have some bearing on what you do here, or are you set on capturing Walsh for reasons all your own?"

She frowned, bent to catch up a handful of soil and let it trickle through her gloved fingers. "Ah! You would talk of dirt after all." She would not look at him, gazing instead at the far horizon. "I've my own reasons," she said. "Land is one among them."

Miles felt an impatience with such coldly practical reasoning. "Life is surely too short for such a bloodless approach," he said, his voice shaking with emotion. Lester's death had hit him hard. He had expected life to respect the pattern and timing of his own making. He had expected to be there at his uncle's passing. "What of love?" he asked, almost hating her as she coolly struck down the green stalks that lined the edge of the field and spoke so reasonably, so coldly of land as a good reason for marriage.

"Do no emotions stir when you consider the prospect of marriage, other than this lukewarm lust for land?" he asked, without the slightest hint of diplomacy.

She flinched, ceased her destruction of the plant life, and turned to glare at him through narrowed eyes. "You cannot know what it is like to be homeless and penniless, sir, else you would never have made such a cruel remark. Is land not enough for you? It is enough for me. Certainly many marriages are based on far less. Land I understand. Love I do not. Land lasts through all eternity. Can you say the same of love?"

"We ourselves do not last for all eternity in this mortal form, Miss Ramsay." Miles could not disguise the contempt in his voice, nor the anger in his gesture as the clod of earth he held between his fingers was cast from him. He bent to raise another handful, and as it sifted through the fingers of his glove, he took her hand, and removing the offensive quirt from her grasp, he pressed the dirt into her palm instead, curling her gloved fingers around it.

"Can you really hold on to land, Miss Ramsay? Can you curl up to it at night?" With leashed passion he dropped the quirt and drew her into his arms. "This land you crave cannot caress your cheek." The tip of his finger traced the edge of her cheek so gently she closed her eyes.

He drew her closer. Her fingers were still clenched around the dirt he had pressed into her hand, but it slipped away, no matter how tightly she clutched. His eyes, his arms, his voice would not allow her to slip away so easily. "Land cannot kiss you."

He could, and did.

She did not pull away. In fact, she opened both her hands and her mouth to him. The dirt she had been clutching fell unheeded onto the toe of his boot.

And yet as abruptly as she succumbed to his arms, she thrust herself out of them, her hand to her mouth, as if to stop its yearning. "Damn," she swore. "How dare you?"

"I dare"—his voice caught—"because I have fallen in love with you. Surely you must have noticed?"

Chapter Seventeen

Aurora was overwhelmed by a feeling of panic. There was something most compelling, quite invigorating in fact, in being told one was loved! Miles Fletcher was in love with her! Could it be true? The words knocked her back a step. She was not prepared for love. Love would make a mess of things. Was this love? Was love what she wanted and needed? She had to admit a certain tenderness for Miles. He made her pulse race whenever he was near, and her lips were constantly preoccupied with the promise of his kisses.

The hand she had lifted to her mouth dropped to her breast. The corner of the unopened letter crackled beneath her hand. The letter, yet unread, with all its implications, held them apart. She must remain strong. She must remain true to her purpose. Her family was faced with ruin. Her future was uncertain unless she acted decisively and with haste. Aurora saw no other way to save herself, no other way to rescue her family than in Walsh. Surely it was dangerous to change direction this late in her race against time.

Thus, with a weak laugh that had nothing to do with being amused, she denied the love he claimed to feel for her, protesting, "You must not say such a thing when you know I mean to marry Walsh."

He closed his eyes, as if to shut out her rejection before opening them again with a wry laugh, saying, "If I could return to you your land and rid your family of all obligation of debt, would you be interested in marrying me, Miss Ramsay?"

"Such a question does not merit an answer," she snapped.

"Does it not?"

The question hung heavily between them.

Aurora swallowed, uneasy with his insistence. Would it make a difference? Should it? It should not, but it did, and she was not one to pretend otherwise.

She tried to lighten the tension of the moment with humor. "My dear Mr. Fletcher, could you transact such a miracle, I would marry you in a trice. But, you cannot, can you?"

He made no such admission, merely looked at her with such a piercing gaze she thought he must see within her to the source of her every thought and motivation.

"Come along," Miles said with a smile that did not in any way reach his eyes.

"Come along where?"

His face had a closed look about it, a sadness that worried her, though she did not like to admit it, even to herself. The polished veneer she had noted the first time she had met Miles Fletcher, had slipped. She was not sure exactly what emotion she was reading, but that he was feeling something powerful was not to be denied as he strode to the shady spot where his horse was grazing. He threw over his shoulder as if it were the most natural course of action, "If you spoke in all seriousness, you must come and marry me. We shall hie to Gretna Green before the dew is dried." He mounted the animal and sat staring down at her, his eyes dark and broody, his veneer of light humor almost back in place. "If you spoke in jest and still mean to snare Walsh"—his eyebrows rose comically—"we must work on your dance steps and then get you to the mating of the mare."

Aurora frowned as she climbed into the saddle without any assistance offered. She was depressed and confused by Fletcher's hollow proposal, by his ready acquiescence once again to help her to capture Walsh's attention. Surely if a man loved her, as Miles Fletcher had just claimed to love her, if he meant to marry her, as he had also suggested, he would not so readily move on to dance steps with which she might impress another!

Was the man an unconscionable flirt, a sarcastic wit and nothing more? Was his mention of the mating of the mare meant to serve as insult? He ran hot and cold with her. She should have expected as much. His own sister had warned her against him. What was it she had said? *He is a dangerous fellow where hearts are concerned. You must not take anything he says too much to heart—else you will suffer as much as any other female who has mistakenly believed my brother might love her for more than a moment.*

How foolish she was to have offered her lips to a man who offered in return no more than pretty words and a few heady moments of passion. Despite the wisdom of her caution, Aurora was troubled with a feeling of emptiness. She had the strange sensation that something vital and rare was slipping away from her, perhaps forever.

By the same path taken earlier, they returned to Holkham Hall. Once again a stop was made at the temple in the woods.

"I mean to share this letter with my brother," Aurora said.

With a cool nod that acknowledged her words for the dismissal she intended them to be, Miles let her go. He was disappointed and angry—with Aurora—with himself. He had meant to tell her all. He had started to explain. What stopped him now but his own bruised pride?

"Do things go well with your goddess sublime, Miles?" Grace asked when he reined in his horse near her easel.

"They do not." Miles grimly studied his sister's painting.

"Do you not like it?" Grace asked.

"No, I do not."

"What a pity. I think it is one of my better paintings." She sounded offended.

Miles shook off his sour mood. "It is not the painting makes me frown, pet."

"I am relieved you should say so." She studied him pensively, as if awaiting some other response.

Miles's eyes widened. There was no mistaking the moment caught here in translucent color. Two figures sitting in the shady portico of the Doric temple, one with red hair and a fan in her hand, the other a dark-haired fellow who leaned toward her, as if to kiss her. These two looked remarkably familiar.

"I say! What's this?" Miles muttered sliding from the saddle. Just how much had Gracie seen of the kisses he had lavished on Miss Ramsay?

His sister feigned innocence. "A watercolor, Miles. Surely you have seen one before?"

"You know what I mean. This looks very much like me, and that can be none other than Aurora Ramsay." He stabbed his finger at the painting.

"Watch it." She slapped at him with her paintbrush. "That bit is still damp."

"Do you mean to toy with me, Gracie? Do you mean to start vicious rumors?"

"Rumors? Not at all! I do but hope to capture a bit of truth in my poor paintings."

"Truth? What truth is this then?"

She wagged her paintbrush at him. "The truth is you have fallen in love with our Miss Ramsay and she with you. Why do you not ask her to marry you and be done with this farcical pursuit of poor Walsh?"

"I have asked her."

She blinked in disbelief, her paintbrush falling from her fingers. "But this is wonderful!"

He interrupted before she could embarrass him further. "Is it? She thought I was toying with her, so do not toy with me as well, Gracie. I shall have this painting when you are done with it."

Frowning, Grace bent to retrieve her paintbrush. As she rose, she gave him a measuring look. "I am sorry, Miles. I have promised it."

"To whom?"

"To Miss Ramsay. She spoke to me of it only this morning when she and Walsh rode by."

Walsh! he thought in disgust. Was Walsh to have both this painting and its subject? His gaze sought out Aurora beneath the trees. She bent her head to talk to Rue.

"Miss Ramsay wants the painting does she? Can she afford such a thing?" He bit the words off.

Grace, had he but noticed, took unusual interest in his remark. "We did not speak of price," she said. "Is there something wrong with the Ramsay finances?"

"Deeply wrong," he said. "As wrong as anything else connected with a Ramsay. And a great deal of it is Uncle Lester's doing."

"Uncle Lester? Whatever do you mean?"

Another letter is come!

Aurora said no words to that effect, merely withdrew the missive from her pocket and fanned her face with it as though suffering from the heat. Rupert was beside her in an instant, withdrawing from the company of his new friends and limping to a secluded spot where they might be private.

"What does it say?" he asked with the same sort of dread she had felt in first receiving the letter.

"I don't know. I waited to open it with you beside me," she said softly. "But you must not show either concern or anger no matter how much you may feel it." Aurora cracked the wax seal and unfolded the page. "This is too public a place to reveal our feelings. I would not have it said that any hint of this latest fiasco in our lives might be construed from our behavior here."

Rue chuckled nervously as he hung his head over her shoulder to read along. "Then you must stop chasing after Walsh, now, eh?"

Aurora did not know whether to laugh or to throttle him. Rue's snide remark on top of Miles Fletcher's hints to the same effect were the least of her troubles. She was still feeling undone by the wounding proposal from Fletcher.

"Oh, I say! What nerve Jack has!" Rue growled as they deciphered what was written. "He makes the mess and we are to clean it up. Dashed insolence! How can he think to ask us to find buyers for the sheep and cattle while we are here?"

"Jack does not think. He just does, Rue. He always leaps

first and then looks to see what damage he has left behind. The man is a mountain goat."

"Dear God! Only listen to this bleating madness and see if it does not make you furious."

Aurora read:

> *"It appears the wheezing old gaffer who won our house, lands and living, cocked up his toes no more than two days after beating me. I am living high on the hope that his heirs are not yet aware of the old gent's winnings. With luck they never will be."*

"Well?" Rue asked expectantly. "Are you as shamed as I am? Our mountain goat would skip out on his debts."

Aurora exhaled heavily, her eyes burning with unshed tears. "Is Jack truly so devoid of honor? How can he shirk all responsibility, all obligation so completely? I do not understand the turnings of his mind, though he is my own flesh and blood."

Rue nodded. "I know. He would have us rely on deceit and wishful thinking. Even for Jack this sinks to a new low."

Aurora handed him the letter—her mind, her heart, her very soul gone numb. It would appear she had less time than she had imagined before they were paupered. She shook herself. Time was against her. It was indulgent in her to waste it. "Is there anyone among your new acquaintances who is looking for cattle or sheep?"

"Gad!" Rupert swore softly.

"What?"

He was gazing at her with earnest, open admiration. "You would have made a marvelous soldier, Aurora."

From Rupert there could be no higher praise. She smiled grimly, her confidence returning. "We are reconnoitering buyers then. I do not mean to go down without a fight."

"Buyers. Yes." He squinted at the gathering beneath the trees. "How about Fletcher? Did you not tell me he had recently come into a patch of land? He would seem the most likely prospect."

Aurora sighed. Her chest hurt when she thought of asking Fletcher. "I hate to beg favors of him," she murmured.

"But why? I think he would leap at the chance to curry favor. He has as much as told me so."

Aurora passed a hand over her lips and thought of bitter words concerning love and land. "It is precisely for that reason that I am loath to ask the man."

Chapter Eighteen

Aurora began her second dancing lesson with Miles Fletcher with a sense of trepidation. He had boldly claimed he loved her this morning. Gad, he had gone so far as to ask her to marry him! Now he seemed eager to help her win the interest of Lord Walsh—a rival. Aurora tried to find some method to this madness. Did Miles mean to seduce her this afternoon? There was no denying the heightened tension between them. That she had additional pressures from the letter just received—that he seemed angry with her and a trifle cold, only increased that tension. She would have liked to have asked him if he were interested in buying some of her livestock, but found she could not. Tension stood like a wall between them.

Despite the strained feelings, perhaps in part because of them, Aurora felt desires that were new to her, desires that involved the interplay between a man and a woman: glancing, talking, touching, laughing, and—dare she acknowledge the thought again—kissing. She could not stop imagining Miles meant to bend his head to hers again, to seek out her lips with his own. She watched and wondered and tried to concentrate her thoughts and desires on Walsh.

She failed miserably in the endeavor. She could not untangle the image of Miles's mouth from her memory. Walsh did not have the effect on her that Miles did, and yet she remained resolute in her intention to continue her pursuit of Walsh. Such course made sense to her intellect, if none at all to her emotions and sensibilities.

Miles Fletcher refrained from pressing himself upon her, though he had ample opportunity. They practiced dancing—as close as a man and a woman could decently be, their bodies gliding together and apart in growing harmony, their rhythms matched. On occasion his breath whispered across her cheek or along her neck. The clasp of his hand at her waist heated almost to the burning point and his gaze fastened on her lips time and again, but he did not kiss her nor did he say anything in any way suggestive.

Aurora tried to concentrate on the need to sell her sheep, on her need to secure Walsh's interest before her brother's folly became common knowledge. She tried to think of the future, but her mind perversely focused on nothing more than the moment, this moment she spent in Miles Fletcher's arms. She wanted him to kiss her again. She forgot all troubles while kissing. She could believe herself loved when her mouth yielded to Miles Fletcher's. She found herself thinking of little else, other than the placement of her feet, and the movement of his shoulder beneath the palm of her overheated hand. She did at one point test his resolve by ever so nonchalantly swinging her head toward his as they danced. For a spellbound moment their mouths were temptingly close. Surely he would kiss her now.

But with an insouciant smile and a strange sadness in his eyes, he merely gazed at her a moment, their breaths intermingling, so proximate were their noses, before he said mildly, "Is it not time for the mating, Miss Ramsay?"

For an instant what he said made no sense to her. Mating? What intimacy was he suggesting? Then, gaze flying to the case clock in the corner of the room, she broke away from him.

"I am late!"

Before she could race from the room, he held out his arm to her. "Come," he beckoned, "I will escort you to the barn."

To the barn they went—a silent, rather awkward walk until they encountered Tom Coke, also on his way to the covering of Lord Walsh's prize mare.

"Interested in the breeding, are you?" he asked them openly.

Miles nodded. "Tell me, sir—for I consider you our resident expert—what, in your opinion, constitutes sound breeding practice? Suppose for example you had a mare who could run like the wind and knew one end of a turnip from the other."

"We are talking horses here?" Coke laughed.

"Hypothetical horses," Miles assured him. "Now, would you put that hypothetical horse with an animal who also understood turnips, or with a stallion who danced well, dressed impeccably, and recognized at a glance the difference between Greek and Etruscan pottery?"

Aurora blushed furiously.

"Very interesting horses you're breeding here." Coke was gentleman enough to studiously avoid looking in her direction.

"Hypothetically interesting horses," Miles agreed.

"Have these horses equal pedigree?"

"Let's assume they have."

"Well then, sir, I would breed the two that have different strengths."

"I see." Miles held the barn door open to Aurora and his host. His blue eyes sparkled mischievously as she passed.

After such pointed hypothesizing, Aurora was rather relieved to part company with Miles Fletcher. Once inside the barn she went immediately to Lord Walsh's side.

"There you are." He was pleased to see her but undeniably distracted. "I had begun to think you might not come. I hope you do not mind my not standing here with you, but I must oversee the arrival of the mare."

Before she could assure him she was quite all right on her own, he was away, his focus on the horse. Aurora positioned herself so that she might best observe the proceedings. In doing so, she realized that she was the only female present. Having seen many a mating before, her singularity in this respect would not have bothered her, had someone been there to stand beside her. Alone as she was, there was an uneasiness in the men around her whom she acknowledged with eye contact or a tip of the head. A circle of space widened around her like a buffer. Aurora began to feel both uneasy and alone.

She marked Miles Fletcher and Tom Coke standing just opposite her position, and as was so often the case of late, the instant her gaze touched upon Fletcher, he turned to look directly into her eyes.

The stallion was brought in then, huffing and snorting, his tail high—drawing all eyes, except Fletcher's. Aurora looked away and then back again. Still, he stared at her.

There came a mental turning point for Aurora in the uneasy silence into which the observers fell as the mating ensued with a grunt from the stallion and a squeal from the mare. There was inherent in this urgent, almost violent coming together of animal teeth and hooves and flesh, the essence of the union she herself meant to accomplish in linking herself to Lord Walsh and his land. This thrusting covering of one beast with another brought flying through her consciousness the image of a pregnant ewe, gone glassy-eyed beneath the stroking hands of her shearer. She was reminded of the suggestive paintings in Tom Coke's attic and the rather tragic story connected to the painting of Coke that had been given to him by a lovelorn princess.

The rhythm of this mating echoed the rhythm of Miles Fletcher's tongue as it had thrust between her lips in kissing her with such passion her knees had turned to water. This was the unnerving part of the marital expectations she had hidden away in the back of her mind. She would bear her husband's children. She was to serve as the vessel for his lust. That thought, in connection with the cold-blooded connection she intended to consummate with Lord Walsh sent a wave of nausea coursing through Aurora. She stared into the staring, slightly panicked eyes of the mare and panicked herself.

She turned her back on the mating, and the men who stood observing it. She strode from the barn, her head high. The air was too close, the press of men and the animal smell too strong. She had to get away.

*　　*　　*

Stampeded by doubt, she plunged out of a doorway straight into her brother.

"Hallo! What's the matter?" Rue's face was a picture of concern. "You have not been talking to Grace, have you?"

"Grace?" He was looking at her far too intently. She wanted to lay her head upon his shoulder so that his arms would encircle her with a feeling of security and affection. She wanted him to tell her their troubles were over, not that there was some new calamity to overcome. "Is there more bad news?"

He stopped his staring. In fact, she thought he avoided her gaze. "She was looking for you. Said something about doing magic on your hair."

Aurora sighed in relief. "Is that all? I was so afraid you meant to tell me more bad news."

He was frowning at his crutch. "Bad news? No, no . . ." He seemed for a moment uncertain just what it was he meant to say. "Quite to the contrary. You'll be pleased to hear I've located a fellow who will have our pigs."

Aurora smiled and straightened her shoulders. "That is good news. I'm ashamed to say I've nothing along those lines to report, favorable or otherwise."

"No matter," he said decisively, lines of worry still digging furrows in his forehead. "I intend to line up a buyer for the cattle and your sheep ere the ball begins."

Aurora reached out to touch his hand and was surprised that he should flinch, so unexpected was the contact. She had never seen him so driven. His fervor was moving. "You ease my mind, Rue. Now, where did you leave Miss Fletcher? I must give her plenty of time to work magic with my hair."

"We . . . she was in the pleasure garden when last I saw her." He avoided her eyes so assiduously in mentioning the place, that Aurora wondered what pleasures her brother and Miss Fletcher had been enjoying in the pleasure garden.

Aurora investigated the place thoroughly: the boathouse, the grottos, pavilion, and hermitage. Grace was no longer to be found in the gardens.

Still seeking her whereabouts, Aurora went inside. She got no further in her search than the Green State Bedroom's reception room. There she sat and gazed at the painting of the young Tom Coke dressed in silver and salmon satin and tried to find answers to the questions that the breeding of a pair of horses had raised—that and a sense of peace. She understood this painting today as she had never understood it before. She stared at the statue of the lovelorn Adriadne, stared at the shattered architectural bits that represented the broken dreams of a princess. She understood completely the reason why this painting had been commissioned. Her own dreams seemed shattered today.

Miles Fletcher had her rattled. The letter from her brother had her rattled. The mating in the barn had her rattled. The trend of her thoughts was confused. So focused were her thoughts on the painting and how it mirrored her own life that she started with surprise when Grace Fletcher placed a comforting hand on her shoulder and sat down beside her.

"It is a sad painting," she said softly. The look in her eyes would seem to ask again of Aurora if she was all right.

Aurora sighed. "Yes, quite tragic."

"What would you have done, had you been in her shoes?"

Aurora was uncomfortable with such a question. "Whatever do you mean?"

"Well, if you were promised to a titled and moneyed gentleman twice your age for whom you felt little respect and no love at all—would you marry him, or run away with a younger man, without future, whom you loved despite his lack of prospects? Would you choose security, which would be sure to satisfy your family's desires, or passion and possible poverty to satisfy your own?"

The question too closely mirrored the dilemma that Aurora herself was debating. "What would you do?" She sought safety in turning the question.

Grace smiled a knowing smile and responded with such a lack of hesitation that Aurora was convinced she must have given the question prior consideration. "I would, without a doubt, run away with love," she responded. "I would risk censure, disdain, public outcry, and potential poverty. There is no question in my mind that true love, and thus true happiness, is worth the risk. Would you not agree?"

Grace turned from her examination of the painting to study Aurora. Aurora continued to study the painting, rather than meet her searching look.

"Answer me this then, if you have no opinion. Are you still interested in the watercolor I did at the temple? Would you care to have it, Miss Ramsay?"

Aurora could no longer avoid eye contact. "Yes, but I thought your brother . . ." she could not continue.

"He is in love with you, you know," Grace said matter-of-factly. "He cannot bear to look at my watercolor. He tells me it pains him now that it is finished. He has quite wounded my ego in saying so, as you may well imagine."

Aurora frowned. She made every effort to keep her voice from sounding too forlorn. "You warned me against your brother's charm. Those words have rescued me on more than one occasion. You were right you know. Miles is so charming, I have at times come very close to forgetting myself." She gave Grace's hand a pat. "But, as you suggested, I have carefully guarded my heart. It remains safely intact."

Grace stared at Aurora openmouthed. "Dear God! Is it my doing that you hold him aloof? How stupid of me. You see, I was wrong, dreadfully wrong. I have done my brother an injustice in assuming he would never lose his heart."

"Whatever do you mean?"

"I knew he would fall in love with you. Miles falls in love with anything beautiful and he declared you sublimely so the very first time he laid eyes on you. But, this is different. I have never seen him caught in Cupid's clutches before. He has promised—vowed—to make you happy, no matter how miserable it leaves him. He will marry you to Walsh, you know, if Walsh will have you, though it breaks his heart to do so—and for no other reason than that he would see you happy. Do you feel nothing for him?"

It was Aurora's turn to frown. "I am not sure. At present, my emotions are a tangle."

Grace passed a hand over her stomach with a strangely knowing smile. "Love can knot one up inside," she admitted.

Aurora laughed harshly. As Grace regarded her with narrowed eyes and puzzled brow, she said, "To love or love not. That is the real love knot, is it not?"

Chapter Nineteen

Grace was as focused in her work on Aurora's hair and subtle application of makeup as if she were painting a watercolor. "A dusting of powder"—she patted Aurora's nose and forehead with her hare's foot—"the barest hint of perfume . . ." She ran the crystal stopper of her perfume bottle along Aurora's neck.

"I have been meaning to ask you, Grace." Aurora reached up to halt the movement of the other young woman's hand. She sat before the mirror in Grace's room, studying her likeness in the mirror. A beautiful stranger looked back at her.

Grace regarded her with curiosity. "Yes?"

Aurora swallowed hard and forced the question from her lips. It would not do to go on wondering. "Do you mind?"

Grace's narrowly plucked brows rose over eyes almost as blue as her brother's. "Mind what?"

"About Walsh?" Aurora watched every shade of emotion that passed over Grace's features. "I know he is one of your suitors."

Grace was still a moment, perhaps too still. She wielded the hare's foot again with such vigor that Aurora was obligated to close her eyes.

"Not at all," she heard Grace say a trifle too emphatically, her enthusiasm almost aggressive. She sounded cheerful, but powder flew too freely for Aurora to verify if her expression matched her voice. "I am the type of female who marries for love or not at all. I would, without hesitation, elope to Gretna Green were the right gentleman to ask. I have known Walsh forever. He would not think of requesting such a thing of me, nor would I go with him if he did." Grace rattled on. "We practically grew up side by side, you know, so of course I am fond of him and wish him every happiness. If he finds that happiness with you, how could I object? I am grown fond of you—and your brother, Miss Ramsay. It is as if we have known one another for ages. We converse so freely, on the most intimate of topics . . ."

For a moment Aurora could not be certain to whom Grace referred. Was it Rupert she conversed freely with, or herself?

"I have begun to think of you in the light of a sister," Grace said. "I wish you happiness as much as I wish it for Walsh. Only tell me that he will make you blissfully happy and you have my every blessing. My brother . . . as you know, is grown undeniably fond of you. You may depend upon him to further your cause, if it will secure your happiness. Will Lord Walsh secure your every marital desire, Miss Ramsay? Please tell me it is so, for I could not wish anything but happiness for you."

Aurora felt as if such questions weighed heavy on her soul. She could not in good conscience answer in the affirmative. She wished to marry Walsh because it made economic sense, not because it made her happy. The two of them would make amiable partners, not passionate ones. She would be lying to this woman if she said otherwise. And yet, Grace expected an answer and deserved one as well. What she said, therefore, was not a lie at all, but as much of the truth as she dared reveal.

"I believe I should be completely lost without him." Her voice and manner were light, but she spoke in all seriousness. She did believe herself lost without Walsh. Certainly all hope of retaining her land and livestock was lost without him.

"I am relieved you should say so," Grace said, her eyes searching Aurora's. "There, I am done." With a decisive nod she set aside the pots and powders she had been delving into and aggressively dusted Aurora's shoulders and lace with a feather duster. "You are splendid," she breathed, and as her brother had arrived in that moment to escort them downstairs, she turned to him for verification. "Isn't she splendid, Miles?"

Miles was himself splendid. Dressed very much as he had been the first time Aurora had seen him—in formal, black swallow-tail coat, Cossack style pantaloons, and gleaming black pumps—his stock was impeccably tied high under his chin with the diminutive knot of the *Sentimentale*. His waistcoat was white damask, a subtle touch of romance that seemed all the more poignant after their afternoon's conversation. There was a sadness about his eyes, she thought, a tightness about his lips, that impressed her far more than what he wore.

When he turned those sad blue eyes to gaze at her, she was suddenly shy of her own unfamiliar grandeur. "What do you think?" she asked.

His smile was very warm as his gaze traveled over her, but his words chilled her. "No doubt you will attract Walsh's eye. You are sublime."

Sublime? Was that not the term Grace claimed Miles had used on first seeing her? Aurora was uncomfortable with praise. That she was looking far better than usual she would not argue, but sublime? Never before had such time and care been associated with her preparation for any night's entertainment. She had been bathed and scented. Her hair had been curled in a thousand tiny ringlets all bunched at the crown of her head but for kissing curls at temples and brow. A coronet of pearls that Grace had loaned to her and a multitude of narrow ribbons wound their way through the gathered hair.

Aurora glanced once more in the mirror. She looked splendid on the outside, but felt not at all splendid on the inside. There was no splendor in cold-bloodedly planning the snaring of a man she respected but did not love. There was no splendor in being ably assisted in that snaring by the man she had begun to care for, and there was no splendor in his lowered opinion of her for doing so. Her future seemed entirely lacking in splendor. She was being led, she felt, like the mare to a mating.

*   *   *

Aurora Ramsay was, Miles thought, like a lovely golden bubble this evening. A fragile, glittering, iridescent bit of perfection that floated away from him in the wind of her own perverse direction—a lovely bubble that would burst and be gone if he reached out to touch her. She delighted him, as much as any child is delighted by a soap bubble dancing in sunlight; she disappointed him, too, by her very transience. He was in no mood to help further her plan to capture Walsh; he was in no mood to be delighted by her. Yet the love of beauty that was so much a part of him could not be denied any more than the promise he had made to his uncle. He would see her happy, see her future secured. Then he would leave all memory of how she took his breath away this evening behind him.

The shades of amber and gold in which he had directed her parchment-colored evening gown to be rebodiced and draped did not just suit Aurora, they *were* her. She was the dawn. Her hair was the promise of sunshine, cascading in a mass of shining curls over one shoulder and bound with amber ribbons. It begged to be touched, as did her shoulders, fashionably bared, unbearably fair but for the gold dust of her freckles. Her breasts too, beckoned brazenly from the lowered bodice. God, he thought had not created anything more amazing under the sun and the moon—she was his desire personified.

She turned around before him, her skirts belling, seeking his approval and yet not really requiring it. He could tell she was buoyed by her own self-confidence. Her eyes, when they strayed to the mirror, seemed both pleased and unconvinced by what looked back at her from that glittering surface.

"A masterpiece," he said softly. The strength of his voice grew. "You are tonight, Aurora Ramsay, a picture of perfection."

She stopped pivoting before him, her chin raised, her green eyes almost golden in the light. They looked on him for a moment with a sadness that made his heart ache. In their depths, and in her words, there was a sort of farewell and the knowledge that this beauty he beheld was only skin deep. How could she pursue the fate she so boldly sought and still remain beautiful within?

"Framed," she said, her voice strong. "I am but framed tonight, sir." She held out her elegantly gloved hand to him. "You said you would set me in silver, sir, like a work of art. You must display me now, for all the world to judge."

He had no idea of the thought that ran through her head as he gathered up her hand was *like a prize cow*.

Together they went to the statue gallery, from whence came the sound of music.

Heads turned when the threesome entered the crowd. Conscious of that fact, and conscious, too, of the reason for so much focused attention, Miles made a point of breaking a path through the crowd, languidly traversing the length of the room with an occasional pause to nod to this one or exchange a few words with another.

Miles felt justifiable pride in the stir they created—chest-swelling pride that shoved aside his disappointment. Pride filled him up and spilled over in a broad smile and a protective hand and eye in guiding both Miss Ramsay and his sister through the press. Miss Ramsay was the primary reason for the wave of whispering that followed their passage.

The fire within her had been stoked to full flame. No one could ignore such golden, glowing heat. It was ablaze tonight. All eyes that turned in her direction must recognize the change. Of all the women in the room, Aurora Ramsay shone the most. Heads turned when she passed. Tongues wagged. Men who had never given her a second glance, now looked after her with hunger painted on their features. Women who had deemed her beneath their notice, had no choice in the matter this evening. Aurora lit the room like a glittering chandelier. Many would not gaze directly at her brilliance; others were mesmerized by her shine.

Miles basked in Aurora's glory, the moment all the more poignant because he was aware that this light in his life might soon be carried away by another—that this glowing, candle-flame creature shone for Lord Walsh, not him.

Miles led Aurora onto the dance floor.

*   *   *

Aurora was distracted by the stares, distracted by a crowd of faces all swiveling to follow her passage. She was distracted by one face in particular. Lord Walsh's handsome eyes were as fixed in her direction as anyone else's, though he had linked arms with Grace Fletcher in preparation for the dance. So much focused attention so suddenly was vastly discomfitting. Aurora was used to people looking at her because of her hair and freckles, but the looks were generally judgmental ones. The looks turned upon her this evening were very different.

There were those who turned to look at her and smiled, admiration plain in their expressions. Other's mouths dropped open in awe. There were men, and women, too, who looked at her and as swiftly looked away, unwilling to be caught in the act. Some of the gentlemen stared at her with a penetrating boldness that made her long to slap them. It was not entirely pleasant to be the center of attention. Envy, lust, and annoyance reached out to her with unexpected force. She felt self-conscious in a way that had never troubled her before. It was as if she took center stage in some strange impromptu drama when she followed Miles onto the dance floor. Why were so many eyes turned her way?

"Do they expect to see me fall again?" she enquired of Miles. "Is that why they leer?"

Miles ignored the room. He spared not a single glance for anyone but her. "Relax," he said softly. "They do but stare at a thing of beauty."

She could not relax, but his words, his very attitude steadied her. His demeanor, of all those who filled the room, was the same as it had always been. His eyes had always turned to look at her with latent humor and unqualified admiration. They did so now, just as his hands guided her in exactly the manner they had for several days.

Stiffly, she followed his lead.

"Relax," he said again with so gentle a tone she wanted to fall against him, that he might support her entirely. She resisted the temptation, but her movements loosened a little. "Excellent," he breathed. "You are far more fluid when you relax."

Aurora did relax. It was not the light, undemanding conversation that stilled the turmoil of her thoughts and soothed her fears, nor was it the hypnotic familiarity of the movement of their bodies. It was after all the look in Miles Fletcher's eyes that filled her with both peace and confidence. Beneath the gentle tone of his voice, deep within the level gaze that settled on her, there was the subtle hint of deeper feeling, of an emotional pull. The telling warmth, affection, and openness steadied her self-confidence and shook her resolve with regard to Lord Walsh.

As if to remind her of that purpose, Miles said gently, "Walsh has not taken his eyes from your face since we began the dance. Might I suggest we join my sister and her partner when the music stops? Walsh will want to ask you to take the floor with him, I'll be bound."

Aurora was injured by the question. How could he suggest such a thing if his feelings were what she supposed? How could he look at her so? Perhaps she was wrong. It would be best for all concerned, she thought, were she wrong. And yet, that she might so misread him stung her.

"By all means," she said briskly to hide her pique. "Let us join your sister."

Proud and miserable, Miles watched the predicted exchange between Lord Walsh and his protégée.

He had worried that Aurora's head would be turned too far by such attention. His worries were unfounded. True, Aurora held her head high, and part of her radiance came from the glow of self-confidence that suffused her person, but the rudest stares of the room could not penetrate the shield such self-confidence leant her. She floated, it would seem, just a little above them all—tethered to the arm of the man she had so long sought. It was clear by the very possessive light in his eyes and the grip of his hand on her arm that Walsh meant she should not float away.

She broke away from him however, just long enough to say, "Thank you."

Miles gazed into her shining eyes and had no choice but to smile. "What is it you thank me for?" he asked.

She raised both brows with surprise. "For restoring to me my pride," she said simply. "I never dreamed I would be able to enter this room with equanimity again, much less to meet the reaction you have conjured up."

He took her hand and kissed it. "My pleasure," he said. "You will, of course, invite me to the wedding?"

She laughed and bit down on her lip to stop the outburst, eyes sparkling. "I've yet to receive a proposal, sir."

"From Walsh." He pointedly reminded her of his own proposal to her with the remark.

Her eyes lost a little of their fire. Her mouth grew serious. He tried to smile as if it did not matter. The smile did not feel at all natural.

She slid her hand from his. "Of course." Again, she braved his displeasure with humor. "But, you have yet to return to me my land and relieve my family of the burden of its debts."

"What?" Her remark caught him off guard.

She shrugged. "You have, no doubt, forgotten the promise you made to that effect. It was, after all, a promise made in the middle of a cornfield." Miles frowned. Her remark was meant to be taken in jest, but there was too much ugly truth in this lighthearted exchange.

"I am a man of my word," he said with a forced smile. "May I crave the honor of another dance before the evening is out? Perhaps then we will have a moment to discuss this cornfield business."

She agreed as he bowed over her hand. Walsh claimed her and she was gone.

Grace had been watching his exchanges with Aurora with signs of confusion. "I am puzzled." Her voice was low when she linked arms with him. "How can you go on pushing Miss Ramsay into Lord Walsh's way when you are in love with her? Is it for Walsh's sake you taught her to dance? Is it all for Walsh and this stupid promise to Uncle Lester? How can you fall out of love as nimbly as you have fallen in?"

Miles stood quiet a moment watching the young woman he wished to marry step confidently onto the dance floor, moving gracefully through the dance in the beautiful gown he had redone for her, on the arm of a gentleman whose face he would like to pound. "I have not fallen out of love, Grace."

Grace had drawn breath to begin on him again, but this quiet remark stopped her, mouth open. "You love her then? But, Miles, I do not understand. You continue to help her to throw herself in the arms of another man. It makes no sense."

He sighed. "I do so in the hopes that she will sooner come to the realization they do not suit."

She blinked in disbelief. "I have never heard more foolish nonsense. Why do you not press your own suit if you really care for her?"

Was he foolish? Miles wondered.

"I have never been more seriously in earnest in all of my life, Grace. I will win her in my own way. You must not interfere. She has set her mind on Walsh. I would not be the one to convince her he is not the man for her."

"No? And who better?"

"She must convince herself," he said firmly.

"My dear brother," Gracie said, shaking her head, "you are a fool not to use your considerable talents of seduction if she is indeed the one you would have. Do you comprehend the noteworthy power of your smile? Of this dimple?" She pinched his cheek. "You have only to crook your finger at the girl and she is yours. You have only to promise her the land her brother so foolishly gambled away."

He smiled a careful smile as he watched Aurora skim around the room on the arm of the man she had told him plainly she meant to marry. "I am determined, Gracie, that she should not be looking always over her shoulder, wondering if she would not have been happier as Lady Walsh. I am determined, too, that I shall not win her with nothing more than a handful of dirt."

Gracie sighed. "Your intentions are honorable. I sincerely hope you do not lose the love of your life because of them. I would certainly not let opportunity slip so easily through my fingertips." Her eyes lit up with a fire Miles was unused to seeing. "When love claims me, I will run away with it," she said.

Chapter Twenty

Aurora had got what she wanted. She was dancing with Lord Walsh, dancing with grace and confidence. There was no chance of landing on the floor this time.

"You look marvelous," he said. "You have done something different with your hair."

Aurora almost laughed, so greatly did his remark understate the matter. She was transformed top to bottom. Time and effort had gone into her every word, move, every stitch of clothing on her person. All was exactly as she had hoped, dreamed, and planned. Even Lord Walsh was exactly as she had imagined. He was proud and handsome and well-versed in all the matters that had once seemed so very important to her happiness.

They conversed with complete compatibility, discussing the value of root crops and the latest improvements in plows and cultivators. Walsh held forth on the value of walled gardens, greenhouses, and the hemming of open fields with shrubbery. As he spoke, his eyes warmed. Aurora could not recall inspiring such a glow in their morning gallops.

"You really do look lovely this evening, Miss Ramsay," he said.

How ironic that she should be regarded with admiration by Walsh when she could not remember a time when she felt less deserving. Her contrived beauty this evening had become a torturous sort of misery. *Why was this man not drawn to me without my turning myself inside out?* she wondered, and as she wondered, her gaze cast about the gallery looking for Miles Fletcher. The happiest moments of the evening seemed spent. Unaware of the value of their time spent together, she had allowed it to slip through her grasp.

Miles Fletcher stood across the room from her, his attention fixed on the face of a gold pocket watch he had just flicked open with his thumb. In the instant Aurora looked at him his gaze rose from the face of the watch to hers, as though he was conscious of her presence despite the distance that separated them. Time seemed to freeze. Watch in hand, he stared at her, a trace of longing in his gaze, a hint of sadness in the set of his mouth. She felt as if he must be able to hear the quickening of her pulse from across the room, so loudly did it pound in her ears.

The moment slid by with exquisite languor.

Aurora's lips lifted in the beginning of a smile, but before it could dimple her cheek, Miles Fletcher closed his hand around the gold watch and looked away. Time thawed in a rush. He tucked the watch into its pocket.

Aurora reminded herself of all the reasons why it had been so important to win Walsh's attention. She thought of his land, of her land, of any land. She reminded herself of her brothers' expenses, of the stock she must sell because of them. Was any of this as important as she had imagined? Did the weight of any of it compare to that of a pair of blue eyes meeting hers across a crowded room?

Perhaps it was the dance that made her peevish, Aurora thought. She and Walsh did well enough, but there was not the special, gliding rhythm that she felt in her dances with Miles Fletcher. There was not the humming vibrance between their hands, nor the strange connection of thought that had them moving as one. She looked for such a connection in Lord Walsh. She had expected that much and more. She wanted it to be there—but the feeling was undeniably absent. She felt awkward in the arms of the gentleman she meant to marry.

"You have been practicing, Miss Fletcher," her partner observed with a look of approval. "I am most impressed."

Aurora admitted she had indeed been practicing. She should have been pleased Walsh noticed the changes in her, but with every indication of his increasing favor, she felt as though a great weight crushed inexorably down on her. With each passing minute, she felt stretched and flattened, a victim on the rack of her own misjudgment.

The music stopped. Walsh offered to fetch refreshments. Aurora thanked him, her gaze drawn to one after another of the fine marbles that lined the walls of the gallery. These exquisite nudes—gods and goddesses in polished marble—reminded her of Miles. He had meant to show them to her. That he had never done so reminded her of the paintings in the attic. Fletcher's words echoed in her mind. *Such passion should not be shut away in the attic—ignored.*

Aurora focused on the letter she had received from Jack.

"Are you in the market for some sheep, my lord?" she asked Walsh when he returned to her side, glasses of sherbet in hand.

"Not at the moment," he said without hesitation.

"Cattle then?" She sipped at her drink and tried not to rush the matter. "This would seem to be a superb setting in which to locate excellent stock. Do you not agree?"

"Oh, indeed. It has been. I have filled all of my requirements quite nicely. Are you in the market for stock? I can recommend several excellent fellows to you who still have prime animals available."

Aurora's heart sank. The sherbet seemed suddenly wincingly sweet. "I do appreciate your kind offer, but I am interested in locating buyers rather than sellers. I have some excellent creatures for sale."

"Ah! That is another matter entirely. Have you asked Fletcher if he will not take them off your hands? It would seem the most logical solution."

Miles Fletcher was the last man on earth Aurora wanted to ask favors of. She thanked Walsh for his suggestion and made a promise to herself that she would ask every other man in the room before she asked Fletcher to buy her stock.

She kept that promise. Her dance partners, and there

were many, were each of them asked the same question. "Are you in the market for some fine livestock?"

Berney Brampstone, youngest son of the Earl of Brampstone, who complimented her on her grace in dancing, claimed he had no use for her animals and suggested, "James Gant was looking for cattle and Miles Fletcher would seem the man to ask about your sheep."

The baronet, Gant, was interested both in buying bulls and in examining intently the low cut of Aurora's neckline. His eyes rarely lifted to the level of her face as he spoke. He had no interest in her sheep whatsoever. "Not a sheep man, my dear. You must chase after Lester Fletcher's nevie for that. He's just come into Lester's properties you know." Having said as much, he froze a moment, openmouthed, before with an explosive laugh, he said, "But of course, you of all people would know that better than anyone."

Aurora blushed. Had she been so indiscreet in her interaction with Miles Fletcher that everyone guessed her true feelings of affection for him? Did this man think her so deep in Fletcher's pocket that she was informed of his financial circumstances? Fletcher had said no more to her than that he was due to come into a patch of land. Who was this Lester Fletcher on everyone's tongue? Had he died to leave Miles an inheritance? Could this be the bad news Miles had received from London this morning—the news that had brought such sadness to his deep blue eyes?

"Shame about Lester popping off suddenly the way he did," Tom Coke said when she tried to find out more. "I suppose his funeral will send Miles and Grace scurrying back to London."

Aurora made sympathetic noises, reminded of how little she really knew about Miles Fletcher. She had had no idea Fletcher stood to inherit riches and land.

"Quite an upset to his elder brother," Lord Montgomerie informed her. "But no surprise to those who knew the old gent. Miles indulged his every whim. I am told he outfitted Loughdon Hall with several exceptional friezes from Greece."

"I believe his uncle collected Flemish tapestries," someone else confided. "I have heard that the dining hall at Loughdon is lined with them."

Yet another informed her, "The gardens at Loughdon, though small, are said to be quite magnificent due to the addition of a number of exotics Miles imported from overseas."

Everyone seemed prepared to extoll the virtues of Miles Fletcher and his inheritance of Loughdon Hall. Few were interested in making purchases of her livestock, but as the evening dragged on and her throat went dry praising the value and quality of her own stock, Aurora managed to wring commitments from first one and then another for all her cattle, two flocks of geese and any number of pigs. The sheep however, none would have, at any price, and it was in her flocks that Aurora saw the greatest potential for profit.

Still she hesitated to ask Miles Fletcher if he cared to have them, though his name had been recommended to her a dozen times and more. He had already done so much for her, too much perhaps. It was awkward, too, that he had asked for her hand and she had refused him. Surely she need not rely on him for anything more.

Lord Walsh hung at her elbow when she was not trotting around the dance floor. She fluttered her fan and batted her eyelashes, valiantly trying to stir some spark between them. Something vital was missing in their exchanges. She could not immediately put her finger on what it was, but their conversations became an ordeal. There was no conflict to fire them, no impassioned exchange of heartfelt beliefs. They agreed too completely. Her head grew weary of nodding. In short, the two of them together were unutterably boring.

There was no spark, no sense of surprise or adventure to this evening—a sense she had grown to anticipate in her exchanges with Miles Fletcher. In Walsh she found a mirror image of herself. Their very souls seemed cut from the same cloth. There was no real potential for growth in such a relationship, no hope of happiness.

Aurora had vowed to herself that she must forget Miles Fletcher, that she must concentrate on Walsh. Strangely, in ignoring Miles she became aware of his every movement and in concentrating on Walsh, she found herself wanting nothing more than to ignore him.

Walsh evidenced no inkling of her growing boredom.

"I must admit I find it quite remarkable that you and Miles Fletcher stand on such cordial terms," he said. "I do not think I would be so understanding were our roles reversed."

"Roles, my lord?" For the first time that evening Lord Walsh completely captured Aurora's attention. What had roles to do with her relationship with Miles Fletcher?

"Had the man inherited my land, I do not think I could stand to be in the same room with the fellow, much less on friendly terms with him."

Aurora was still confused. Inherited her land? Her land? Like a puzzle, all the pieces fit together, whether she wanted them to or not. Clarity hit her like a blow. Miles Fletcher's inheritance, the one everyone was so hesitant to mention in her presence, included her land. Fletcher's uncle was the old gent who had bested her brother at faro. There could be no other explanation, and yet this explanation stuck in her throat. Aurora looked across the room at Miles Fletcher, and as had happened several times before that evening, he looked up in almost the same instant and locked eyes with her. The hurt and dismay she was feeling must have evidenced itself in her expression.

"Are you all right, Miss Ramsay?" Walsh's voice sounded as if from a distance. "You are looking unreasonably pale."

Miles Fletcher, as concerned as Walsh, broke off conversation in midsentence and took a step toward her.

Aurora could face neither of them. With anger and anguish warring in her breast, she could not say a word. Almost at a run, she fled the room. She must locate her brother. If anyone might be depended on to help her through this mess, it would be Rupert. She managed to control all tears, to hold back all feelings in connection with this stunning sense of betrayal until she reached Tom Coke's library. Her hand was on the doorknob, her heart lurching up into her throat, when a voice called her name.

It was a footman.

"Are you Miss Aurora Ramsay?" He approached with caution, as if aware that she was not in a mood for conversation.

"Yes," she said stiffly, reigning in her passions.

"Mr. Rupert Ramsay bade me give this to you." He handed to her a screw of paper, folded in the manner that Rupert favored for his most personal confidences. Aurora looked at it with a sense of confusion. What had Rupert to say to her that he could not say to her face?

"Do you know where Mr. Ramsay is to be found?" she asked as she took it in her hand.

She thought the blankly respectful demeanor of the footman's expression faltered for an instant. "No marm," he said crisply, his eyes downcast.

Aurora was too distracted by the strange manner in which her brother chose to convey this message to her to stay the footman's exit. Had he been one of her own servants, she would have insisted he explain whatever it was he held back from her. As it was, she chose instead to enter the library, certain she would find Rupert there to explain it all himself.

The library was deserted.

There was only one light glowing in the golden gloom. Aurora crossed the room to it, unfolding the screw of paper from Rupert as she went. This unusual communique from her brother seemed somehow more ominous in the vast, ill-lit emptiness of the room where she had expected to find him in person. The wound of betrayal she suffered at Miles Fletcher's hand seemed to bleed into the moment, coloring everything she touched. Her hands were uncertain with the screw of paper. Twice she tore the page. The light flickered with her approach, as if it too was made uncertain by her very proximity.

With trembling hands she smoothed the folds in the paper and held it to the light.

My dear sister—

By the time you read this, Miss Fletcher and I will be well on our way to Gretna Green.

Chapter Twenty-one

Aurora's hands shook too much to continue reading. Her legs managed to carry her to a chair. There they folded beneath her and she sank into the downy comfort of featherstuffed brocade. A tear slid down her cheek and then another. She was on the verge of abandoning herself to a flood of emotion when a scratch came at the door and it was opened to admit a man's head. "Miss Ramsay?"

She expected it to be Fletcher. For an instant she convinced herself it was he, and with great strength of will, she blinked away her tears.

"Yes," she said, her voice shaking only a little.

"Have I upset you in some way, Miss Fletcher?"

It was not Miles Fletcher who pushed open the door and crossed the darkened room. Lord Walsh had followed her here.

Aurora crumpled the letter in her hand. "It is not you who upsets me, my lord," she said thickly, her voice lower than usual, its tenor unsteady.

"Are you ill then?" His voice was appropriately concerned. That concern threatened Aurora with tears.

"Not ill, sir. I am merely at wit's end."

Walsh took her hands in his, and pressing her back into the chair, knelt beside the arm of it, saying calmly, "You must tell me what has driven you there."

Aurora slipped one of her hands from his and pressed it to her forehead. "My life is a tangle, sir, a tangle so snarled I no longer think I can begin to unknot it."

"Perhaps I can help. Can you begin to tell me?"

Aurora looked into the beseeching kindness of his face

and felt her spirits sink. She was a fraud for conniving so coldly to marry this man. Lord Walsh had begun to care for her, he had perhaps even lost his heart to her, just as she had lost her heart to Miles Fletcher. She felt no single spark of desire within her for this man, though she had intended to marry him, given the chance. "I am betrayed, sir," she said, "betrayed by passion gone awry."

"Passion, Miss Ramsay?" He seemed transfixed by the word.

"Yes." She could no longer look into the fascinated eyes that regarded her, without despising herself. "The most unruly of emotions, sir. Do not let passion betray you. I warn you."

"I am quite confused, Miss Ramsay."

How much could she tell him after such a statement? She must explain herself to some degree. "It was passion . . ." she began, "a passion for winning drove my brother to gamble unwisely, risking all I hold dear. His passions, sir, would abandon him, and the siblings he was meant to care for, to a life of disgrace and penury. I am betrayed, sir. Betrayed by everyone, and it breaks my heart."

"Who else dares to so abuse you, my dear Miss Ramsay?"

"My friend, sir, a gentleman I had come to care for as much as any of my brothers . . ."

"Mr. Fletcher," he guessed.

She closed her eyes on the tears that threatened to burn tracks upon her cheek once again. "He never told me . . ." She opened her eyes, and blinking very quickly, her mind set against the emotions that threatened to overcome her, she stared at the mosaic above the mantel, the lion and the leopard. She had wondered once who was the lion, who the leopard in the strange and moving relationship she shared with Miles Fletcher. There was no question now. His teeth marks were on her throat. The wrenching pain of his deception threatened her ability to speak.

"He never told me it was he who was to have our land," she said. The words tasted bitter in her mouth. Their meaning burned even more bitterly in her soul. "I have been betrayed," she said, stiffening her spine, "by a man I took for a gentleman—one whom I trusted above all others. My own unruly passions, I am ashamed to admit, led me to believe him genuine in his concern for my well-being. But in all the time we shared"—her voice broke and a single tear spilled onto her cheek—"Mr. Fletcher never saw fit to tell me of his role in my family's undoing. He has, I think, betrayed me most cruelly. My brother and I had so come to trust him and his sister, that Rue has succumbed completely to his own passions. He has, and I know it must pain you to hear this, my lord, run off to Gretna Green with Miss Fletcher."

Walsh frowned and remained completely quiet for so long that Aurora feared he was harder hit by this news than even she might have imagined.

"Are you all right, my lord?" she whispered. "I know you care dearly for her."

He tried to smile and failed. "We are both betrayed by passion, it would appear, Miss Fletcher. I have known for many years that Grace Fletcher did not share my feelings." He laughed dryly. "One might say my passion for her. And yet I continued to deceive myself, to believe that with time and patience the fire that burned within me might warm her to me. I had, you see, no interest, not so much as a glance to offer any other female who crossed my path, until you thrust yourself upon my attention. Perhaps we two can untangle the knotted affair that passion has made of both of our lives. I would offer you my hand in marriage, Miss Fletcher. Will you take it, I wonder?"

Miles had gone to Aurora's room when she dashed from the ballroom, thinking he might find her there. He meant to explain. He was sure from her expression she had discovered what he had so long intended to reveal to her. She was not to be found in her room however, so next he had tried her brother's quarters, which had even more of a deserted air. Only then did it occur to him she might take refuge in the library. The door was half open when he arrived, but he was drawn up short by the touching tableau that played itself out in the circle of light thrown by the only lamp that illuminated the room. Aurora Ramsay was perched on the edge of a gold damask chair, her hair glittering like flame in the lamplight, and at her feet knelt Walsh, his hands wrapped around hers. He had the look about him of a lovelorn swain. Could this be the proposal that Aurora had claimed all along she intended to illicit?

Miles was devastated by the thought, and yet he could not believe the posture of these two meant anything else, for as he watched with breaking heart, Walsh leaned forward to kiss his love upon the lips, and she made no move to elude his passionate intent.

Stunned and disheartened, Miles collected himself enough to take himself off to his own rooms. It was there that he found the note that his sister had left explaining that she and Rue Ramsay were on their way to Gretna Green.

Aurora returned to her own rooms not much later, her head whirling with the enormity of what it was that Lord Walsh offered her. He had asked her to marry him. He meant that they two should work his lands together, side by side, just as she had imagined. She need no longer look forward to a pauper's future. She need no longer worry about money or debts, or a mad fit of gambling relieving her of all her possessions. All that she had dreamed, all that she had hoped for, was to be hers.

And yet, she could not be content in the offer. She entered her room with but one thought in her mind, a thought so consuming she swept past the note that littered the floor by her door. To the escritoire she went. Pen and paper she drew forth. Furiously, she scribbled a note.

Do you mean to go after them? was all it said.

Having allowed but a moment for the ink to dry, she leapt up and would have dashed as quickly out the door had the note on the floor not caught her eye.

It was from Grace.

> *My dearest Aurora—*
> *I hope you do not mind my addressing you so, we shall, after all, call one another sister when next we meet. I hope you do not object to such a future. I am supremely confi-*

*dent, you see, that great happiness will come of this run-
away marriage. Never has a man so suited me as dear Rupert does suit me—not in position, perhaps (a factor to
which my eldest brother and guardian was sure to object),
not in wealth, (another matter that is sure to anger
Matthew), but we will not allow our overflowing passions
be stayed by such poor objections. In all other ways two
hearts could not be happier, no nor better suited. I know
that somewhere in your heart you will understand our haste
in marrying. The death of my uncle threatened to return me
to London. Once there, under the sway of not one, but two
elder brothers, I feared my desires would become subordi-
nate to those of my guardian. Life's a tangle and we must
each see our own way to unknotting it. I close this letter
with the hope that you will not see fit to separating the tangled strands of happiness that bind me, heart and soul, to
your brother.*

*As a token of my deep and lasting affection, I leave the
painting you so admired in the temple in the woods.*

Aurora had sat on the edge of her bed to read this letter.
She fell back now, across the coverlet, looking from the
scribbled line she had meant to shove beneath the door to
Miles Fletcher's room to the passionate lines that touched
her heart far more than she would have imagined. With a
heartfelt sigh, she balled up the single line she had written
and tossed it across the room. Lunging from the bed, she
returned to the escritoire and pulled forth a clean sheet of
paper. No words flowed from her freshly dipped quill however, and at last she returned it to the standish. Hands trembling, she drew forth from the drawer in her wardrobe
where she kept her undergarments, the love knot that Miles
Fletcher had twice given her.

As she stared at it, the tears she had held back so dili-
gently throughout the evening flowed freely from her eyes.
She could not interfere in her brother's chosen road to happiness when her own way was so confused. With a sigh,
she tucked the love knot into its bed of white linen and
closed the drawer on it and her tears. Resolutely she took
up the quill again and dipped it in the inkwell.

Assuming you are not already on the road to Gretna, and as we are soon to be sister and brother-in-law, we should, I think, meet and make our peace with one another.

The note was finished and her hand upon the door when a great pounding on its panel gave her a dreadful start. What now? She opened the door. Miles Fletcher, caped and gloved, waited with the impatient air of a man in a hurry to be elsewhere. He looked surprised she opened the door to him so quickly. The air between them seemed charged with tension and things unsaid.

"Mr. Fletcher!"

"Did I startle you?" His eyes searched her expression with an urgency that only served to increase the tension between them.

"I was on my way to give you this." She handed him her note.

Quickly he scanned the lines. His jaw tightened when he came to the end. Tucking the note into his breast pocket, he said gruffly, "I'm after them." He swallowed hard. "Do you care to come with me?"

Her mouth dropped open. "Are you asking me to run away with you?" Hope leapt high in Aurora's breast.

"I am."

She smiled wistfully. "Thank you, but I cannot." She bowed her head. "Lord Walsh has this evening proposed to me."

He sighed, and though he made no movement, it was as if he stepped away from her. He blinked, arranged his face neatly and said very politely. "I see."

She caught his arm. "I do not think you do."

"No?" He looked down at the hand on his arm. She felt compelled to remove it, so cold was that look.

"It would be too cruel if both of the women this man has proposed to, ran away to Gretna on the same evening," she said.

"Cruel? Yes, I suppose it would be." His jaw seemed very tight. "Am I to wish you happy, Aurora? I dare call you Aurora, you must understand, because you are, as you have yourself pointed out to me, soon to be my sister. I hope you find nothing to object to in such boldness."

She shook her head. His tone was biting. Not at all polite.

"Your goal is met. Is it all that you had hoped for?" He clipped off every word as if with scissors.

She could be as biting as he. "Do you ask because you care, *Miles*"—she placed subtle verbal emphasis on the use of his first name—"or because you feel you owe me some form of recompense for your uncle's good fortune at cards?"

He met her accusation with silence, jaw working. "You know," he said at last. "How long have you known? Is this why you never asked me to buy your sheep?"

She frowned. He meant to talk of sheep?

He frowned as well and drew forth his pocket watch. "This is not the time to explain, or to beg pardon." He slid the watch back into its pocket. "I was wrong not to tell you, myself," he said simply. "I was, quite selfishly, afraid the knowledge would interfere significantly with our getting to know one another."

"It would surely have done that," she admitted, still peeved. The tension between them increased.

"I wanted very much to get to know you better," he said so softly she almost did not hear him.

"Do you mean to put a stop to the union of my brother and your sister?" she asked bluntly, wary of this softness to his tone.

He chuckled humorlessly and squeezed the fisted head of his cane, so that the leather of his glove made a strained noise. "Never that. No, I mean to put my stamp of approval on their joining, if I can get to Gretna Green before the wedding ceremony is ended. There should be some semblance of order, of familial approval to the proceedings."

"You surprise me."

"Do I?" He regarded her with an intensity that surprised her again. "I would sooner chase after my own happiness than that of my sister's divination." His voice and manner left Aurora with the unsettling impression he referred to her.

"Oh," she said softly. Tension hummed between them like the notes of a violin.

"I must be off." He distanced himself from her with the words as much as his former remark had brought him near.

She was disappointed. "Until you return then," she said. She could think of nothing better.

He nodded, shot her one last searching look, and set off down the hall. Aurora was troubled by a feeling of finality to this separation.

He did not look back, though she stood waiting, hoping he would. She closed the door on the empty hall with a feeling of such loss, such emptiness, her heart ached. She stood pressed against the door, trying not to cry, biting down on her lip and beating helplessly with her hands on the sides of her skirts.

Bang, bang, bang! Someone pounded on the door at her back. Recognizing the rhythm of that tattoo, she flung open the door.

"Miles!"

"Aurora." His voice was throaty. He pushed into the room. Sweeping her into his arms to kiss her, he tilted the combined weight of the two of them, clasped, against the door, shutting it on the world behind them.

For a supremely satisfying moment they lost themselves in the sensation of mouth upon mouth, body pressed warmly to body. The tension between them ignited in a fire of blind desire, singeing the edges of Miles Fletcher's polite and polished veneer. Possessed of an uncontrollable, almost violent, certainly animal passion—a passion that must consume them both, his beautiful swimming hands were everywhere. His mouth, hot and demanding, melted into hers and then moved on, to brand temples, throat, and breast with the searing power of his desire.

His control was not completely and irrevocably departed. With a groan, he wrenched himself away from her. "I really must be off."

"Must you?" she whispered, her lips tingling, her body alive with such desire she wanted more than anything to stay his leaving her ever again.

"I must," he said firmly, his control returning. One more kiss, lightly, upon the tip of her nose, and he was gone.

Chapter Twenty-two

Aurora was impatient in her wait for Miles to return. Of Coke, every day, she asked, "Has Mr. Fletcher come?"

And every day came the same answer. "I am sorry to say, my dear Miss Ramsay, he has not."

Aurora felt the absence of Mr. Fletcher, like the absence of a tooth. She could not stop worrying over it. As much as she noticed Miles Fletcher's absence, the other guests at Holkham Hall, noticed the absence of her brother. With Rue gone, Aurora was placed in the very awkward position of being single, female, and without a proper chaperone. Her position became an awkward one. Even with the Cokes and their daughters to champion her singular state, she became the object of unwanted attentions from any number of the male guests.

Aurora wrote to her brothers. While she waited for their response, Walsh became her stalwart defender, assuming the role as if he had a right to it. He, among all of her swains, showed no inclination at all to take advantage of her brother's absence.

"Will you kiss me, my lord?" She asked him outright on one of their morning rides.

He seemed surprised at her request, but obligingly pulled his horse beside hers, that they might lean toward one another.

Aurora shut her eyes and presented her lips to him. She had imagined this moment many times, not the part where she asked him to kiss her, of course, but ever since Miles Fletcher had blessed her lips with the wonder of his mouth, she had wondered what it would be like to share just such an exchange with Lord Walsh. Her imagination was far more exciting than reality. Lord Walsh's salute to her lips was no more moving today than it had been on the evening of his proposal. She had suspected that might be the case, but had needed verification.

The sound of riders approaching drew them apart.

Walsh sat back in his saddle, leather creaking. His expression was as troubled as the kiss he had given her. "Why did you want to kiss me, Miss Ramsay?"

She studied the horizon. There were three gentlemen on horseback headed in their direction. "I was looking, my lord, for something I cannot describe . . ."

He seemed suddenly interested in the stitching on his glove. "Something you have found elsewhere?"

"Yes." She could not lie to him. "I wish it were not so, but I have fallen in love with another . . ."

He looked up with a sigh. "I am not entirely surprised," he said evenly.

"No?"

"No." He smiled at her. "And I like you too much, Miss Ramsay, not to wish you more luck with Fletchers than I have enjoyed."

There was no time for Aurora to respond. The riders drew near, the horses breathing hard.

"Making an offer to our sister, are you?"

Aurora recognized the decisive voice even before she turned in the saddle to find her brother Roger astride the big black gelding that took him everywhere. Beside him, glaring at her rather more fiercely than she was accustomed, sat two more of her brothers.

"When is the wedding?" Jack asked pointedly.

"Wedding?" Aurora was confused.

"There is going to be a wedding after a display like that in broad daylight." Gordon sounded as if there would be no arguing the matter.

A strong breeze kicked the trees along the roadside into uneasy motion as Miles returned from his mad dash to Gretna Green, his coach besplattered, his horses bone weary. Another spring shower threatened and Miles's watch had become part of his hand. He glanced at it now, before leaning out of the coach window to glare at the darkening sky.

"Faster." He banged his fisted cane on the roof of the carriage. "The rain will catch us."

The roads to Gretna Green and back had been dreadful, the weather uncooperative. Delayed by rain, he had arrived too late to witness his sister's hasty wedding. All he could think about now, all he had thought about then as he had been flung about the coach, was Aurora.

He had gained but one thing from this trip. He possessed now a better understanding of the strength and courage with which Aurora Ramsay met the recent upsets of her life. Her brothers had regularly played havoc with her emotions, her future, her sense of security and control. His sister had, just this once, with his and he was wrecked by it.

Yet, Miss Ramsay managed to meet such upheaval with aplomb. She held her head high. She even managed to improve herself. There was something remarkable in such fortitude, he decided, something noteworthy in her grace under pressure.

Miles had not weathered well his pursuit of Grace and Rupert. He was, in fact, a sad sight to behold. He had not slept or eaten with any regularity. He had not taken enough clean clothing with him to withstand the rigors of rain and muddy roads. He had not had a shave this morning. He felt shaken, a state with which he was not at all comfortable. His sister seemed to have disappeared into Scotland without a trace once her name was writ in the parish register. Strangely, he did not particularly care. Grace had made her choice. Surely she would not find it an unbearable one. She and Rupert knew they might come to him and receive his blessing once the deed was done.

Matthew was going to be livid—but what did it matter? What did any of it matter? All that mattered to Miles now was returning to Aurora.

His coach sped onto Coke's property only to find its progress delayed again, not once, but many times as a steady stream of carriages rumbled down the long drive away from Holkham Hall with the same scudding speed that the clouds rolled across the sky. The shearing was done. The sheep gamboling across the green of the fields, were a whiter, lighter, less-fleecy bunch than those he had seen upon his arrival.

Miles ran a hand along the stubble that roughened his jaw. He could do with a fleecing himself.

As his coach approached the channel looking dark and mysterious under the lowering sky, he felt tempted to jump in. He needed a bath, a shave, and fresh clothes, but more than any of these, he needed and wanted Aurora.

There were, unbeknownst to him, come a number of obstacles to stand in the way of his getting what he wanted. His coach, when it pulled into the drive, was descended upon first by a horde of servants come to do their jobs, and then by a horde of redheaded gentlemen come to do their best to make his arrival a memorable one.

Ramsays, several of them, had arrived in his absence.

"Are you Miles Fletcher?" One of the three men inquired aggressively, his breath far too fetid with brandy for such an early hour. His ruddy cheeks and nose would seem to indicate he was in the habit of drinking far more than was good for him.

Miles stuck his hand toward the gentleman and stuck his nose somewhat out of the direct line of his brandied breath. "Are you one of Miss Ramsay's brothers?"

The fellow seemed surprised he was so easily identified. He declined to shake Miles's hand, thrusting his own in his pockets as he said gruffly, "We've come to hash things out with you, sir." His manner was defensive, his stance decidedly rude. He was blocking Miles's approach to the hall.

Rakehell, whom he recognized, made a point of agreeing, though he could not look Miles in the eye when he spoke. "We hear you have been cozying up to Aurora during your stay here. Not content with stealing our home from us, would you have our sister, too?"

A spattering of raindrops whipped at them from the wind.

"Stealing your home is it?" Miles hadn't the energy to argue. "Well, Ramsay, as much as I would love to stand in the rain trading insults, we must make an appointment to continue this slander at a later date. I've prior commitments at the moment."

The third gentleman had said nothing at this point. He was the handsomest of the lot, a great, tall fellow with long dark, auburn curls and even darker sidewhiskers and brows above eyes the same deep Wedgewood blue as Miles was used to seeing stare from Rupert's mild expression. These eyes were bright and watchful, not at all mild, despite lids held at a deceptive half mast, as if their owner were bored with the whole proceeding. He laughed now—he had a pleasant laugh—and held out his hand.

"Roger Ramsay," he said. His every gesture had flair. "May we call on you this evening, sir?"

"You may." Miles agreed. This one, he thought, was perhaps the most dangerous of the lot. His emotions were not on the surface and easy to read like his brothers, like Aurora's. A pity, Miles thought, if the man really was wasting away of the pox. He had a cynical sort of beauty, a subtle air of intelligence and manners that Miles liked.

"Come Jack, Gordon."

Ah! Jack and Gordon were their names. Miles made a mental note.

Roger beckoned his siblings with a negligent wave of his hand. With the same negligence he turned to Miles, his eyes lazy. "By the way, how is Rupert? I understand you and I may now be brothers, if gossip has the story of his recent nuptials straight." His brow arched suggestively.

"He is married to my sister, sir, and as her husband I do not think I would be overstating the matter to suggest he has never been happier."

He smiled at that. "I look forward to meeting my new sister. Rupert deserves to be happy."

"Can you tell me where *your* sister might be found? I must speak to her."

Roger shrugged lazily. "Look for Lord Walsh, sir, and you are sure to find Aurora."

With a sense of foreboding, Miles cornered the first footman he encountered within the walls of Holkham Hall. "Where may I find Miss Aurora Ramsay?" he asked.

The man shook his head. "Couldn't say, sir. Shall I ask around for you?"

"Yes. And please have hot water sent up to my room immediately."

Miles bounded up the stairs, tapping on the panel of Aurora's bedroom door in passing. There was no response. That would have been too easy.

In his own room he flung off his coat, waistcoat, cravat, and shirt. He was preparing to remove his breeches as well when a knock sounded on the door. Thinking it was either the footman come with news of Aurora's whereabouts or the valet with hot water, Miles called out eagerly, "Come in."

His brother, Matthew, opened the door and walked in, his chin set in dissatisfaction.

"Where in blazes has Grace gotten herself off to?" Matthew demanded in the severe tone he adopted when the world did not measure up to his expectations. "I entrusted her to your care, Miles. How could you let her run off to Gretna with a penniless one-legged man? For God's sake, put on some clothes."

He flung his hat onto Miles's bed and sat himself heavily in the most comfortable chair the room had to offer. "I expect a full reckoning of the entire episode."

Miles crossed to the bed, picked up his brother's hat, and returning it to him, said, "I will tell you all after I have had a change of clothes, a bath, a shave, and a most pressing interview with one other person."

Matthew refused to take the hat from his hand. "I've no intention of budging until I have had the full story."

Another knock upon the door. Miles, shirtless, his brother's hat in his hand, shouted "Enter," once again. Surely this knock heralded the entrance of the much-wanted hot water.

He was mistaken. It was his host who entered. "Miles. I see your brother has found you."

"Yes," Miles said emotionlessly as he tossed his brother's hat onto the bed again and delved into his wardrobe in search of clean linen.

"Well, I would not interrupt, but there is a gentleman here to see you who was most insistent I bring up his card. I have him situated downstairs in the library."

"Is he a redhead?" Miles withdrew from the wardrobe, sliding his arms into a clean shirt.

Coke laughed. "He is not one of the Ramsay brothers if that is what you are asking. Here is his card."

He handed a solicitor's card to Miles. It was Uncle Lester's solicitor who waited below.

"Shall I put him off?"

Before Miles could answer in the affirmative, yet another knock sounded on the door.

Matthew made a derisive noise from his chair. "Come in," he shouted.

Lord Walsh popped his head in the door. "Hallo!" he said. "Am I interrupting? I wanted the latest news."

"Come in, come in," Miles waved him in. "I was told you might know where Miss Ramsay is."

Walsh nodded. "She said something about fetching a painting when I spoke with her this morning."

"Painting?" Miles tried to make introductions and puzzle out why the mention of a painting rang a bell with him. "You remember my brother, Matthew?" He waved an arm, as he slid it into a clean waistcoat.

"Of course." Walsh exchanged pleasantries.

Again, the door took a beating. "Come in," sounded a chorus of voices as Miles, his brother, and Tom Coke responded.

Miles, feeling driven like a sheep before dogs, threw a clean cravat around his neck and loosely knotting it, went to open the door.

This time it was hot water. Miles politely held the door open, allowing the servant to enter with his wide-wheeled cart. Leaving his unwanted guests to deal with the water, Miles stepped quietly out of the room and shut the door behind him.

"Miles!" Matthew's call was muffled through the thickness of the door. Hurrying down the hall, Miles studiously ignored the summons inherent in such an utterance. He meant to find Aurora and had a good idea where he might find her. Nothing was going to stop him.

Nothing but the weather. The sky had opened up. The portico was dripping rain when he stepped outside. The wet gave him pause, but for no more than a moment. His coat was upstairs in a roomful of people he did not want to talk to.

"Miles!" Matthew was catching up to him. There was no mistaking his imperious outcry.

Miles turned up his collar. Darting into the rain, he made a dash for the barn.

Propped in the doorway of the Doric temple, her picnic basket beside her, a folded blanket beneath her hips, Aurora fell asleep. It was inevitable that she should. She had not passed a peaceful night at Holkham since her brother had run away with Grace Fletcher. She could not lie down in her bed without being troubled by burning thoughts of her last passionate exchange with Miles Fletcher. But here, in the shaded portico of the temple where she had spent so many pleasant hours, she drowsed in peace. The humming of the bees lulled her, the shushing of the trees in the wind soothed her frayed nerves. A pair of doves cooing high above her head while clouds threw alternate light and shadow over her respite closed her eyes entirely. There was a storm brewing, but no need to seek shelter more comforting than this.

Before she shut her eyes, Aurora had from the doorway she leaned against, an excellent view of Holkham Hall and its reflection in the clouded waters of its channel. She had chosen this place because of its view. She hoped Miles Fletcher meant to return today. She would see the arrival of his coach if he did. Her life would become quite complicated if he did not. Life was a tangle and she had no idea how to go about unknotting it. Her brothers were ready, even eager, either to marry her to Lord Walsh or to take her

away with them. And while she had told them she had other
plans, she could not tell them what or whom those plans involved. Roger might understand, given a great deal of explanation, but Gordon would not, and Jack had come with
every intention of insisting that Miles Fletcher return to
him the land Jack had so foolishly gambled away.

Aurora knew it was also possible, though she did not like
to admit it, that Miles Fletcher would lose his desire for
her. He had made her no promises, offered her nothing of
substance. She had no proposal from him of any kind. She
possessed only the certain knowledge that she loved him
above all others, above all reason. She could no longer
imagine a future without him.

She woke from troubled dreams when the clouds opened
up and drenched the clearing. It was not the sound of rain
pelting the leaves of the trees that woke her; it was the
pounding rhythm of hoofbeats. Aurora started up out of the
void of her lethargy with a strong premonition that something of moment was happening.

A horse raced through the rain-laced clearing, a gentleman in shirtsleeves, and those quite soaked, clinging to its
back. She did not immediately recognize the man. The
horse was one of Tom Coke's. So drenched was the
mounted gentleman, so wet and plastered to his form were
his clothes, that she could read far more of the shape of him
than she was either accustomed to or comfortable in someone of the opposite sex. She was reminded, as the sleek wet
horse came charging toward her, of the paintings in Tom
Coke's attic. There was something larger than life, something wild, even dangerous in this stranger's approach. Aurora stood. Picking up the picnic basket and blanket, she
held them before her like a shield, to face this stranger
standing, rather than in a huddle at his feet, when he flung
himself from the horse's back to take shelter with her beneath the portico.

"Aurora!" Miles Fletcher gasped, combing dripping hair
away from his rain-beaded face with an equally drenched
hand.

Aurora was startled, so changed was the gentleman before her. There was none of the cool, unruffled collectedness she associated with Mr. Fletcher. His blue eyes, framed by wet hair and lashes, had a wild look about them, staring as they did from his unshaven face. His entire being seemed changed. There was about him an urgency, a pent-up energy that seemed to flow from him along with the rain.

"Tell me you do not mean to marry Walsh. Tell me you have not accepted his proposal." His voice was as breathless as his approach.

She studied him a moment as though he were a stranger. "I do not mean to marry Walsh," she said softly, almost frightened by the strange, unfettered wildness she sensed in him.

He smiled and moved toward her, the blue of his eyes glittering wetly like the rain in his hair. "Do you love me then, Aurora?"

She backed into the door of the temple with the feeling she had been cornered by a wet and hungry wildcat. How could he ask her such a question without first declaring his own feelings, his own intentions? "Did you catch up to them?" She hoped to divert his attention, hoped to stop his advance.

He smiled broadly. There was nothing halfway about the emotion that curved his mouth today. "I did not come here to talk about my sister, Aurora."

He continued to advance, still dripping, imminently dangerous.

"No?" Aurora swallowed hard. "Perhaps you mean to explain to me then how you could go on day after day pretending to be my friend, when in reality you had already taken from me that which I held most dear? How could you berate me for marrying for land as opposed to marrying for love, when you had my land in your possession all along?"

"The land is yours, to do with as you will. I would not have it come between us," he said, his eyes never straying from her face. "I will sign it over in your name today if you like."

She backed through the door to the temple, into the domed central chamber. He followed. The sound of rain on the roof was accompanied by the drone of the bees. The smell of honey was strong.

"Did you think to salve your conscience in helping me to win Walsh?" She was not ready to quit her quarrel with him.

He was still smiling. The wildness still looked out at her from his eyes. "You might say that. I came to Holkham Hall specifically to find you—to see that you were not paupered by my uncle's last moment of good fortune. It was his dying wish."

"So you meant to marry me off to Walsh, and then ride away absolved of all guilt?"

He slowed his pursuit of her. "I meant to see you happy. I meant to see your future secure. I came to fulfill your heart's desire and, yes, then I would have gone away absolved of guilt. I had no intention of falling in love with you."

She met his declaration with silence. At last, the words she had hoped to hear. He loved her. And yet, doubt still gnawed at the edges of her peace of mind.

"How can you expect me to believe such a statement when you have done nothing but push me into Walsh's arms?"

His gaze moved past her, lingered a moment and then returned. He smiled at her then so sweetly her heart ached to see it. "Why did you come here today, Aurora?"

She knew what it was he had seen. Grace's painting leaned against the wall. She turned to look at it again. It was really quite striking now that it was finished. There was a light, airy quality to the brushwork, an effect too easily muddied by the novice. Grace was perhaps more talented, Aurora thought, than anyone realized. The temple, created by the very absence of paint, other than a few pale washes to indicate shadow, was pale backdrop to the gathering of happy souls picnicking beneath sunlit trees. It was unmistakably Miles who bent to whisper in the ear of the female who wielded a fan. That female had hair the very color of her own.

Aurora looked at Miles. He had a glint in his eyes that reminded her of the last time they had stood within this temple.

He raised a dark eyebrow. "Did you come for the painting?"

She could not continue to meet his gaze. He read her too clearly. "Grace left it for me," she murmured.

"Would you hang your passion on the wall, Aurora, as Princess Stolberg hung hers?" His voice held so much understanding, Aurora felt like crying or laughing or shouting at him. "Do you love me, Aurora? Please say you do."

He advanced on her again, dripping effusively with every move.

This time she did not back away. She closed her eyes and felt the drops of water, like fingertips touching her sleeves, her skirt, her skin.

"Of course, I love you," she said gruffly. "Why else would I throw myself at you the way I have?"

He threw his arms about her then, soaking her to the skin with his embrace, crushing the picnic basket she still clutched. "Will you throw yourself at me again, my dear?" There was a tenderness in the way he said those simple words, a tenderness that was echoed in the curve of his lips, in the warmth of his look, that filled Aurora's heart to overflowing.

She lifted her free hand to touch the dripping locks of hair that rained moisture onto his nose. She leaned over the basket and kissed away a raindrop as it rolled down his cheek. "For the rest of my life, Miles, if you would still have me."

He closed his eyes, savoring her kiss.

She touched her lips to his forehead, as a second raindrop moistened his temple. Eyes still closed, he clutched her to him, but the basket got in the way of his fervent clasp. He opened up his eyes to shove it brusquely aside. He seemed determined to share his moisture.

"Does this mean you intend to marry me, Aurora?" he sighed into the hollow of her neck. When he spoke he punctuated each word with soft, rain-chilled kisses that trailed coolly down her neck and shoulder.

"It does," she said softly, her grasp loosening on the basket as his kisses sank lower still, testing the boundaries of her bodice. The basket slipped her grasp entirely when rain dripping from his hair wet the fabric covering her breast and he nuzzled the rigid peak of her nipple through the damp fabric.

"There remains but one question, my dear."

He knelt before her and Aurora, rather startled, prepared herself for some new and devastating lesson in lovemaking he now meant to teach her from this position. She was shaken, even vaguely disappointed, when, by his actions, he made it clear his intent was not to assault her with some new form of passion, but to collect the fallen basket and its spilled contents.

"One question, Miles?" She made a game attempt to regain her composure.

"Yes." He gazed up at her, eyes glowing, his face looking faintly pink and freshly scrubbed because of the drenching he had suffered in racing to her side. Aurora's breath caught in her throat, so dear was this face become to her. She was reminded, not of the weasel she had first associated with this gentleman, nor of the popinjay she had been ready to name him, but instead, of a man who sees what he wants and will stop at nothing to possess it.

"What question?" she managed to stammer.

He held up the recovered basket, his eyes bluer than gill flowers.

"Indoors or out?" he asked.

Aurora smiled, aware as she had never been aware before that the sway she felt from this man was easily equalled by the sway she had upon him. He awaited her answer in breathless anticipation.

"In," she replied with a very clear sense of what it was he asked of her. "I think our picnic would be best enjoyed indoors since it is raining. Do you not agree?"

In the time it took the basket to slip his fingers and roll along the floor, spilling its contents for the second time that day, he had swept her into his arms and informed her without another word spoken, that he wholeheartedly agreed.